DARKEST BEFORE THE DAWN

Also by Mike Martin in the Sgt. Windflower Mystery Series

The Walker on the Cape
The Body on the T
Beneath the Surface
A Twist of Fortune
A Long Ways from Home
A Tangled Web

Darkest Before the Dawn

MIKE MARTIN

ottawapressandpublishing.com

ISBN (pbk.) 978-1-988437-13-2
ISBN (EPUB) 978-1-988437-14-9
ISBN (MOBI) 978-1-988437-15-6

Design and composition: Magdalene Carson at New Leaf Publication Design

To my partner, Joan. I am grateful to have you by my side.
Thank you for sharing this adventure with me.

DARKEST BEFORE THE DAWN

ONE

Winston Windflower was surrounded by women. Literally and figuratively. At home, his beautiful wife, Sheila Hillier, was busy minding the new joy of their lives. Amelia Louise was just over a month old, and she was the most beautiful thing that the RCMP sergeant had ever seen. Right in front of him was a gaggle of ladies from the Grand Bank United Church Women. He was finishing up the latest in a series of seminars the local Mounties were conducting on how to make your home safer.

The sessions were in response to a series of break-ins around the Burin Peninsula in recent months. There had been ten reported in Grand Bank alone. This was concerning to the locals who were used to living in a community where you never had to lock your doors at night. It was disturbing to the RCMP as well because they had no idea who was behind this latest crime spree. Usually, that was the easiest part of their job.

Break and enters were often carried out by drug users looking for quick money for hits or professionals who would stake out a home or business that had particularly valuable assets. There were random robberies for other reasons, too, but ten in one small town was more than unusual. What was even stranger was that houses had been broken into, and nothing appeared to be missing.

That had startled the RCMP and scared the local women who had come out tonight to hear about double bolts and security systems.

"We never had to lock our doors around here," said Mabel Bennett.

"Who is doing this, Sergeant?" asked Rachel Mahoney.

"Is it drugs?" asked Barb Pritchard.

Windflower was trying to respond but the questions kept coming.

"They don't know yet," came a voice from behind him. Windflower turned to see who had come to his rescue. It was Betsy Molloy, his administrative assistant.

"The whole detachment is working on it, and they'll find them," continued Betsy. "The Mounties always get their man," she stated confidently.

That seemed to assuage the gathered women, who parted to let the RCMP officer slip through. He nodded and smiled as he politely refused all offers for coffee and cake and squeezed his way out of the church hall.

Outside, he exhaled a sigh of relief and breathed in the first warm night air of spring. It was early June, but the weather had been unseasonably cold for this time of year. There'd even been morning frost up until a few nights ago. Tonight was calm and beautiful and mild. Windflower hoped that would be a harbinger of warmer days ahead. But he had learned from living in this part of the world that unpredictable was the norm when it came to weather. The good news was that if you didn't like the weather at the moment, you only had to wait about an hour and it would be different.

He didn't really care about wind or weather tonight. He couldn't wait to get home to see Sheila and their baby. He drove home quickly and was welcomed by yet another female in his life, Lady, his five-year-old collie. She was still a puppy at heart despite her age and wanted to jump and play with her master. Windflower pacified her with a pat on the head and a Milk-Bone biscuit and ran upstairs.

Sheila was putting a new pink onesie on the baby who was looking at her mother.

"She knows who you are," said Windflower, creeping in behind her. The baby moved her eyes towards him.

"I think she knows you, too," said Sheila. "Come and say hello."

Windflower sat on the bed next to Sheila and grazed his baby's cheek with his finger. Then, he touched her tiny fingers, and it felt like she was trying to grab on to him. It may have been reflex, but Windflower was overjoyed at her reaction. Maybe she does know me, he thought.

As he was pondering this question, Amelia Louise closed her eyes and was soon fast asleep.

"Put the kettle on, and I'll be down in a minute," said Sheila, who picked up the baby and carried her to the bassinet next to the bed.

"Okay," said Windflower. "I'll take Lady out for a quick spin too."

Windflower went downstairs where Lady was waiting none too patiently for him. Her spirits lifted when he grabbed her leash after plugging in the kettle.

"Let's go girl," he said. She didn't need to be told twice. Lady was quite happy to sniff and snort her way all along the roadways in Grand Bank. She did her business and barked at dogs on the route to let them know that she had the best master in town. She was disappointed when Windflower took the short way back home. But once there, she was quite content to lie at his feet as he sat in the living room with Sheila.

"So, tell me all about your day," said Windflower.

"It's not very exciting," said Sheila. "Eat, poop, sleep. Repeat. But I'm not complaining. We have a beautiful, healthy baby girl."

Windflower smiled. "Well, I couldn't be happier, with her and with you."

"Thank you, Sergeant. What's happening out in the big world of Grand Bank? How did your meeting go at the church?"

"They're worried. Can't say as I blame them."

"It's a big shift. Especially for those who have lived here all of their lives. What is going on?"

"Don't know yet, but as Betsy says, we always get our man."

Sheila laughed. "Good thing Betsy was there. She's always helping out with the church ladies."

"She certainly helped me out tonight. We'll figure it out. We always do. In the meantime, lock the doors when I'm not around. I don't want anything happening to my two favourite ladies in the world."

"Make that three," said Sheila, laughing again, as Lady pushed herself up against Windflower for one more rub.

He started to stroke her when his cell phone rang. "Boss, it's Jones. We've got a situation. We got a call about a shooting up near the seniors' club."

"Injuries?" asked Windflower.

"A teenager," said Jones. "I'm on my way."

"I'll be over in a sec," said Windflower.

"Bad news?" asked Sheila.

"I'll call you," was all he said back.

Sheila didn't ask any more questions. They liked a layer of insulation between his police work and their personal lives. He gave her a peck on the cheek and patted Lady as he left to drive to the seniors' club, hoping for the best and fearing the worst.

The reality was somewhere in between.

TWO

There were lights flashing and a large group of people gathered near the Grand Bank 50+ Club. RCMP Constable Rick Smithson was in charge of crowd control and barely managing. Windflower walked over to him, and the crowd shrunk back. Smithson smiled his thanks while Windflower went to talk with Constable Yvette Jones, who was dealing with the paramedics. She nodded to the paramedics and came over to him.

"What have we got?" asked Windflower.

"Levi Parsons, 15, is in the back," said Jones. "He's got a busted-up shoulder, but it could've been a lot worse. Someone saw him come down here a while ago with a shotgun. They thought he was shooting birds. He may have been doing something else."

The ambulance drove off with its lights flashing to the Grand Bank Clinic.

"What do you mean?" asked Windflower.

"There's a note," she said, pulling a plastic bag out of her pocket. "The paramedics found it near the young guy."

Windflower peered through the plastic. He couldn't make out a lot from the scratchy scrawlings, but it looked like a letter.

"Make me a copy and leave it on my desk," he said. "Then store the original. Have you read it?"

"Yes. I'm no expert, but I'd say it looks like a suicide note. It's a description of what Levi Parsons thinks about his life and his prospects. None of it good."

"So, he came down here to end it all?"

"Or draw attention. I've seen both in Thunder Bay and back home in Dartmouth. Either way, it's not good."

"He must be pretty desperate. It's hard to imagine things being that bad here in Grand Bank."

"It could be anything. Depression and suicidal thinking are more common than you'd think in small communities. And this is the time of year for it, too. The end of the school year means that the kids will get scattered and won't be able to support each other. Some of them will be graduating into an adult life or college, and that scares the heck out of them. They don't have great ways of coping except to drink and smoke pot, which aren't that helpful."

"You seem to know a lot about this." Windflower was learning more about his constable all the time, it seemed. "We had our share back home in Pink Lake, but the situation here is nothing like that," he said.

"It's what's inside that counts. And social media and cell phones spread bad news pretty quickly. You probably didn't have Facebook and Snapchat back then."

"We most certainly did not."

Windflower thought about the work ahead. "I'll leave you to clean up the site," he told Jones. "Get Smithson to talk to all the neighbours around here to make sure we didn't miss anything. Are you comfortable talking to the parents?"

"I can," said Jones. "But I'm thinking that they might want to talk to someone with a bit more authority."

"Okay," said Windflower. He knew what she meant. Jeremiah Parsons was a sombre man. Some might call him religious, and he certainly was. But he was also a severe-looking man. Windflower knew him as a carpenter who mostly worked out of town. Mostly, because he had fallen out in some way with nearly everyone else in Grand Bank over the years. Windflower had seen him dozens of times. But he had did not remember ever seeing him smile. Not once.

Tonight was no exception. When Windflower walked into the clinic waiting room, Jeremiah Parsons was not in a good mood. His scowl permeated the area like dank smoke. His wife, Charlene, whom Windflower had met only on a couple of occasions, brightened when she saw him, as if he might have good news to bring. But that dampened under the glare of her husband.

Parsons stood to meet Windflower. He was a large man, in height and girth. Towering over the RCMP officer, he blocked the view of his wife, but Windflower made a point of greeting them both by their first names. If anything, that seemed to make the husband even grumpier. "What's goin' on, Sergeant? When are you going to clean up this town, get rid of them drug dealers, and lock up some of these vagabonds?" he demanded to know.

Windflower ignored the interrogation. "How is your son?" he asked.

At that question Charlene Parsons broke down sobbing and was merely muffled by her husband's dark stare. "He'll be all right," said Jeremiah Parsons. "He needs a touch of the switch and a week of prayer and hard chores. That'll get the devil out of him."

"Has he been having trouble at home or in school these days?" asked Windflower, trying to move the conversation back to a more helpful level. "Do you know if he's been drinking or using drugs?"

At the last question, the mother almost collapsed but was revived by her husband's loud voice. "That's what I've been talking about," said the father. "He's been doing drugs and hanging around with those heathens listening to the devil's music. I'll take care of my son. You take care of the rest of that scum. Or I'll do the job myself."

Before Windflower could respond, even if he could have thought of something appropriate to say, Jeremiah Parsons grabbed his wife by the arm, almost lifting her out of her chair. "Come on, we're going," he said.

Charlene Parsons resisted her husband's pull. She looked directly at Windflower. She didn't speak, but Windflower knew that look. He'd seen it before. It was a non-verbal question that asked if he would back her up. He nodded.

"I'm going to stay with Levi. You can go if you want," she said, pulling her arm away from her husband's grip. "He shouldn't be alone in here."

Jeremiah Parsons blew by Windflower like a gust of red-hot smoke and, with one more dangerous glare at his wife, he was out the door and into his truck in a flash. Windflower and Charlene Parsons watched in a kind of stunned silence as the truck peeled out of the clinic parking lot.

"Have you heard what's going on with Levi?" asked Windflower.

The woman stopped shaking, clearly grateful to be able to focus on her son again. "They told me that he had a separated shoulder. They were going to strap him up and probably keep him overnight.

I don't want to leave him."

"That's perfectly understandable. We don't need to talk about it tonight, but Levi does need help, Charlene."

"I know. But Jeremiah is so stubborn and set in his ways. I've taken Levi myself to St. John's to see a psychologist a few times. But now he's forbidden that, and there's no real services here in Grand Bank."

"We think he may have tried to harm himself." Windflower spoke slowly, unsure how well Charlene could take the news.

"Jeremiah said that it was an accident," she said. "Levi didn't say anything."

"He wrote a letter . . ."

Windflower would have liked to continue the conversation, but the nurse beckoned them over from the reception desk.

"The doctor says that your son is fine and they're moving him into a room for the night," the nurse said. "He'll be in room 117, just down the hall if you want to wait for him there."

"Do you want me to stay with you?" asked Windflower. "Or I could send someone over."

"No, thank you, Sergeant," Charlene responded. "You've done enough already."

"Okay. Someone will be over to talk to you tomorrow. We'll need to get a statement from Levi as well."

The mother nodded silently at this last request. She started to leave and then turned back to Windflower. "Can I see the letter?" she asked.

"I'll bring it over in the morning," Windflower said as he watched Charlene Parsons slowly walk down the hall. It might be better for her to be alone with her son tonight, he thought. It would certainly be better than going home right away to her husband. This way she could really talk to the young man. He certainly needed someone to talk to.

When Windflower arrived home, the lights were off downstairs and Lady was curled up on her blanket in the kitchen. She rose expectantly when she saw him, but all she got for her loyalty was an opened back door so she could do her business. She completed that quickly and was soon back in her comfy bed. Not long after, Windflower had that same pleasure.

THREE

It was not a long sleep. Amelia Louise made sure of that. The mid-night's sleep interruption seemed to make everyone cranky but was soon replaced by smiles and laughter from the newborn's parents. Once she had been fed and changed, the baby seemed happy to just be held by her mom and dad and provide them with endless joy.

Soon, the newborn drifted off to sleep again. Sheila lovingly placed her back into the bedside bassinet and cuddled into Windflower, who had made a point of jumping into bed as soon as he could. They, too, quickly fell to sleep and were grateful that no one stirred until the morning light streamed into their bedroom. Sheila fed the baby while Windflower went downstairs to see to their other child.

Lady greeted him with her usual enthusiasm. He put the coffee on to perk, grabbed her leash, and set off into the bright spring morning. To Lady's obvious pleasure, they took the long route all the way up to the edge of the pathway that led to the Cape. Windflower let her off the leash and watched her pure enjoyment at being able to sniff all the new scents of the earth coming alive again after the winter. He allowed her to wander up the path, then called her to come back.

Reluctantly, the collie turned away from the Cape and bounded down the hill towards him, nearly knocking him over at the bottom. Windflower laughed and together they strolled down through the sleepy town on their way back home. He filled her bowl and got her fresh water. He poured a cup of coffee for himself, then took one up to Sheila and sat on the bed with her to admire their beautiful baby girl for a bit.

Sheila then took out the baby bath and put a little water in it to wash Amelia Louise while Windflower went downstairs for his morning rituals. He took out his smudging kit. It contained his earthenware smudging-bowl, sacred medicines, and two feathers, one for smudging and an eagle feather that had belonged to his grandfather, a chief of his nation. He didn't use the eagle feather anymore because it was beginning to fray. But he brought it with him when he was home because it reminded him of his ancestors and the path that they had travelled. He hoped they would be with him on this journey as well.

Lady followed him out and was doing her own explorations in the backyard as he mixed a small amount of the medicines in the bowl. Adding some reindeer moss that grew plentifully near Grand Bank, he lit the mixture. Soon smoke was swirling out of the bowl, and he took his smudging feather to pass the smoke over his head and around his body. He paused near his heart to ask that it be made pure and then under his feet to help guide his path.

Once he had finished smudging, he said his prayers, which were almost always thanks for the blessings he had received, and for others that they might find peace and courage in their lives. He had a lot to be grateful for this morning. At the top of the list were Sheila and his new daughter. He was thankful for Sheila's calm and steady influence in his life, even when things were difficult for him as often was the case in his line of work.

She was also the brains in the family and the main reason they would soon be re- opening their refurbished B&B. Thinking about that almost took Windflower off into the world of what else needed to be done before the grand re-opening in a few weeks. But he stayed focused on his prayers and made sure to add Eddie Tizzard to his list. Eddie was still recovering from being shot just before Christmas last year. He had made great progress and had finally made it back to work, although still under a light-duty sentence, as he called it.

Windflower finished his morning routine with a few prayers of thanks and blessings for his ancestors, friends, and allies who were continuing to help him in his life and his work. Then he laid down some tobacco for young Levi Parsons and his family, making sure to include his stern father in his intentions. He might need the help most of all.

Windflower packed up his supplies and felt a cool breeze. He looked up and around to see the familiar swirl of fog starting to creep into Grand Bank.

Fog was a familiar but not necessarily welcome visitor in these parts. It lurked out in the Atlantic Ocean, waiting for any opportunity to come ashore. The wind, another ever-present factor in coastal Newfoundland, was its partner in crime. The fog was the thief, taking away the heat of the sun, while the wind drove the getaway car. Together, these two were almost never good news.

Windflower called Lady, who reluctantly abandoned the new growth and life fascinating her this springtime morning and followed him inside. He poured himself another cup of coffee and went upstairs where he could hear Sheila softly singing to her daughter. He slowly crept inside the bedroom and watched as the two people he loved most in the world welcomed the morning together. Sheila noticed his presence and smiled.

"She is beautiful, isn't she?"

"She's perfect," said Windflower. "Just like her mother." He sat on the bed next to them and kissed the baby's cheek.

"Good morning," he whispered into his daughter's ear.

"That's your daddy," said Sheila.

Windflower grinned from ear to ear. "I was going to make some scrambled eggs. You want some?" he asked.

"Yes, please," said Sheila. "I'm famished. I'm so happy looking after her that I sometimes forget to eat."

Just then the baby closed her eyes and with a great yawn went to sleep. Windflower left the bedroom quietly and quickly and went to make breakfast. Fifteen minutes later, Sheila and Windflower were enjoying their eggs and toast while Lady patiently waited in the event anything fell within her jurisdiction underneath the table.

After they had finished breakfast, Windflower told Sheila about Levi Parsons.

"Oh my God," said Sheila. "Did he really try to kill himself?"

"He came pretty close. I don't know what's going on, but he's in trouble. We'll need to get him some help."

"I've been worried about our young folks for a while. Council put in a request for a mental health worker over a year ago, and we've been told we're on a waiting list."

"I thought the mayor of Grand Bank would have more pull than that," teased Windflower.

"I've been a bit busy," said Sheila, not quite irritated but close enough to it that Windflower could sense he was near the edge of trouble.

"I don't know how you do it with so little sleep," he said. "You're amazing."

"I'm going to have a nap this afternoon. But I have to go over to the B&B this morning to check with Beulah on supplies. Are you still cooking this weekend?"

"I'll do Saturday and Sunday. I'm glad we decided to do this staged opening. Cooking without having room guests is a lot less work. It's fun, actually."

"Once we open fully in July, it will be crazy. We're almost fully booked for July, and I noticed that there are a number of requests for August to respond to on the Airbnb account."

"I still have a bit of touch-up painting to do upstairs. I hope I can get it all done in time."

"It seems I'm not the only one who needs some help." Windflower nodded his agreement.

"You know," said Sheila, "I was thinking about hiring a student for the summer to help out around here and over at the B&B. Why not see if Levi Parsons is up for it? Give him something to do."

"That's a great idea." Windflower gathered their empty plates and put them in the dishwasher. "If his shoulder is not too beat up," he said, "it might be good for him and us. You, my dear, are not only beautiful, but pretty smart, too."

Sheila smiled, and Windflower knew he had navigated back to the relationship safe zone. It was tricky, but he was learning.

"I've got to get cleaned up and over to work," he announced.

"And I've got a date with a washer and dryer. Pretty exciting lives."

"I wouldn't want any other," said Windflower. He went upstairs and showered and shaved. When he came back down, dressed and ready for work, he called out his goodbyes to Sheila who was in the basement laundry room.

"See you, tonight."

FOUR

The fog had not merely blanketed Grand Bank. It had swallowed it up completely. He was glad he was in town and not on the highway this morning where the lurking danger of roadside moose made driving dangerous at all times and potentially deadly on a morning like this. He pulled his Jeep into the Grand Bank RCMP detachment parking lot at the same time as another RCMP cruiser.

"Good morning, Harry," said Windflower.

"Good morning, boss," said Constable Harry Frost, returning from his last highway run of the shift. Frost was now the second-longest serving Mountie in the area, after Windflower. In the middle of his career with the force, Frost was scheduled to be shipped out later in the month. He was being transferred to Portage la Prairie in Manitoba, near Winnipeg, which was much closer to his hometown of Brandon.

"It's brutal out there," said Frost.

"Any moose?" asked Windflower.

"I didn't see any, but you know they're out there. You can almost feel them."

"I know what you mean. You almost expect to see them when you come over every hill. At least we've managed to slow people down a little."

"Yeah, you can notice that people are paying a bit more attention when they come to the reduced speed zones we set up. And not just when they see us," Frost laughed.

Windflower laughed too. "Anything exciting happen overnight?"

That was their running joke. Almost nothing exciting ever happened in Grand Bank, and that was quite fine with Windflower.

"Nah. After the incident with the kid, it was pretty smooth. I'm going to miss this place. I know that it will be much busier where I'm going. I kinda like the rhythm, the pace of life here. It would be a good place to raise a family. How's that daughter of yours?"

Windflower's face brightened when he thought of Amelia Louise back at home. "She's great," he said. "I couldn't be happier."

The two officers were sitting in the back drinking their coffee when they heard another vehicle speed into the parking lot and stop very quickly. "Tizzard," they both said together.

Soon after, Corporal Eddie Tizzard appeared in the doorway with a package of partridgeberry muffins under his arm.

"I brought a snack," he said.

"You always have a snack," said Frost. "If I ate like you, I would be 300 pounds."

"You gotta look after yourself," said Tizzard. "Everything in moderation."

"Is that your new motto?" asked Windflower. "It must be for going forward purposes, since it looks like you already ate two of those muffins."

"I was hungry," said Tizzard. "Dad told me it's better to eat a lot when you have it, before you really want it. That way you're sure never to be hungry."

"Did he really say that?" asked Frost as Windflower grabbed a muffin and walked away laughing.

Windflower was wading through his paperwork when Tizzard knocked on his open door.

"Got a minute?"

"Come in," said Windflower.

"I know I'm supposed to be on a reduced schedule, but I'm going crazy here, boss. Can you talk to the inspector and at least get me back into the rotation?"

Windflower looked at the young corporal and smiled. "I'll talk to Ron. But I think this is out of our hands. You have to get medical clearance and then HQ has to sign off."

Tizzard sighed. "Look, you can see how healthy I am. I'm even working out at the gym. And my appetite is back."

"I don't think you ever lost your appetite, Eddie. Even when you were knocked out. I think the first thing you said when you woke up was, 'What's for breakfast?'"

"Is there anything you can give me?" Tizzard pleaded.

"How about some research? We need some info on how we can get more mental health services in this region. Can you find somebody to talk to in the provincial government and see what the possibilities might be?"

"I can do that. Is this about the young guy last night?"

"It is, but there may be more problems in this community that we don't know about. If there's one kid in trouble, there are likely at least a few more."

"I'm on it, boss. Thanks." Windflower didn't see Tizzard leave, but the whole office shook when he peeled out of the parking lot.

"He didn't slow down much," said Frost, peeking into Windflower's office to say goodbye.

"That's just who he is," said Windflower. "Slow is not really in his vocabulary."

Frost waved goodbye, leaving Windflower a few moments alone to think about his young friend and how close they had come to losing him. "I'll take him at any speed," he said to himself.

FIVE

Betsy arrived in the office right at eight o'clock. She popped in to see Windflower. He handed her over a pile of paperwork that he'd managed to plough through. She smiled and handed him over a new stack.

"Sorry," she said.

"The bane of my existence."

"Did Levi Parsons really try to kill himself last night?"

"Is that what people are saying?" Windflower asked in response. He knew that if anyone had the pulse of the community, it would be Betsy.

"That's what I heard," she said. "Why would a young person do something like that?"

"Well, we're not really sure what happened yet. I'm going over to talk to the family later this morning. But sometimes young folks don't have enough hope, or they have problems that they can't seem to work out on their own."

Betsy thought about that for a moment. "I don't know if I should say anything. But that man is awfully mean."

"Jeremiah Parsons?" asked Windflower.

"He got religion from his father. Old Abe used to be a preacher of sorts. He never had a formal congregation or church. Used to hold services in his house and then he would take his family with him while he did a summer revival tour all over the province. Everybody was afraid of the old man. I guess Jeremiah followed in his footsteps."

Windflower smiled. Betsy could always be relied on for information.

"That can't be a very fun place for a teenager," he said. "Anyway, we'll know more later. Thanks for re-filling my pile. And thanks for your help in extricating me last night."

"You're welcome. We have to look after each other."

How true is that, Windflower thought as he heard Constable Rick Smithson on his way in.

"Morning, boss."

"Good morning, Constable. Did you find out anything from your interviews?"

"Not too much," said Smithson. "A couple of people saw the kid walking down towards the brook. They saw him carrying a hockey bag. We found it in the water. His father identified the gun and wanted it back. Kind of insisted. I told him we needed it for the investigation. He was not real happy with us."

"I suspect not," said Windflower. "Do you have it locked up in back?"

"Yeah. There was one more thing from last night. One of the people I talked to said that they heard a cat crying in a house down on Tim's Lane. She said it's been going on for a few days and that the place stunk.

"Were the SPCA called?" asked Windflower.

"I don't know. Doesn't sound like it."

"I guess you should go over and check it out then. Do you know whose house it is?"

"It's a guy by the name of Jacob Crowder," said Smithson, looking at his notes.

"He's the computer guy, isn't he?"

"Yeah, that's the guy. He's got a sign in the window saying computer repairs , but I've never seen anybody in there. As a matter of fact, I've never even seen him. Have you?"

"That's interesting. But no, I don't think I have," said Windflower, now scratching his head as he tried to remember if he had ever seen Jacob Crowder. "Go check it out," he told Smithson.

Smithson left, and Windflower thought about the computer guy for a minute. That's more than interesting. That's weird. He decided he needed to see a Grand Bank expert about the matter—Betsy.

"Do you know Jacob Crowder?" he asked Betsy, who had removed her headphones when she saw him coming.

"I know the family and a bit of the history," she said. "His grandfather, Albert Ryan, was from here. That's his house over on Tim's Lane. Apparently, he was lost at sea on a boat called the Edith M. Prior. Everybody around here knows about the boats that went down."

"Any family left around?"

"There was a daughter, Elizabeth, who married a man named Bruce Crowder from Ontario. She moved away from here and the house was left to run down. About a year ago, young Jacob showed up and started fixing it up."

"Do you know everything about Grand Bank?"

"I've lived here my whole life. I make it my business to know my community. My mother was a school teacher and she said that we had to remember our past because it might predict the future."

Windflower nodded. "So why haven't I ever seen Jacob Crowder?" he asked.

"I think he has a phobia of some sort," said Betsy, with some confidence. "I don't know that for sure, but he's never out. He orders his groceries by phone from Warrens and they deliver to him. The boys over there say that he gave them a credit card to pay for his orders but he won't open the door, so they leave everything outside. Sometimes he gets equipment and stuff from St. John's and all over, but that comes by mail or gets delivered by the taxi."

"Have you ever seen him?"

"Not in person. There's always noise and music playing, and I think you can hear someone moving around in there."

"Thanks, Betsy. Smithson is going over to take a look at the place. Someone said they heard a cat crying."

"I didn't know he had a cat," said Betsy, walking away perturbed.

Windflower shook his head. He had bigger things to deal with, including three very confused and troubled people in the Parsons household. He wasn't looking forward to it, but that was his job. It also felt like something bad or difficult was starting to stir in Grand Bank, where seldom did much of anything stir. But when it did, it really did. "When sorrows come, they come not single spies, but in battalions." He tucked the copy of the letter from Levi Parsons into his pocket and drove over to see the Parsons family.

SIX

Jeremiah Parsons lived with his wife and son in the same small fisherman's house that his father, and his father before, had lived in. It was up on the hill near the edge of town, a bit apart and above the rest of the community. Jeremiah had started out as an inshore fisherman, like his predecessors, but that was all gone in the collapse of the cod fishery. He got some cash from the government as part of the readjustment package but hadn't really been able to find anything productive since that. His wife was the main breadwinner now, and Windflower had seen her from time to time at Sobeys where she worked as a cashier.

That must be grating on him, too, thought Windflower as Charlene Parsons opened the door and invited him in. He gave her a copy of the note from last night and watched as she slowly read the letter. She didn't say a word and then rose to get her son from his bedroom.

Levi Parsons had sleep in his eyes and his arm in a sling when he stumbled into the kitchen. He looked dazed, but not surprised to see the RCMP officer sitting there.

"Good morning, Levi," said Windflower, opening his notebook and laying it on the table in front of him. "I need to ask you a few questions. How's your arm?"

"It's okay," mumbled the boy.

"What were you doing last night with a gun down by the brook?"

"I dunno."

"Levi, this can all go away really quickly if you help me. If not, there will be more questions, and this will just go on. You're not going to be in any trouble if you cooperate," said Windflower, hoping he sounded convincing.

The boy looked at his mother to check her reaction. She nodded to go ahead.

"I guess I was pretty upset. I didn't know what to do. I was confused. I thought maybe . . ."

He was interrupted by the back door blowing open. All six foot seven and 300 pounds of Jeremiah Parsons rushed through at full speed. "What's going on here?" he shouted at all of them, with particular attention paid to Windflower.

"I'm interviewing your son," said Windflower. "We need to know what happened so that we can close off this incident and get your son some help."

"My son don't need your help," said Parsons. "His family and God will look after him."

"It's good that he has your support," said Windflower. "But he may need some outside help, too." Despite himself Windflower could hear his voice get louder, and he was sure that his complexion was showing his impatience as well.

"You need to start praying, boy," thundered Parsons. "Stop smoking those drugs and give up your sinning ways. Ask God for forgiveness."

Levi Parsons looked terrified and ran from the room with his mother close behind. Windflower stood and faced the giant in front of him.

"You can do what you want with your religion, but your son may need help. He may have tried to kill himself last night. And he may do it again. Next time we may not be as lucky," said Windflower as calmly as he could.

Parsons looked like he was ready to explode when Charlene Parsons came out of the bedroom. "Please sit down, Jeremiah. Sergeant Windflower may be right. We have to get Levi some help."

Jeremiah Parson's eyes started to bulge, and he opened his mouth to speak, but no words came out. He sputtered and then stormed out of the kitchen as quickly as he had arrived, slamming the door nearly off the hinges on the way out.

Windflower looked at Charlene Parsons, a little incredulous that she had managed to quiet the beast in her kitchen. She clearly had had to do that before. She was good at it.

"Jeremiah is a lot of smoke but not much fire. He knows we're right, but he can't admit it. He won't stand in the way. Can we talk about how we can get Levi the help he needs?"

"Sure," said Windflower.

"I'll put on some tea." With that, Charlene Parsons plugged the kettle in and got two china cups out of the cupboard. Then she took a cherry pound cake out and cut a large slice for herself and one for her guest. Windflower might have thought of refusing, but that didn't seem to be an option. Instead, he thanked his hostess and tasted what might have been the best cherry pound cake that he'd ever eaten.

"This is amazing," he murmured. He tried to eat it slowly but managed to almost inhale it anyway. Charlene rose to take his plate for another piece, but this time he did manage to say no.

"Thank you so much, that was delicious,' he said.

The lady poured them both a cup of strong black tea. She put milk and sugar out, but Windflower preferred it just the way it was served.

"Have you noticed anything different about Levi recently?" he asked.

"Levi has always been a quiet boy, a bit of an introvert and a loner. He was never much for games or sports. He always liked music, and when they started a band in school a few years ago, I'd never seen him happier. He would lug his clarinet everywhere with him and play it by himself in his room all night. I thought Jeremiah was going to go out of his mind."

"It's nice to have an activity you enjoy," said Windflower, finally able to take more than a sip of the scalding hot tea.

"Yeah, he seemed happy. Then last year they cancelled the band program at the high school. Levi was devastated. He became withdrawn and grumpy. He wasn't himself. He started hanging around with an older crowd, and they were doing a bit of drinking down under the wharf. When Jeremiah found out about that, he was not very happy and started making him stay home when he wasn't at school."

"Did that work?"

"Not very well. As soon as Levi could, he would sneak out, and then his father would be roaring around town looking for him."

"Was he drinking very often?"

"I don't think so. But there was also some pot involved. I know it's not good, and it's not part of my generation's idea of fun, but it's not really that bad is it?"

Windflower did not want to respond to that question. He had no good answer, at least as an officer of the law. Instead, he turned the subject back to the father. "I'm guessing that your husband wasn't happy about the pot," he said.

"Oh, my God, no," said the woman. "That's when he went nuts, completely bananas. I'm a religious person, and I believe in God and asking for God's help, but we need to get a bit of help from here on earth, too, don't we?"

"What about the teachers or counsellors at the school?"

"Some of the teachers are nice, and the principal is doing what she can, but I don't think Levi trusts them. They're the ones who told us about the drinking, you see. And there's more than our Levi getting into trouble. He seems to just listen to some of his friends, and I don't think they're in any better shape than he is."

"We're going to see what we can do about getting some more support here," said Windflower. "It sounds like we can all use a bit of help. Are you okay, Charlene?"

"I'll be fine, Sergeant. Please get some help for Levi, okay?"

Windflower nodded and walked silently back to his Jeep. He was still thinking about the Parsons family when he arrived back at the detachment.

Betsy waved to him when she saw him through the window. "Smithson called," she said as her boss walked in the door. "He wants you to meet him at the Crowder house. He said he found a body."

SEVEN

Windflower drove over to Tim's Lane near the brook and saw Smithson standing outside looking like he'd lost his best friend.

"What have we got?" Windflower asked as he got out of the Jeep.

"There's a dead man in there," said Smithson, spitting it out as if he had been holding it in for hours.

"Walk me through what you've done since you got here," said Windflower. Then, noticing a few neighbours had started to gather around at the sight of two RCMP vehicles, he pointed back to his vehicle. Both officers got inside.

"I came over like you suggested. There was no sign of anything going on. I was about to leave when I heard the cat. It's still in there." He started to freeze up, and Windflower urged him on.

"Was the door locked?" he asked.

"It was," said Smithson. "But I went around the back and found a window I could jimmy. I hope that was okay."

Windflower nodded. "What did you see inside?"

"Well, the first thing was the smell. You can catch it even out here. In there, it would choke you. I almost threw up. Like rotting meat and garbage and poop all rolled in together. I covered my face and started to look around. The cat came out to inspect me and then ran into the bedroom. It's still in there, as far as I know." Smithson paused and took a deep breath, as if he was trying to get more clean air into his lungs.

"What else?" asked Windflower, trying to keep Smithson going.

"He was slumped over in his chair in the kitchen with the computer open in front of him on the table. It was still on. But he was dead. I'm sure of that. There's blood everywhere, boss."

"Okay. I want you to secure the scene outside. Tape off the entrance and put cones in the driveway. I'm going to call the paramedics and get backup. Can you do that?"

"Yes," said Smithson. "I can do that."

"Once we get backup here, I want you to go to the detachment and write up your statement. Got it?"

"Got it," said Smithson who was already getting out of the car to start his assignment.

Windflower called Betsy and got her to get both the paramedics and Doctor Sanjay on the way. He also asked her to get Frost and Jones in as soon as possible. They would need everybody on deck for something like this. It wasn't often they had a dead body of any sort to deal with in Grand Bank, let alone one involving the possibility of foul play.

Whether it was foul play was still to be determined. But the stench inside the house was foul indeed. It was a cold and heavy smell that hung suspended inside the house as Windflower walked into the kitchen area. If possible, it increased in intensity as he came closer to the body. He wanted to see the scene for himself, but he didn't stay one second longer than necessary. He saw the blood that Smithson described. It was a very dark red, almost black. Dried and matted all over the deceased. That he was dead would have to be confirmed by the paramedics and Sanjay, the coroner, but he agreed with Smithson's initial assessment. Not much doubt about it.

As he left, Windflower made some mental notes. No weapon or sign of struggle. That usually meant that the attacker or attackers were known to the dead man, or at least invited in. And no obvious weapon near the body or under the table. That might rule out suicide, but he was getting ahead of himself.

Heading for the door, Windflower tried not to run but certainly walked quickly to get outside so he could really breathe again. He was surprised see Tizzard talking to Smithson in the driveway.

"Need any help, boss?" asked Tizzard.

"You're not supposed to be out here like this," said Windflower.

Tizzard shrugged his shoulders.

"Okay. Smithson, you go back and fill out your report. Tizzard, you're on the perimeter."

When Smithson had gone, Windflower turned to Tizzard. "You're going to get me in trouble," he said.

"I'm not going to do anything. Just sit in the driveway and keep the snoops away," said Tizzard.

"Make sure that's all you do," said Windflower, trying to sound serious, but not fooling anybody, including Tizzard. He didn't have any more time to worry about it before the paramedics arrived with their lights flashing and siren blaring.

"If people didn't know there was something going on before, they sure do now," said Tizzard. Windflower ignored him and went to the ambulance.

"There's a body inside," he told the supervisor, Lillian Saunders, whom he recognized from many other incidents around town. "It won't be pleasant. We'll have to get forensics, but that's going to take some time. He hasn't been pronounced. I think Doc Sanjay is on his way, too. Do you guys have a camera?"

"Yeah," said Saunders. Then, to the young man who was accompanying her, she said, "Get the camera and be careful when you come into the house. We'll try not to disturb anything if we don't have to."

After the two paramedics were inside, another vehicle pulled up outside the residence, and a small but lively man with a black doctor's bag jumped out. He and Tizzard were engaged in what looked to be a friendly conversation when Windflower walked over. "Sorry to break up the party," he said a little more sternly than he intended. Whatever his intention, the other two men paid scant attention and continued their chat.

Finally, the smaller man clapped Tizzard on the shoulder. "Good show, my man," he said. "Sergeant Windflower, how's she goin' b'y?"

Windflower had to smile at Vijay Sanjay's Newfoundland-style greeting. He was an irrepressible good spirit, as well as a great friend. They had shared good times and bad together as outsiders in this small community, but more good than bad. That was almost guaranteed if Doctor Sanjay was involved.

"I am well, my friend," said Windflower. "A tad perturbed by our young corporal who is supposed to be home recuperating."

"I think he looks in great shape," said Sanjay, to Tizzard's glee. "I would recommend that he return to full duties. It would be good for his morale."

"I'll pass that along," said Windflower dryly. "We have a dead body inside. No obvious weapon. But lots of blood. There's quite a smell, too."

"I'm not worried about the smell," said Sanjay as he took his black bag and walked into the house. "You've never been to the slums in India, have you? Crowded, open toilets and sacred cows wandering around everywhere. It's the first thing a Westerner would notice. Me, I'm Bengali. Doesn't bother me."

Windflower shook his head.

"I got this here if you need to go back," said Tizzard, after Sanjay went into the house.

Windflower scowled but nodded okay. "Nothing. Do nothing. I will send someone to take over soon."

"I got it," said Tizzard.

Windflower gave him one more look and then drove back to the detachment.

EIGHT

"Oh, my God," said Betsy. "Was Jacob Crowder murdered?" she wondered out loud in the direction of Windflower.

"I don't know that he was murdered," said Windflower. "Doc Sanjay is still looking at the body, the last time I checked. But he's certainly dead."

"People have been calling in already," said Betsy. "One of the neighbours saw the police cars. Now everybody knows that something is going on. They're speculating that it's murder."

"They can speculate all they want. Right now, we have a death and we'll work through the process. We haven't even got a certified death yet," said Windflower.

Betsy handed him his messages. He scanned them quickly. There was one from Inspector Ron Quigley in Marystown and another from Sheila. He decided to call his home boss first.

"Hi Sheila, what's up?"

"Winston, can you pick up some diapers on the way home? I didn't know a creature this small could make so much poop."

Windflower laughed. "Oh, the joys of being a parent. I'll drop them off sometime today, but we've got a problem that I have to deal with right now."

"That's too bad," said Sheila. "I was hoping you could drop by for lunch. I've got a pot of pea soup going. I'll leave it on the stove, so you can get some whenever you can come by."

"Thanks, appreciate it. We've had a suspicious death that I have to look into. But I'll pop by sometime this afternoon."

"We're not going anywhere," said Sheila, not asking any more questions. She knew that her husband would tell her what he could when he could. "I love you, Winston."

"I love you, too, Sheila."

Windflower hung up the phone, missing Sheila and her pot of pea soup, and called Ron Quigley in Marystown.

"Good morning, Sergeant. How's the beautiful town of Grand Bank today?"

"Morning, Ron," said Windflower. There was no need for formality between the two long-time friends. They had known each other and worked together too long for that. "Well, as I look out the window, I'd say Grand Bank has disappeared into a giant fog bank. But other than that, I am well."

"How's that beautiful baby of yours?"

"Both mother and daughter are absolutely gorgeous and doing well, thank you. The same can't be said, however, for one Jacob Crowder. He is lying dead at his kitchen table, surrounded by blood, most of it his by the looks of it. Doc Sanjay is there right now. I'd say, judging by the aroma, that he's been dead a couple of days. Not likely self-inflicted."

"In Grand Bank? Nothing much ever happens in Grand Bank."

"I know. And we had a young guy kind of attempt suicide last night. I'm not sure if it wasn't simply a cry for help. But, it's not good. It seems like things go along swimmingly and then everything breaks open at once. I'm kind of afraid to see what's next. It's like 'Hell is empty and all the devils are here.'"

"Trouble does seem to come in bunches. We've had some mental health issues with young people over here as well. What do you think is going on?"

"I'm no expert in this, but I'd say that some of our young folks don't see a great future for themselves. And even though they have all the latest tools and gadgets, they don't seem very happy. And I think they're bored. I asked Tizzard to do some research into mental health resources, and I know the Town is doing the same thing."

"That's good. Keep Tizzard busy. He's driving me crazy to get back to work on a full-time basis."

"Can you do anything about that? Move it along? He seems ready."

"Paperwork and medical approvals," sighed Quigley. Windflower could hear the exasperation in his voice.

"I'll make some more calls today," promised Quigley, now anxious to move onto another topic. "In the meantime, the reason I called you is to tell you I've got a new second-in-command, at least for the short term."

"That's not going to make Tizzard happy," said Windflower. "That's his job."

"He might be, when he finds out who it is. Carrie Evanchuk," said Quigley.

"His girlfriend, Carrie? How'd you swing that?"

"She applied, on compassionate grounds, to be closer to Tizzard. I guess she's had the request in since she was here at Christmas. It came to me and I said yes. She'll be here next week and will stay until the end of the year."

"Wow. I'm guessing he doesn't know."

"No, and keep it under your hat for now. I talked to Carrie this morning, and she'll call him herself. And keep me posted on the Crowder case. If it's murder, then we'll have to work with the media. We can look after most of that from over here if you send the info. Anyway, I have to go. 'Brevity is the soul of wit.'"

"I will. Thanks, Ron. Talk soon."

Great to have a boss who shares one's love of the Bard, thought Windflower. It doesn't make things easier, but it does make them more pleasant.

"Doctor Sanjay is on line one," came Betsy's voice over the intercom.

"Windflower."

"I thought you would like to be the first, after me of course, to learn that Jacob Wayne Crowder, aged 31, died of massive hemorrhaging after being stabbed repeatedly."

"How long has he been dead?" asked Windflower.

"A couple of days, for sure. I'll give you a better estimate after the examination. Can I give the green light to remove the body?"

"Sure," said Windflower. "Thanks, Doc."

After he hung up, he called Betsy into his office. But she was already on her way. She stood in the doorway of his office with her notepad. By the look in her eyes, he knew this was going to be a long day.

NINE

We need to find and notify next of kin," said Windflower.

"I believe Elizabeth Crowder is living in Brampton," said Betsy. "His father has been dead many years. Elizabeth was back a few years ago by herself for a visit. She said it was her good-bye tour. She came in by taxi and stayed with one of her cousins. I think she's a model or something. There may still be a few Ryans around, but most go by their married names now. I can get the contact info from them."

"Can you call forensics?"

Betsy raised an eyebrow at Windflower. "I called them when the incident was first reported. I know it takes time for them to get here. Corporal Brown called back. Here's his number," said Betsy.

"And the media?"

"There's lots of them calling already. I told them that Marys-town would be putting out a statement. So, I suspect they're lined up over there waiting for news."

"You are the best, Betsy. Let me scribble down a few notes and I'll get you to write it up and send it over. Thanks very much. I'm sure we could never get by without you."

Betsy beamed at her boss and went off to carry out her tasks with a broad smile across her face.

Windflower wrote up the basic information to be included in the press release. Betsy would make it legible and Media Relations would put it into the proper format. He'd have to deal with the media later, he knew, but this would give them time to properly set up the investigation without being pressured.

"What's Betsy so happy about?" asked Jones.

"She's just happy in the service," said Windflower. "We could all learn from Betsy about improving our attitude."

"Okay," said Jones, more reluctantly than Windflower would have hoped. "How can I help?"

"We need to make sure we keep the scene intact," said Windflower. "Can you go and relieve Tizzard and tell him to come back here? Have you seen Smithson?"

"He's a bit shook up. Being the first on the scene is always difficult. I don't think he's done that before," said Jones.

"You have?" asked Windflower.

"Back home and in Thunder Bay," she responded. "It's never easy, but you get used to it somehow. Just part of the job."

Windflower nodded. "Okay, thanks. Can you give this note to Betsy? I've got to call forensics."

Jones left, and Windflower picked up the phone and called the number Betsy had given him.

"Brown, here."

"Good morning, Ted. How's she goin' b'y?"

"That's good, Winston," said Corporal Ted Brown of the RCMP Forensics Unit. "Pretty soon you'll be a real Newfoundlander."

"I've been here almost ten years," said Windflower. "Surely I've paid my dues by now."

"You get my vote," said Brown, laughing.

"So, where are you guys today?"

"We're finishing up a crash on the highway near Avondale. A young man and his girlfriend went off the road. Both died. It looks like he might have been texting. That's why they called us. They want the pictures and evidence for their campaign."

"That's tough," said Windflower, taking a deep breath. "When can you get over here?"

"I've got the backup crew coming to pick me up later today. We'll be there tonight and ready to go first thing in the morning."

"Great. I'll have some people there to help out."

Tizzard was Windflower's next visitor. He heard him speed into the RCMP parking lot and come to an abrupt stop. Windflower could recognize Tizzard's driving style every time. Fast and faster was his motto, and his injuries from last year's shooting, as severe as they were, did not slow him down one bit. That shooting had shaken Windflower to his core. Tizzard had located a desperado high on coke and on the run and had taken three bullets for his troubles. But he was clearly on the mend.

"Carrie's coming to Marystown," he blurted out when he saw Windflower.

"I heard from the inspector this morning. That's great news."

"And I'm starved. I'll buy you a bowl of soup."

"You're always hungry," said Windflower with a laugh. "I'd love some soup. You can tell me all about Carrie."

Minutes later the pair were walking into the Mug-Up café. It was noisy and warm from the mingling of people and cooking, and to Windflower's grumbling stomach, it smelled great. The small café grew quiet as the Mounties found the last remaining table. They may have been hoping to overhear a tidbit of news from the cops about what everybody was talking about—a murder in Grand Bank.

But the Mounties talked about the women in their lives, which reminded Windflower he had to pick up diapers on the way home. Usually, he would have a chance to play with Amelia Louise or take her for a spin around the block in her stroller. But not today. Much more grim tasks lay ahead. But he was happy to share in Eddie Tizzard's good news. He needed it.

Tizzard almost didn't make it last year and here he was, looking as good as ever and talking as fast as he drove his car. He only slowed down when Herb Stoodley came to take his order. "I'll have moose soup and a roll please, Herb," said Tizzard.

"Same for me," said Windflower. "And a cup of coffee. How's Moira?"

Herb and Moira Stoodley were the proprietors of the Mug-Up. They had bought it from Sheila, who sold it after a serious car accident, and the two couples were close and fast friends.

"She's in the back, slaving away. I get the easy job of standing out here and looking pretty," said Stoodley. "How's that precious child of yours?"

"She's a doll," said Windflower. "Some days I think I'd like to quit my job and stay home with her."

"You can do that now," said Tizzard. "You can get paternity

leave so that the father can stay home with the baby. You can take half or more of the time off and get most of your salary while you're doing it."

"Is that right?" quipped Stoodley. "Are you thinking about having a baby any time soon?"

"Carrie is coming back here, at least to Marystown," said Windflower. "Maybe there's something Eddie's not telling us."

Herb Stoodley walked away laughing while Tizzard turned a bright red in his chair.

"I'm glad Carrie is coming back," said Windflower. "And I talked to the inspector this morning."

"What did he say?" asked Tizzard. "Can I go back to work?"

"He said he would check again. He thinks it's just paperwork. By the way, it looks like you're already shoving your way back in."

"Inching is more like it," said Tizzard. "My Dad said that it was okay to nudge but not to take advantage. That's my strategy. By the way, some of the locals have a theory floating around about the late Jacob Crowder."

Tizzard paused and waited for Windflower's reaction.

"Spill the beans, Eddie," said Windflower as Herb Stoodley came back with his coffee.

"Patience is the companion of wisdom," replied Tizzard.

"Is that your Dad's saying?" asked Windflower.

"Nope," said Tizzard. "It's Saint Augustine's." But not wishing to run out his luck with his old boss, he quickly added, "There's a ghost."

"A ghost?" asked Windflower, almost spitting out his coffee. "A ghost killed Crowder?"

"Two people who live on the street came up to me while I was there. They said it was the ghost lady."

"The ghost lady?" Windflower was anxious to hear more. "What are you talking about?"

"Folks in town have seen a mysterious lady walking around late on foggy nights. When they try and talk to her or approach her, she runs away. Disappears into the fog. They think she's evil and that she's brought evil on our town. Now she's killed young Crowder," said Tizzard.

"I don't know where people get all this," said Windflower. "But there are no ghosts, and science and Doctor Sanjay will determine what happened to Jacob Crowder."

"I'm only telling you what they told me," said Tizzard as their soup arrived.

Windflower shook his head and blew on his soup to cool it. There was little more said as the men dug into the thick chunks of meat and sipped on the hearty broth in their moose soup. The rolls were homemade and oozed steam when they broke them open to butter them. Windflower thought about asking for another one but then reserved himself for the possibility of dessert.

When Herb Stoodley came back to get their empty bowls, Windflower inquired about the options for an after-lunch treat.

"We've got cupcakes and a few kinds of cheesecake," said Stoodley. "No fancy cupcakes, just vanilla and chocolate. But there's strawberry, red velvet, blueberry, and chocolate-peanut butter cheesecake."

"I'll have the chocolate-peanut butter," said Windflower, feeling particularly pleased that they had his favourite. "How about you, Eddie?" he asked.

"I'll have the blueberry," he said, after thinking long and hard about his choices.

Stoodley came back with their desserts and topped up Windflower's coffee. The lunch crowd had thinned out, so he sat down with the Mounties and poured himself a cup.

"Shocking about young Crowder," he said, trying to pry what information he could from the police officers.

Tizzard started to speak, but he could feel Windflower's energy, like a hand on his shoulder. So, he stayed quiet and let the prying comment pass.

Windflower finished the last crumbs of his cheesecake and sighed. "That was sum good b'y," he said. The other two men laughed. Then he spoke to Stoodley's question. "Did you know Jacob Crowder?" he asked.

"I think I met him twice," said Stoodley. "Once when he first arrived around here. And then another time he asked me to hold a parcel for the taxi to take into St. John's. But he never came by to eat or even to have coffee. I only knew he was in town when I saw his van in the driveway."

"There was no van in the driveway, boss," said Tizzard.

"A Dodge minivan. Blue, fairly new, Newfoundland plates," said Stoodley.

"That's helpful," said Windflower. "Better than ghost stories."

Tizzard looked miffed, but was pleased when Stoodley intervened.

"There's a long history of ghosts in this area," said Stoodley. "Most people believe in them, too. It's what happens when so many men and boys get lost at sea. They want to believe that they are coming back to visit them. The most famous ghosts are women, though."

"Really," said Windflower, always interested to hear more about the town's history.

"Charlotte Harris was the wife of George C. Harris. His father, Samuel Harris, built the Harris House across the street. The son and his wife both died in the same year, 1954, but it's said that Lottie still walks the floors late at night to watch out for men who might come back from the sea. Nobody lived there for years because of it, and finally they turned it into a museum."

"What about the B&B?" asked Windflower. "Any ghosts in there we should know about?"

"I thought you would've known the history of that place, since you bought it," said Tizzard.

"I know some of it," said Windflower. "Just not all of the folklore. I know that it was built by Captain John Thornhill, who originally lived on Brunette Island across the way. I also know the story about him building his house with lumber from a shipwreck and that it eventually became a hotel."

"All of that is true," said Stoodley. "But you know the house. Didn't you see that it had no master bedroom? Apparently, Captain Thornhill and his wife, Diane, used to move around the house and use whatever bedroom their guests didn't want. It's said that Diane Matthews, the ghost lady, still walks around every night looking for a place to sleep."

Tizzard looked at Windflower as if to say "I told you so," but wisely kept that idea to himself.

"Thank you, Herb, for the fine lunch and the history," said Windflower. "But we've got to get back to work."

The two RCMP officers paid their bill at the cash and went back outside to enjoy the sun, which had finally managed to break through the fog.

"I want you to check on the van," said Windflower.

"Does that mean I'm part of the investigation?" asked Tizzard.

"It means that you find the van," said Windflower. "That's it. Now I've got to go pick up some stuff and drop it off at the house. I'll see you back at the shop."

Tizzard still went away happy, speeding off before Windflower had even opened his Jeep's door. Windflower smiled and drove to Shoppers Drug Mart. He picked up a large box of diapers and drove to his house. He was hoping for some playtime with Amelia Louise, but Sheila had nodded off on the couch, and the baby was also asleep in the bassinet downstairs. He watched them quietly for a few minutes, then walked out into the kitchen where the aroma of Sheila's still-hot pea soup almost made him want to sit down and have a bowl. But he was full of the cheesecake, so he headed back to work.

TEN

Constable Harry Frost was talking to Betsy when Windflower arrived. “Anything new?” asked Windflower.

“Smithson is gone home, said he wasn’t feeling well,” said Frost, almost with a smirk.

“There’s nothing funny about being upset at seeing a dead, decomposing body,” said Windflower. “It’s a natural reaction. Why don’t you go over and relieve Jones? I need her to talk to the principal at the high school.”

“I could do that,” said Frost.

“We need somebody more sensitive at the school,” said Windflower, annoyed. “And I want you to stay over there until the forensics guys get there. They won’t start until the morning, but Corporal Brown might want to take a look around.”

Frost left and Betsy gave Windflower his messages. There were five from the media and one from Ron Quigley.

“I guess they’ve been calling,” said Windflower.

“Those are only the ones who left messages. I hope Media Relations is on this,” said Betsy.

“I’ll talk to the inspector,” said Windflower. “I don’t want to talk to any of them until forensics has a chance to look around. Anything on next of kin?”

“I’ve got a number for Elizabeth Crowder. I was guessing you’d want to talk to her.”

Windflower didn’t want to talk to the dead man’s mother. That was the last thing he wanted to do. But that was his job. Better get that out of the way first so he could give the information to Marystown.

He called the 905 number that Betsy had given him.

"Hello," came a woman's voice on the end of the line.

"Good morning. Is this Elizabeth Crowder?"

"Yes, who's calling, please?"

"It's Sergeant Winston Windflower calling from the RCMP detachment in Grand Bank. I have some sad news for you. Something has happened to your son, Jacob. He's dead." It was cold and it was fast, but Windflower knew from experience that it was better this way—for him and for the person he was calling. There was no good way to deliver bad news, especially this type of bad news.

He waited for a reaction but heard nothing on the other end of the line. "Are you okay, Ma'am?" he asked, as gently as he could.

Finally, he heard a long sigh from the other end of the line. "I'm okay," said the woman. "A little surprised, but not totally shocked."

"What do you mean?"

"I haven't seen Jacob in a long time. We aren't close. It's a long story, but he became more than I could handle or help. But he did call me about a month ago. He asked for help."

"What kind of help?"

"Money, as always."

"Did you give it to him?"

"No, we were long past that discussion. He was always scheming. Scams, I called them. I suspected he was going to use the money to buy drugs or pay off his dealer again."

"Did he have a problem with drugs?"

"You should know. He's been in jail."

Windflower paused. He should have checked Crowder's criminal record. He made a note. "What did he say he needed the money for this time?"

"Something about an international trading system and developing a new form of currency. I didn't really understand. Was he murdered, Sergeant?"

"We don't know that yet. We've just started our investigation. I can call you when I know more."

The woman had nothing more than "okay" to say to that.

Windflower said goodbye and hung up the phone. Well, that was interesting, he thought. Normally, people want to know what happened, and it was not unusual for Windflower to have to comfort people. Elizabeth Crowder almost expected the news and didn't seem too upset by it, either. People handle grief in their own way was his best explanation. That would have to do for now.

He called Betsy and got her to put Jacob Crowder's name into the national database for criminal activity, charges, and convictions. Then he phoned Marystown and got patched through to Inspector Ron Quigley.

"Good morning, Sergeant. I hope you have something to give me to feed the media. They are howling at my door."

"Good news then, Inspector. I can confirm the name of the deceased. He is Jacob Crowder, resident of Grand Bank, age 31. I'll have more once we get effects back from the clinic."

"Next of kin?" asked Quigley.

"Mother, Elizabeth Crowder. She's in Ontario. Didn't seem surprised or even upset at the early demise of her son. She says he has a record. I'm checking that out."

"Well, we don't know what goes on behind families' walls. He may have given her reason to doubt his good will."

"Kind of sounds something like that. Anyway, Brown is coming tonight, and they'll be on the ground tomorrow. We should know more once they have a look around and we get the report from Sanjay. All we have so far is a dead body and some ghost stories."

"I love ghost stories. Sometimes there is an element of the truth in what people say, even when they talk about things like magic or ghosts. 'There is no darkness but ignorance.'"

"True, 'But modest doubt is call'd the beacon of the wise.'"

"Touché," said Quigley. "I have to go feed the wolves."

ELEVEN

Windflower was feeling particularly pleased with himself, having out-dueled his superior officer, when he heard what he thought was a cat outside his window. When he got up to investigate, he soon realized that it was inside and being chased around by Betsy and Jones, who was back from the crime scene.

He saw a blur of black and gray whiz by him and scoot into the kitchen. He calmly walked to the kitchen and closed the door.

"What's going on here?"

"It's a cat," said Betsy.

Windflower turned to Jones.

"I was standing outside the Crowder house and I heard her scratching the door. When I opened it she ran out. I thought she would run away, but she just sat there shivering and looking at me. So, I brought her here. We have to feed her at least," said Jones.

"I think you have to catch her first," said Windflower. "Then give her some water and get her some dry cat food from the store. Feed her a little at a time, even if she wants more. And check her for fleas."

"Where'd you find out so much about cats?" asked Betsy. "I thought you were a dog person."

"I'm a man of many talents," said Windflower. "Like an iceberg. You can only see what's on top."

Both women rolled their eyes as Windflower opened the door.

The cat ran right between his legs and he almost fell over trying to grab her. Luckily, Jones was a bit faster and managed to grab the cat's collar as it went past. She expertly pulled the cat up by the ruff and held it in the air meowing to be released. Betsy opened the door to one of the cells, and Jones laid the cat inside and closed the door.

"I guess cat catching isn't one of your many talents," said Jones. "I'll go get the cat food."

"Come see me when you get back," said Windflower as he walked back to his office. Note to self, he thought. Engage brain before speaking.

Jones was soon back with a bag of dried cat food along with a box and kitty litter. She and Betsy were cooing over the new detachment addition as the cat ate hungrily and drank its fill. They were even more sympathetic when the cat threw up all it had just consumed. They made it a bed with a blanket and watched it curl up and fall to sleep.

"No, we're not keeping the cat," said Windflower when Jones came into his office. "It can stay tonight and tomorrow you will take it over to the animal shelter. Some family will get a fine pet."

Jones started to protest, but Windflower held his hand up in the universal sign for "Stop talking because no one is listening." She got the message, held her tongue, and sat down in front of him.

"I want you to go over to the high school and talk to the principal and the guidance counsellor. Do they still call them that?"

"I think so. They did in Thunder Bay," said Jones. "Is this about the Parsons kid?"

"Yes. But I also want to know if they're having other problems and what kind of supports they have. The Town Council is doing the same thing. But ask around about Levi Parsons and if they knew he was in trouble."

"I suspect that if one kid is in trouble, there are at least one or two more," said Jones. "That was the way it was in Thunder Bay. It was like they fed off each other's negative energy and anxiety. There was a comfort in not being alone with the pain. Sometimes that energy turned bad quickly. We had a number of copycats."

"I saw the same thing back home in Pink Lake. That's why we need to take whatever action we can now. There might be other young people at risk."

Jones stood to leave. "Are you sure we can't keep her? We think her name is Molly. At least that's what was on her dish. Not that there was any food in it." Before Windflower could get his hand up, Jones continued. "Just for a couple of days. Nobody will adopt an older cat like this—they all want kittens. We'll look after her, and we'll find a home for her, I promise."

Windflower thought about saying no, but now that he knew the cat's name, it was a bit harder. He knew Jones was right. Older cats would be put to sleep if no one claimed them after a while. "You have until after the weekend," he said. "On Monday the cat's gone, one way or another. Someone will still have to take her over to the vet in Marystown and get her checked out."

"I'll do that tomorrow," said Jones. "I'm going over to see Carrie anyway."

"Is Evanchuk here already?"

"She gets into Marystown in the morning. She's in St. John's tonight. This will work out perfectly. Thank you so much, sir."

Windflower didn't have any chance to react to this last comment before Jones had scooted out to tell Betsy the good news. She must have been pleased, too, because when Windflower left a while later, she gave him a huge smile. Windflower recognized that as the "he finally did the right thing" smile. He didn't get it often, but when he did, it was a big deal. He managed to get out before Betsy could formally thank him with one of her momma hugs and was soon on his way back home to see Sheila and their beautiful daughter.

He said a quick hello to Lady, with a promise of more later. He could hear Sheila taking the baby out of her little bath. She called him upstairs, and he carried Amelia Louise in her towel back to their bed. He looked directly into her eyes and wondered if the baby knew he was her father. It didn't matter. She was simply amazing.

He was grateful that he had this time with his wife and baby awake at the same time. He was also grateful that Sheila didn't ask him right away what was going on at work. He needed this special time just to survive right now. His sanity might depend on it. He got to put the baby powder and clean diaper on his daughter and to tuck her into a pink sleeper. She looked happy and grateful, too.

"She is such a blessing," said Windflower as he handed the baby back to her mother.

Sheila smiled and nodded her agreement. "We are pretty lucky." Amelia Louise seemed to agree as she yawned the longest yawn a little baby could make. Both Sheila and Windflower laughed as their daughter closed her eyes and went back to sleep.

"So, how was your day?" Sheila asked, after she had put the baby back into her bassinet.

"Let's have a cup of tea," said Windflower. "And maybe a bowl of that pea soup, if there's any left. It's been a long day."

TWELVE

"I don't even know what day it is," said Windflower.

"Wednesday," said Sheila. "Although all the days kind of blend together. I only know it's Wednesday because yesterday was the council meeting. Let me warm up the soup."

Sheila turned the soup on and cut up a small basket of crusty bread. She placed that, along with a cheese plate and some butter, on the table. Windflower took a piece of bread, buttered it, and added a large chunk of Five Counties cheese on top. When Sheila put the teapot on the table, he poured them both a cup.

"Jacob Crowder is dead," he said after he finished his first piece of bread and reached for another. "Did you know him?"

"I don't think I ever met him," said Sheila. "I knew the family, of course, but they moved away a long time ago, even before he was born. What happened?"

"I think he was murdered. We found him in his house. He must have been in there a few days. It wasn't pretty. Young Smithson found him. He's pretty shook up."

"I can imagine. It's strange that I haven't met him. Can't even remember seeing him. That's weird. I'm the mayor. I know everybody."

Windflower laughed. "I've never seen him either, except for today. Anyway, that will keep us busy for a few days. And I went over to see the Parsons family today."

"How did that go?" asked Sheila as she passed him a bowl of pea soup.

"The kid is scared, the mother is upset, and the father is angry. They will all need help."

"We don't have the supports for any of them in this community. I know we're a small town, but without help, we're going to be in big trouble.Bigger than what we have now. I've got the staff looking into getting more resources, but I'm thinking we might want to have a community meeting about it."

"That's a great idea. Jones is going to the high school, and I've got Tizzard checking out resources as well. Maybe we could partner up for the meeting with the clinic. I know Doc Sanjay would be interested. And I almost forgot to tell you, Carrie Evanchuk is being assigned to Marystown."

"Wow, that's great news. Eddie must be happy."

Windflower took a sip of soup, but it was still too hot to drink. He settled for another piece of bread and cheese, this time the Stilton with the mango pieces that was his absolute favourite.

"I haven't talked to him about it, but I bet he will be," said Windflower. He's been a bit lost being off work, and this will help. I'm happy for him. And, I think we have a new cat."

"What? I didn't think you liked cats."

"It's not that I don't like cats. I don't think they like me. They always stare at me like they want to do me harm."

"So, you're afraid of cats." His wife wanted to get right to the point.

"I'm not afraid," Windflower protested. "It's just that I think that they know what I'm thinking. Anyway, it'll only be for a few days until we find it a new owner."

"That's what you said when we got Lady."

"This will be different. Now, can't a man eat his bowl of soup in peace?"

Sheila laughed and went upstairs to check on the baby.

Windflower finished his soup and sopped up the last drops with the remaining piece of bread. He went upstairs and watched over Sheila's shoulder as she lay on the bed and watched their daughter sleep. He curled up behind her and held her as he felt her slowly drift off too. When she was asleep he went downstairs where Lady was waiting, not very patiently, for her share of his attention.

Windflower and Lady took a walk down to the beach and followed the narrow path that led up through the cove towards the Cape. The Cape was once a popular hiking path that had been officially closed for a few years because a previous town council had decided they didn't want the liability of the steep and rocky terrain.

But some people still used it as part of their daily or weekly exercise regime.

Many years ago, it had been the main and closest route between Grand Bank and Fortune, and many weekends teenagers from both communities used it as their gateway to the local dances. There was a more formal pathway then, big enough to allow a horse and carriage to bring supplies from the bigger town of Grand Bank over to Fortune. This evening the traffic was much lighter, with only Windflower and his dog at the bottom and a couple of stragglers making their way down from the peak.

Lady would have been quite happy to run up the trail to greet them, but Windflower didn't have that kind of time today. Instead, he put her back on her leash and led her back towards the main road. They walked down through town, which made Lady very happy. She seemed to relish the idea of showing her master off and even enjoyed the barks and yips that marked their passage. They were about to take their usual turn down towards the brook when Windflower pulled her back and led her up Tim's Lane.

Frost was in the driveway and there were several neighbours gathered round him. Frost shooed them away when he saw Windflower coming down the lane.

"Everything under control?" asked Windflower.

"It's good," said Frost. "I was talking to some of the neighbours. One of them said that a car would often arrive at night. But whoever came would be gone by the morning. They never got a good look at them because it was too dark."

"What kind of vehicle?" asked Windflower.

"A panel van. Said they thought it looked like a rental." said Frost.

"What about Crowder's van?"

"Didn't say. I can ask around."

"That'd be good," said Windflower, pulling Lady back up the road and towards home. They passed along by the wharf and then the old B&B. Windflower paused and looked up. He thought he saw a shadow pass by an open window and then realized it was only a curtain blowing in the wind. Even though it was a mild Newfoundland evening, he felt a cool breeze in his hair. It's probably just the fog, he thought. Just the fog.

THIRTEEN

Windflower tip-toed upstairs where both his girls were gently sleeping. He smiled at them and left as quickly as he could. Lady got a rub on her belly and a Milk-Bone biscuit. Everybody was safe now, he thought, as he headed back towards work. That, in itself, was a great comfort.

Tizzard was sitting with his feet up on Windflower's desk when he arrived. He quickly put the phone down and stood up. "How's it going, boss? I was talking with Carrie. She's coming over this weekend. Isn't that great news?"

"It is indeed," said Windflower. "You should come over for dinner at the B&B."

"You're not going to make anything vegan, are you?" asked Tizzard. "A man could starve on that stuff."

"No," said Windflower with a laugh. "I was thinking about fish and chicken and some salad and vegetables. You don't mind if we have a few veggies, do you?"

"Nah, I guess that would be all right."

"Did you make any headway on the vehicle?"

"The neighbours say that they haven't seen it for a few days. They thought Crowder was away."

"That's what Frost heard, too. There may have been another vehicle visiting that house. Might be a rental van."

"If they rented it on the island, it's pretty easy to track. I can get Betsy on that in the morning. She's a crackerjack at that stuff."

"Good. What about your mental health research?"

"Not much. It's not an area that our government has invested much money in. Eastern Health has a mental health unit in Marystown and recently opened a walk-in clinic. But when I talked to them, they sounded understaffed and overwhelmed."

Jones walked in while the two men were talking. "That's exactly what the principal said. They have one counsellor for over 200 students," she told them.

"And they're now focused on the opioid crisis and trying to keep people alive," added Tizzard. "Their biggest problem is that they have no resources for awareness or prevention. So they just lurch from one emergency to another."

"Sounds like us," said Windflower.

"They're worried over at the high school," said Jones. "A 14-year-old overdosed on her mother's sleeping pills. She's okay, but they think that others might be in similar trouble. They know that once one kid does something like this, it gives others an idea."

"What about Levi Parsons? Did they know what was going on with him?" asked Windflower.

"They said he was different. I think they meant he was gay. But he hasn't told them that, so they're not going to out him."

"Wow," said Windflower. "I can understand why he wouldn't tell anybody. His father would go crazy."

All three RCMP officers were silent as they contemplated that situation. "Okay," said Windflower, breaking the reverie. "Jones, I want you to take the lead on this. Get Tizzard's contacts and see if we can't get someone from Eastern Health to come in and talk to us. Not only us, but the clinic, and the Council, and the high school, and anybody else who is interested in improving mental health services in this community."

"What about me?" asked Tizzard.

"You're not technically at work," said Windflower. "Plus, I thought you'd want a few days off with your girlfriend."

Tizzard almost blushed and started to stammer. Windflower cut him off. "You keep looking for Jacob Crowder's car, and I might let you help out forensics."

Both Tizzard and Jones went away happy. Finally having a few minutes to himself, Windflower started thinking about one of his other favourite things: food and, more particularly, what he would need for his cooking on the weekend. He loved eating, but he also loved cooking. He turned on his computer and opened some of his special cooking links. One of the best was by the famous chef Jamie

Oliver. Windflower had had great success using his suggestions. They were tasty, well presented and, best of all, relatively easy to prepare.

He scanned the list of recipes and checked the ingredients. One of the challenges of living in a small community was not being able to get arugula or many fresh cheeses. But he could get fish and he could get chicken. He found a fish soup, along with a nice-looking fennel salad, on the Oliver website. Then he switched and got a few more recipes to try out. There was a red curry shrimp dish and chicken with garlic and tomatoes. He added one more pasta dish to his recipe list and now he at least had a plan.

He was contemplating all that delicious food when the phone rang. It was Frost.

"Sarge, I wanted to let you know that the forensics guys are here. At least Corporal Brown is. He's having a look around. Thought you'd want to know."

"Thanks," said Windflower. "I'll be right over."

When he arrived, Frost was talking to several men who were standing by an unmarked white cube van. Windflower recognized them as the forensics crew. Frost pointed inside. Windflower waved hello to the forensics guys and walked into the house.

The stench was still pretty awful. He saw a man with a mask and white overalls and assumed he was Brown. He motioned to him and went outside to breathe.

"That is pretty ripe," said Corporal Ted Brown after he took off his mask. He rolled down his overalls to cool off. "Warm, too."

"See anything?" asked Windflower.

"Not too much," said Brown. "We'll start in the morning. I like to start by having a quick look around first. Sometimes something will hit you when you are by yourself. I did notice that it's pretty quiet. Lots of blood but not much of it spread around."

"What does that tell you? No struggle?"

"Maybe. But it also could have been a surprise. The dead person probably wasn't expecting this to happen. Who was he?"

"Loner. Guy by the name of Jacob Crowder. His family was from around here. We're not really sure what he was doing. Something on the Internet. Can you guys have a look at his computer?"

"Sure. We've got a crackerjack techie. Loves playing around with that stuff."

"Great. Did you guys get a spot to stay?"

"We're at Granny's up the road. We were hoping to stay at your B&B, but they said it wasn't open."

"First of July for the rooms. But we're open for dinner on the weekends."

"We'll be gone by then, I hope," said Brown with a laugh. "Anyway, we're going to Fortune for fish and chips. Wanna come?"

"Can't tonight, sorry. See you in the morning." Windflower turned to leave. "Can you do me a big favour?" he asked Brown. "Park your van in the driveway and put the tape up outside? That way my guy can go home."

"Sure, no worries," said Brown. "See you in the morning."

FOURTEEN

Windflower told a relieved Frost that he was off the hook for sentry duty and followed him back to the detachment. Jones and Tizzard had left for the day, and Frost was on the evening shift until Smithson came in around midnight. Frost went out to do his first tour around town and a quick highway patrol. Windflower finally had the place to himself.

Almost alone, anyway. He had just started to work on his stack of paper when he heard her. He walked down the hallway towards the cells and Molly the cat was sitting in her cell staring back at him. Her eyes almost glowed, and she mewed at him in a soft, almost pleading manner. Windflower checked, but her food and water bowls were nearly full. Then he realized what was going on. She was lonely.

He opened the door, and she stayed there, perfectly still. But when he reached out his hand she came towards him, gently and slowly. She rubbed herself against his leg and purred as he stroked her neck. She looked up at him, and if a cat could smile, she smiled at Windflower. That's when he realized he might soon have another female in his family.

Molly followed Windflower back to his office and wandered around, exploring her new surroundings. She was still there when Frost came back from his rounds.

"Got a new pet, boss?" he asked.

"She's only staying for a few days, 'til we find her a new home," said Windflower, almost stammering.

Frost picked up on that cue and smiled. "Looks like she's pretty comfortable here."

"I was just taking her back into her cell," said Windflower, as he picked up the cat and carried her back down the hall. He placed her on her bed inside the cell and, despite himself, couldn't resist giving her one more rub before he closed the door.

He was back in his office when he heard someone at the detachment front door. He walked out as a paramedic was leaving and Frost was carrying in a clear plastic bag.

"Crowder's possessions," said Frost. "Should I bring them over to Brown?"

"Make a copy of the list and give it to me," said Windflower. "Then pop it over to the truck."

Frost returned with the paper and handed it to Windflower. As he started reading it, Windflower could hear Frost leave the parking lot. Various types of clothing, a vaping machine, rolling papers, keys and a key chain, a wallet with ID and credit cards, a small amount of money, and an expired passport. The paramedic who had handled Jacob Crowder's personal effects noted that this passport wasn't Jacob Crowder's. It was a Canadian passport in the name of one Robert Pritchard.

Windflower would have loved to have taken a closer look at this passport. But he knew he couldn't tamper with the chain of evidence. A passport was an ideal document to pick fingerprints from. One would assume that at least two people had handled this—the original owner and Crowder. But there may have been someone else with their fingerprints on their evidence. He highlighted the item on the list and left it on his desk to talk to Brown about in the morning.

What was Crowder doing with someone else's passport? How did he get it? He was puzzling over this passport question when Sheila called.

"Your girls miss you," she said.

"Man, I miss you so much," said Windflower. "Do you know Robert Pritchard?"

"That's a strange question," said Sheila. "I knew Bob Pritchard. He was married to Barb Pritchard. You know her from the church. He died of a heart attack last year sometime. Why?"

"His name came up in an investigation. Not his name, exactly. More like his passport," said Windflower.

"Why would anyone have Bob Pritchard's passport?"

"That's what I'm trying to figure out."

"Well, good luck with that. I called to see when you might be coming home. I had the last of the soup, but I am a bit peckish now."

"I'm starved. I've been so busy that I really didn't think about it."

"I could see what's in the freezer and maybe find something to heat up if you can get here."

"I'll be there soon," said Windflower. It was wishful thinking. Fifteen minutes later he was in the process of shutting down his computer when Smithson popped into his office.

"You're not on 'til 12," said Windflower.

"I saw your Jeep out front and wondered if you had a few minutes for me," said Smithson.

Windflower almost asked if it could wait until morning. Then he saw the hang-dog look in Smithson's eyes.

"Sure," he said. "Sit down."

Smithson started talking and it looked like he was going to cry.

"That's my first time," he said. "Finding the dead body, by myself. I mean, I've seen dead bodies before. It's just that it's been with other people. This one kinda shook me up. And the smell. Oh my God. It was awful. I can't get that smell off of me and I . . ."

"It's okay," said Windflower. "This isn't easy for any of us. You may even have dreams about this for a few days. That's a perfectly normal reaction to a trauma or witnessing one."

"It is?"

"Even for me. It's part of our job; what we do. But that doesn't mean we don't feel it or have reactions to it. We're human. The best thing we can do is to allow ourselves to have these feelings and to talk about them. Just like you're doing right now."

"But I thought people would think I'm weak."

"There is no weakness in asking for help. That's why I'm here. We support each other. I may have to ask you for help sometime."

"Really?" asked Smithson, clearly feeling better about himself.

"Absolutely," said Windflower. "The other secret is to get back on the horse as quickly as you can after a fall. Glad to see you're back at work tonight. But go home and get a rest or watch TV or something before Frost gets back and gets you to do his work for him."

Both men were laughing now. "You know I'm going to miss Frost. He's like my big brother. A bit mean sometimes, but I know he'll look after me," Smithson said.

"Is everything set up for his party tomorrow night at the pub?" asked Windflower.

"Yeah, I've been helping Betsy. We've got some snacks from the Mug-Up and a cake. That was a great gift you thought of. He's always talking about going fishin' on the Assiniboine River when he gets back home."

"Luckily, we found a company in Peterborough that will ship the canoe to him when he gets there. All I had to do was to get him a paddle."

"It'll be fun. Goodnight, sir, and thank you."

"No worries," said Windflower. "Now, I've got to get home before Frost gets me to do his work, too."

FIFTEEN

Windflower and Smithson left together. When he got home, Windflower was greeted by three of his favourite things. Sheila gave him a warm embrace, Lady circled him like a long-lost relative, and the smells from the kitchen drove him nearly crazy.

"What is that?" he asked. "It smells fantastic."

"That's the garlic bread," said Sheila. "It's one of those frozen sticks, but they fill the house quite deliciously, don't they? I've also got a vegetarian lasagna in the oven. But the garlic overpowers everything else. Why don't you take Her Majesty out and it'll be ready when you get back?"

Windflower grabbed Lady's leash and, as hard as he tried, he could not get out the door ahead of her. She scooted ahead while he ran after her with the leash. He managed to catch up to her when she finally stopped, and he hooked her up. The pair had a pleasant, for Windflower, and too short, for Lady, walk around the block. When they returned, Sheila had set the table and had everything ready to go for their late dinner.

Lady took her sentry position near Windflower in case anything fell from the table into her territory, and Windflower sat and smiled at his wife. Sheila smiled back as she put a hefty portion of the lasagna on his plate and added a large scoop of steamed broccoli. She took smaller portions for herself while Windflower poured them each a glass of sparkling water.

Windflower munched on a piece of bread as he waited for his food to cool. "Tell me about your day. Did she do anything different?"

Sheila smiled again. "It's hard to say different, but it's like she's more alive, more alert, maybe even more curious every day. Although the routines are the same, just being with her is such a blessing."

"Do you miss work?" asked Windflower, taking a big piece of broccoli.

"Sometimes. But not as much as I thought. Council stuff is pretty boring. Have you heard any more about mental health services?"

"Jones and Tizzard are both working on getting more information. I asked them to talk to your staff to see if we can't organize a service meeting with Eastern Health and the high school."

"That's a good idea. Let me know if you need anything from our people and I'll push it along."

"Thanks." That was the last word Windflower spoke for the next five minutes as he sampled Sheila's lasagna. When he finished his serving, he thought about asking for more. But even he knew that it was too late at night to eat any more than he already had. He settled for one more piece of garlic bread and drained his glass.

"That, my dear, was an absolutely fabulous dinner. I never knew that vegetarian lasagna could be so good," he said.

"I'm glad you enjoyed it. We really don't need to be eating ground beef. The spices are all the same. I'm not saying it's the healthiest meal, with all that cheese, but it's better."

"It was good. I'll clean up. You go put your feet up."

Sheila kissed him on the forehead and went out to the living room.

Windflower loaded up the dishwasher and put the kettle on to boil. When it was ready, he brought the pot and two cups out to Sheila. They were sipping on their tea, enjoying having the windows open and the light spring breeze blowing through when the baby monitor squawked behind them.

"I'll go get her," said Windflower.

He walked upstairs. Amelia Louise was in full throttle. She had learned how to get what she wanted very quickly with a doting mother and an adoring father. But she quieted down as soon as she heard Windflower's voice calling to her. He could see her searching for him in the darkness, and when he hovered over her, he was sure that she smiled. That was his story, anyway.

He picked her up, laid her on the bed, and took off her damp sleeper. He removed her diaper and wiped her clean, then sprinkled a little baby powder and put on a clean diaper and sleeper from the stack near her bassinet. He watched her stretch and wake herself up. She started to grow restless, and he realized that she wanted her mommy and what only her mommy could give her. He picked her up and carried her downstairs.

"You're getting to be a pro at this," said Sheila. "I didn't hear a peep from her on the monitor."

Windflower handed her the baby and sat across from Sheila. This was more than mere eating, thought Windflower. It was the bonding between mother and daughter that was part of the miracle of human life. He simply stared in amazement and wonder.

"I can talk while I'm doing this, you know," said Sheila.

"I know," whispered Windflower. "But I like to watch. We are so lucky."

"We are, indeed," said Sheila as she started to burp the baby. After Amelia Louise produced a surprisingly loud belch, Sheila laid her on the couch beside her. Windflower came over, and they played with their precious gift until both she and they grew tired.

That night Windflower went to sleep tired but satisfied. He had everything he needed and almost everything he wanted. He drifted off, with Sheila nestled in his arms, thinking that he was the luckiest man in Grand Bank. But maybe it was because there was so much happening in his world, or maybe it was that lasagna, but an hour after he went to bed he found himself awake.

Only he wasn't awake, he soon realized. He was dreaming. He hadn't had many dreams lately. His Auntie Marie told him that usually happened when we got busy and weren't paying attention to things around us. She would tell him to "wake up" by walking in the woods or picking berries, doing the things that brought him closer to the ground and to Mother Earth.

She was a master dream weaver, one of the people who had the gift of interpreting dreams, although his Auntie would say that it wasn't a gift because anyone could learn. You just had to practice. Windflower had spent some time with her and his Uncle

Frank learning to read and understand the symbols that dreams conveyed. His family had practiced dream weaving for generations, and Windflower had picked up enough to start making sense of some of his own dreams.

One of the tricks to master dream weaving was to try to be fully awake while dreaming. This was very hard, especially for Windflower. He told his Auntie he felt like he was being dragged under whenever he tried to do that in his dreams. She told him that was the natural pull of the spirit world which wanted to take him back from the real one. She said that dreams were the pathway between both worlds and that we could decide, when we were ready, which world we wanted to live in while we were sleeping.

Windflower tried to will himself awake as the dreamscape unfolded in front of his eyes. It was winter in his dream, with a blanket of snow covering the ground and dripping from the trees like a Christmas postcard scene. He was standing at the edge of a large meadow. There was no sound and no sight of any other creature, no marks or footprints to mar the perfect beauty of the snow, no sign that anyone or anything else existed.

Then he saw her, far off in the distance, all the way across the meadow. He almost missed her at first. It was a woman dressed all in white, as near the colour of snow as it was possible to get. But around her neck was a blood-red amulet. That's what Windflower saw first as it glimmered in the sunlight. It almost blinded him. He felt drawn to her and started to walk across the meadow. But it was slow going in the deep snow, and he bogged down often. She paid no attention to him until he got a little closer. Then she turned in his direction and smiled. Her amulet glistened in the sunshine. And she was gone. Windflower tried to follow but could not pass through the thick trees at the edge of the meadow. He called out but heard nothing. When he looked behind him, he noticed that, despite his efforts, there were no footprints in the snow.

Then, he woke up.

Sheila and the baby were still sleeping. Windflower thought about the dream for a few minutes. He was confused but not upset. There must be some message in there, he thought, but he was unsure what it was. He was still thinking about that when he fell back to sleep.

SIXTEEN

Windflower heard the baby and then heard Sheila but did not budge for either. He was tired this morning. He only moved when he heard Amelia Louise gurgle. That sound would get anybody out of bed. Sheila had her in her arms and was singing to her.

"I think she likes your singing," said Windflower.

"She's a pretty happy little girl," said Sheila.

"I'll go put some coffee on and take Lady out. I'll make you an egg and toast if you'd like."

"I'd like that a lot. You can go ahead and make me feel special any time you'd like. I'm ready."

Windflower kissed baby and mother and went downstairs. Lady was waiting for him at the bottom of the stairs. And if he didn't feel lucky and loved before, she would more than make up for it. He let the dog out into the backyard and put the coffee on to brew.

He picked up his smudging kit and followed Lady outside. She was quite content exploring the new life that was emerging in the garden. In her earlier years she would have been in the flower beds, digging for all her life. But Sheila had broken her of that annoying habit by giving Lady her own spot where she could dig to her heart's content and not uproot all of Sheila's shrubs and annuals.

Windflower was still a bit bothered by the dream from last night. What did it mean, and what were the messages that he was supposed to hear and heed? That would come, he learned from experience. He could also nudge that process along by talking to his Auntie Marie. She might have some answers for him or point him in the right direction. He mixed up his smudging materials and lit them. While the smoke rose around him, he said his prayers of thanks.

Today, he had much to be grateful for, and he made sure to add all of his fellow officers at the RCMP to this morning's list. He asked that Creator watch over them and keep them safe and that they always have allies on their journey. He gave thanks for Sheila, Amelia Louise and Lady, and somehow another female, Molly the cat, came into his head and his prayers. He prayed that she would find a good new home with owners who loved and cared for her.

Lady came to him as he was finishing up and nudged him to remind him that he still had to take her for a walk. He nudged her back. "I know, I know. I've got to get Sheila a cup of coffee first." He went inside and poured Sheila a cup and put another cupful into his thermos. Sheila was putting the baby back into bed when he came up and handed her the coffee.

"I love watching her sleep," said Sheila as she sipped her coffee.

"Me too," said Windflower. "I'll be back soon."

The fog had slipped away, and the morning mist was burning off the tops of the houses in Grand Bank as Windflower and Lady took their morning stroll. Windflower drank his coffee every time Lady stopped to sniff or carry out an investigation. But they kept up a rapid pace and completed their usual routine quickly. He filled the dog's bowls and put on two eggs to boil. While he was waiting for them, he sliced a couple of bagels and put them in the toaster, cut a pink grapefruit in half, and took out some smoked salmon and cream cheese.

When Sheila came down a few minutes later he was setting the table.

"This is a life I could grow accustomed to," she said.

"You deserve it," said Windflower. "But, 'I bear a charmed life.'"

"That would be true," said Sheila as she spread cream cheese on her bagel and added a slice of smoked salmon. "'I love you more than words can wield the matter, dearer than eyesight, space and liberty.'"

"Very good," said Windflower. "Beautiful, can quote Shakespeare first thing in the morning and make a wicked veggie lasagna. I'm sum lucky b'y."

Sheila almost spit her bagel across the room, she was laughing so hard. "That's a very good Newfie accent," she said when she settled down. "You are one crazy man."

"But your man," said Windflower, cleaning off his plate and

putting it into the dishwasher. "I've got to get going." He kissed her on the forehead and went upstairs. He peeked in at his daughter and smiled at her while she slept. He had to pull himself away and get showered and dressed for work.

"I'll call later," he said, and Sheila stood to say goodbye.

Her embrace was warm and welcoming and once again he had to force himself to pull away. "I have to go," he said. "But I will return. 'The more I give to thee, the more I have to give, for both are infinite.'"

"Thank you. We'll be here, although I'm going over to Marystown with Moira this afternoon. If you need anything for the weekend, let me know."

"Thanks. I'll take a look at my list of recipes." Windflower waved goodbye. He was still smiling to himself about his lot in life when he drove by the Crowder house. There was lots of activity there now. He thought about stopping, but realized he would only get in the way. He drove on and parked in front of the RCMP building.

Betsy was her usual cheerful self, and Jones was chatting with her at the front. Molly the cat was sitting in a wire cage on the floor beside them. The cat started mewing at Windflower as soon as she saw him.

"Somebody likes you," said Betsy.

"We got acquainted last night," he said. "Aren't you taking her to the vet's?"

"On my way," said Jones. "I'm bringing back Carrie, too."

"That's great news," said Betsy. "I love Constable Evanchuk. She's such a nice girl. I'm sure Corporal Tizzard will be very happy to see her."

"Is he around this morning?" asked Windflower.

"Eddie and his dad went for breakfast at the Mug-Up," said Jones. "He said he'd be back later. Anyway, I'm off."

"I'm guessing you have some messages for me," said Windflower.

"Why don't you get yourself a cup of coffee?" said Betsy. "This might take some time."

"I have a feeling this is going to be one of those days, Betsy."

"I'm afraid you may be right."

"You know what, Betsy. Give me 10 minutes. I've got to do something."

SEVENTEEN

Windflower went to the back and got his cup of coffee. He walked back to his office and started writing his email to Sheila with the B&B dinner menu for the weekend. Even if it was busy as heck, he wanted to make sure that he got this to Sheila, who would then add the desserts from Beulah and get it printed up.

He went through his notes.

Soup or Salad
  Spring Salad
  Sheila's Fish Soup

Choice of Entrée
  Thai Shrimp
  Winston's Baked Chicken
  Angel Hair Lemon Garlic Pasta

Then he typed up his list of supplies that he needed to make all that.

2 large bags of frozen shrimp
2 pounds of fresh cod
2 stalks of celery
Fresh thyme
Bunch of red chillies
12 bulbs of fennel or bok choy
Basil
Fish sauce
Angel hair pasta
Garlic

Fresh Parmesan cheese
2 pounds chicken thighs
Fresh kale
A bag of oranges
A pound of fresh almonds
Two heads of arugula (or some speciality lettuce)

He finished his cup of coffee and hit send. The email went off into cyberspace, and Betsy appeared at his office door.

"So, what have we got, Betsy?"

"The media is drivin' me crazy," she said. "Marystown put out the statement and all that did was increase the attention. A lot of reporters want interviews. Do you want to deal with them individually or set up a press conference?"

"We could think about a press conference for this afternoon," said Windflower. "Maybe I'll have something to tell them by then. Did Doctor Sanjay call yet?"

"No," said Betsy. "Should I call him?"

"Yes, and ask him when he thinks he'll have an idea on cause and time of death. Once we know that, we can talk to the media. What else?"

"I've got a printout of Jacob Crowder's record from the database." She handed him some sheets of paper stapled together.

"Did you look at this?" he asked.

"He's been in trouble for a long time," said Betsy.

"I'll take a look at that later. Next?"

"Corporal Tizzard asked me to check in with the rental people about van rentals. I called around St. John's and have a list of all the van rentals for the last three months from each of the agencies." She gave him a large stack of paper.

"Get Tizzard to go through these and see what he comes up with," said Windflower. "Anything else?"

"I need approval for these supplies and decorations for Constable Frost's party tomorrow night. I got a giant card, too, so we can all sign. Do you want to start it off?"

Betsy placed the huge card in front of him. He looked it over quickly and signed his name with a note wishing Frost a great time in his new posting. Then he added a thank you from Grand Bank detachment and passed it back to Betsy.

"Thank you, sir," she said. "Inspector Quigley called, and Corporal Tizzard and his dad want to see you when you get a chance."

"Thanks. Betsy. I'll call the inspector now. Send Eddie and his dad in when they get here."

Betsy left, and Windflower dialed Quigley's number in Marystown.

"Have you seen Crowder's sheet?" asked Quigley when he answered Windflower's call.

"Just got it from Betsy. I'm looking at it now. He's got a history going back almost 20 years."

"And I bet that he was in trouble before that," said Quigley. "People don't graduate high school and become criminals. We just don't track them before that."

"Young Offenders Act." Neither man was much of a fan of that legislation because it restricted access to records, even for youth convicted of serious crimes.

"I'd say he's spent more time inside than out by the looks of it," Windflower continued as he looked over the record. "Mostly drugs and property crime, although his biggest bit was for armed robbery."

"Likely to get drugs. It appears that made use of his time in the joint to better himself—at least technologically."

"What do you mean?"

"I ran him through Interpol as well. It appears he's known to have dabbled in the dark web."

"What's that?"

"It's the underworld version of the Internet. People can go onto the web anonymously and carry out activities without being monitored or easily traced."

"Like drug dealers."

"Or terrorists, or money launderers, or people engaged in identity theft. And according to Interpol, our friend Crowder is wanted in regard to two out of three of these activities."

"We didn't know?" asked Windflower, wondering why he hadn't been alerted.

"Someone in the RCMP knew. But according to what I could

see, they'd lost track of him for a couple of years."

"That's because he was hiding out in Grand Bank for one of them."

"Exactly."

"Well, forensics is here today, and they have a crack technology person. I'll put them on to this. Thanks."

"You're welcome," said Quigley. "I hope you'll be able to feed the media sometime soon. They are growling at the gates over here."

"Same here," said Windflower. "Once I get a preliminary report from Doc Sanjay, we'll do a presser. I'll send you over the info. When are you coming over again?"

"I'll be over tomorrow night for the party. Enjoy your day."

"That's it? No better advice from a son of the Bard?"

Quigley laughed. "Okay. Beware of silent dogs and still waters."

"No danger of either around here," said Windflower, laughing as well. "I have one for you, too. When a fox preaches, take care of your geese." Windflower hung up before his friend could respond. He was still smiling when Eddie Tizzard and his father came into view.

Windflower waved them into his office. "Good morning, Richard. Eddie."

Richard Tizzard walked to Windflower and shook his hand. Eddie nodded.

"You want some coffee?" he asked.

"No b'y, I'm stuffed," said the older man.

"Me too," said Eddie. "Dad and I were talking last night about suicide and mental health issues." He paused to see if Windflower had a reaction to this, but Windflower didn't lift an eyebrow. He was used to both of these men raising serious issues, and almost always in a thoughtful way. He was interested in what they had to say.

"Why don't you go ahead, Dad?"

Richard Tizzard cleared his throat as if he were in a classroom. "Well b'y, the research shows a couple of interesting things about suicide in Canada. First of all, it is one issue that affects many more men than women. Secondly, there are a number of high-risk groups. They include teenagers who have problems at home, gay and lesbian kids, middle-aged men, and seniors, especially over 80. And as you are aware, Sergeant Windflower, Indigenous people are at a high risk, too, especially the young people in remote or northern communities."

"Here in this province, we used to have a low suicide rate compared to many other parts of the country," added the younger Tizzard. "Now, it may have been under-reported." His father nodded at this remark. "But in recent years both the data and the anecdotal evidence show that these rates are increasing and are now more in line generally with the pan-Canadian averages." Richard Tizzard smiled broadly at his son's last statement to show both his agreement and his pride in the younger Tizzard's knowledge in this area.

"We all know that we have a problem with young people thinking about it," said Richard Tizzard. "But it's actually the middle-aged men who are most at risk. When they try it, they are often successful. Most times we don't hear about suicides because the family is embarrassed about it, and they don't want anybody to know. Or men smash their cars into a tree, and everybody thinks they were avoiding a moose. The facts are clear, across Canada and right here in our province. Almost half of all people who die by suicide are men between 40 and 64."

"I did not know that," said Windflower. "I knew that it was a major problem for youth, especially Indigenous youth, but I didn't realize that middle-aged men were most at risk. Why is that do you think?"

"Well, in Newfoundland and Labrador, the decline in the inshore fishery has struck a lot of men and their communities pretty hard," said Eddie Tizzard. "In many cases they're no longer the main breadwinner, and their ego and identity has been hurt. It shows up in other stuff, too. You know, like domestic violence and rising divorce and separation rates."

"It's like they're caught between worlds," said Richard Tizzard. "Some of them feel trapped in their lives and see no other way out. Then, there's all these untreated mental health issues and conditions. Many men are afraid, or too embarrassed, to ask for help."

"And if they did, they would find out how few services there actually are," said Windflower. "Interesting stuff, but why are you talking to me about this?"

"Well, I've been looking at mental health supports, and I was talking to Dad, and it seems to us that we can't only do something for the kids," said Eddie Tizzard.

"We need to do something for the men as well," added Richard Tizzard.

"What do you suggest?" asked Windflower.

"I'm not an expert," said Richard Tizzard. "But I'd be happy to help organize a men's meeting, if you thought that might help. We'd have to get a trained professional to lead it, but I could spread the word around, if you'd like."

Windflower knew that if Richard Tizzard spread the word around half the men in the community would at least listen seriously. "Good," he said to Richard Tizzard. "Let's make that happen."

Then, turning to the younger Tizzard, he said, "I want you to include this in your discussions with Jones and the other people involved."

"Yes, sir," said Eddie Tizzard, and both he and his father shook Windflower's hand. He could hear them in the hallway still talking and planning their next move on their way out.

EIGHTEEN

Windflower was still processing all of this as he drove over to check on the forensics crew. The house on Tim's Lane was a beehive of activity. The forensics people were moving in and out, carrying items into their van where Windflower knew they were being tested for fingerprints and other evidence. He parked outside and waited for someone to come talk to him.

Soon, he saw Ted Brown emerge from inside the crime scene.

"Good morning, Winston, how are ya, b'y?"

"It's goin' good b'y," said Windflower. "Anything yet?"

"Not too much, still plugging away."

"Did you get that bag with Crowder's effects?"

"Yeah, somebody dropped it off. Anything in particular you're interested in?"

"There's a passport in there. Not Crowder's. Can you see who else's prints might be on it? And apparently our man was not simply repairing computers, he was involved in something called the dark web. He's also got a long record with drugs."

"All good to know. I'll have Froude have a look at the computer and see what she can come up with. We're also looking out back for any possible weapons. I'll give you a call if we find anything."

"Perfect," said Windflower. "Have fun."

Brown waved and headed back inside. Windflower had just started down the driveway towards his car when his cell phone rang.

"I hear you're looking for me," said the voice at the other end of the line. "Why don't you stay where you're at and I'll come to you."

"Better yet," said Windflower, "I'll come over. Are you at the clinic, Doc?"

"I am," said Sanjay. "At your service and convenience."

"I'll be right there."

Windflower decided to drive the short distance to the clinic. Then again, everything was a short distance in Grand Bank. Many people still went home for lunch, creating one of the few traffic jams in town. Lunch at home would be nice, he thought, but he knew that wasn't going to happen for him today. Instead, he got out of his Jeep in front of the clinic and walked in to hear the verdict from the town's coroner about the demise of the late Jacob Crowder.

He said good morning to the duty nurse and went down the corridor to Doctor Sanjay's small office at the back.

"Cup of tea?" Sanjay asked as Windflower came in.

"That would be great," said Windflower. "So, what have you got for me, Doc?"

Sanjay poured them both a cup of tea and sat behind his desk. He took out his notebook and put on his glasses. "He's been dead a couple of days, at least 48 hours, most likely more than 72. Both the odour and the decomposition of the body tell us that much. But this is mostly guess work."

"Cause of death is by stabbing, I assume," said Windflower.

"Many, many stab wounds. I can show you if you'd like."

"That won't be necessary," said Windflower, sipping his tea. "Anything else?" He could tell there was by the mischievous twinkle in the doctor's eyes.

"I'd say he was tied up and tortured first," said Sanjay. "There are rope marks on his wrists and what look like cigarette burns on his chest. Fairly new and I suspect, very painful. I would also opine that there may have been more than one assailant."

"Why do you say that?"

"I guess it could be one ambidextrous person. But the stab wounds are of different sizes, and the angles suggest more than one person and that more than one weapon was used. I suppose one person could've switched hands and weapons, but that's unlikely. The knives, and I am thinking knives, were short and effective. Those who wielded them knew what they were doing."

"Professionals?"

"That I leave to the police," said Sanjay. He waited until Windflower took out his notepad and made a few notes. When

Windflower finished, Sanjay turned to more pleasant things.

"Now, how are the baby and mother doing?" Sanjay asked.

"Things are wonderful," said Windflower. "Both are doing well, and I've never been happier."

"That is great news. I know you are quite busy, but if you have time, I have a wonderful GlenDronach Allardice that I've been dying to try. It's 18 years old and ready whenever you are."

"I'd love to try out that Scotch," said Windflower, almost salivating. "Especially if it comes with some of your lovely wife's wonderful curry."

"Repa and I would be honoured to have you visit at any time. Give me the word and she will whip up the finest curry this side of India."

"Thank you, Doc. I'll see what I can do." Windflower shook hands with his friend, and all the way back to his office he could taste that beautiful curry on his lips. He walked into the office where Betsy was on the phone. She pointed to his office to tell him he had a visitor.

He was quite surprised to see who that was.

"Good morning, Winston. How's she goin' b'y?" asked his visitor.

"Uncle Frank, what are you doing here?"

"Is that any way to greet your favourite uncle?" asked Frank. "I came to see my new grandniece. I told you I was coming down this summer. I just got in on the taxi from St. John's."

"Where are you staying?" asked Windflower.

"I'm going over to Richard Tizzard's. Eddie is staying there right now, and he offered to take me out cod jigging. I told you about that, too. Your memory must be going b'y."

"You told me at Christmas that you might come down this summer. I didn't know when that was going to be. You could have given us some notice."

"Since when does family need notice to visit? Back home you can knock on any door and you're welcomed in for a cup of tea. I thought Newfoundlanders were like that, too."

"They are, we are. It's just that we're really, really busy right now."

"Oh, don't worry about me. I'll stay out of your way."

But Uncle Frank never stayed out of the way. The man was always right in the middle of everything. He was an irresistible scamp that no one, especially Windflower, could ever stop loving. He went over and gave his uncle a great bear hug.

"Nice to see you, Uncle. How is Auntie Marie?" he asked.

"She is slow and aging since her stroke, but she is still my beautiful girl," said Frank. "She would've liked to come, too, but she's really not up to it. I am her emissary. She even bought me a new phone with a fancy camera so I could get lots of pictures of the baby."

"I'll call Sheila and see if she's around. In the meantime, go back and get yourself a cup of coffee. You know where it is."

Uncle Frank went to get his coffee and was soon replaced in Windflower's office by Betsy with her trusty notepad. "Anything for me?" she asked.

"Let's set the media briefing up for around four o'clock," said Windflower. "I have some preliminary information from Doctor Sanjay, and maybe we'll have more from forensics by then as well."

"Good," said Betsy. "I'll clean up the room out back and send out the notice. I'll check back in later. Okay?"

"Okay," said Windflower. When Betsy left he started to call Sheila, then texted her instead. It was less intrusive, he decided. She or the baby could be sleeping. A few minutes later, Sheila called him back.

"Hi Winston. What's up?"

"Uncle Frank is in town," said Windflower. "He just got here. He's staying with the Tizzards. I wanted to make sure that this was a good time for him to come over."

"I'm actually leaving right now to meet Moira at the Mug-Up to go over to Marystown. Why don't I pop by?"

"That would be great," said Windflower. "I can get to see you both, too."

"How's your day going?"

"From crazy to frantic. But I'll be okay. How's yours?"

"A little slower, that's for sure," said Sheila with a laugh. "When the highlight of your week is going to the supermarket in

Marystown, it's pretty slow. But I know this is a very special time—time we'll never have again."

"True. See you soon."

Windflower walked to the back where Uncle Frank had a cup of coffee, a handful of Purity Jam Jams, and a captive audience in Harry Frost. They were sharing fishing stories, with Uncle Frank talking about whoppers he had caught in Northern Alberta, and Frost telling tales about pike and walleye monsters in the Assiniboine.

"Sheila will be over soon with the baby," said Windflower.

"Frosty was telling me he's going back to Manitoba soon. I might have to go visit him. I'd love to fish those rivers again, just one more time."

"You'd be welcome any time," said Frost.

"That's more like it," said Uncle Frank to no one in particular, but Windflower still felt the hairs on his neck rise up.

Frost got up to leave. "We'll see you tomorrow night," he told Uncle Frank.

"I wouldn't miss it. I love a party," said Uncle Frank.

As Frost left to go home, Windflower and Uncle Frank went to the front to talk to Betsy. Soon afterwards they saw Sheila wheeling her pram up to the door of the RCMP detachment.

NINETEEN

What a beautiful girl," said Uncle Frank as he held Amelia Louise in his arms. "Winston, get a picture of me on my phone." He passed it over to Windflower who took a few shots of Uncle Frank and the baby, and then with Sheila, and finally after summoning Betsy's help, a picture was taken of the happy family all together.

Sheila hung around for a few minutes to visit, and then Moira came to *Southern Gazette* who wanted a shot of him with the poster that Betsy had prepared. Then Windflower made his excuses and snuck out of the room. He walked down the hall and closed the door to his office. Tizzard came by shortly afterwards and knocked gently before opening the door a crack to get permission to go ahead in.

"That was great," he said. "Was that picture Betsy's idea?"

"Yeah, she's pretty great, eh?"

Windflower and Tizzard stayed inside his office until the last of the media had left. Then, Tizzard went off to start his work going through the bag of documents that forensics had brought over. Windflower started in on his paperwork but felt drained and distracted. He needed a break. He walked out to the front and told Betsy he was going out for a while. He wanted to go see one of his favourite females, Lady.

Lady was pretty happy to see him. She was curled up on her bed when she heard the door open and in a flash was at his feet. Windflower patted her on her head and put her on her leash. They went outside and she needed no orders to jump into the back of his Jeep. She didn't know where they were going, but it looked like she could care less about their destination. She really was just happy to be with her master.

"Let's go up the trail," said Windflower. There were no objections. He parked the car at the back of the clinic and let the dog out. She was off and running like a shot. But she always circled back to make sure that he was on the way. Windflower smiled at her unbridled joy. He needed to be out in the trees, in nature. His Auntie Marie had told him that men, particularly Indigenous men, needed to be out amongst the trees, that it wasn't good for their souls to be surrounded by concrete and asphalt.

Windflower agreed. He loved walking up this nature trail that had been so lovingly crafted and maintained by the locals. The path had been there forever. It led up through an area where folks around here had their vegetable gardens years ago, all the way up to the top of the hill where the first radio transmission tower had been built. It was also a favourite route for both young lovers and blueberry pickers, each looking for pleasure in the quiet and isolation so near to the busy bustle of their town.

A rabbit darted across their path and Lady started to run after to investigate. But she came back quickly when Windflower called her and was quite happy to resume her position a few steps ahead of him on the smooth trail. They walked near the top and paused at the lookout. Windflower gazed down over Grand Bank. He was always grateful when he looked out over his newfound community, nestled in between rock and ocean, waiting for him to come home again.

The pair strode quickly down the hill and, after a quick pause for several drinks in the brook, Lady and Windflower were back in the Jeep and on their way home. He put Lady inside and paused for a moment in his vehicle to give thanks for all of his blessings and for the brief respite in his busy day. Now, back to work.

When he arrived at the detachment, both Betsy and any signs of the media presence were gone. In their place was a laughing trio that Windflower could hear as soon as he opened the front door. He walked to the back where Jones, Tizzard, and Carrie Evanchuk were enjoying each other's company and the remains of a box of doughnuts. The cat, Molly, was lurking beneath the table.

"I hope you saved one for me," said Windflower.

"Boston cream," said Tizzard.

"You didn't buy them, Eddie," said Evanchuk.

"Thank you to whomever I owe the pleasure," said Windflower. "And welcome back Constable Evanchuk."

"Nice to be here," said Evanchuk.

"Carrie's got my old job," said Tizzard. "Until I get back, of course."

"Be careful," said Jones. "She might be better than you. She's certainly smarter."

"And much better looking," said Windflower. "So, big plans for tonight?"

"Not for me," said Jones. "I need to get some shut-eye. I'm doing a double tomorrow. I'm hitting the sack early. So's Molly."

"Everything check out okay with the cat?" asked Windflower.

"She's good," said Jones. "But no luck so far in finding her a new family. Are you sure you don't want a cat?"

Windflower looked at her without responding.

"We'd take her, but my dad is allergic," said Tizzard. "We'll probably have a quiet night in, too. But first, Carrie offered to help me go through some of the evidence. What do you think this is all about?"

"I'm not sure," said Windflower. "But like most things criminal, it's almost always about the money. Find the money link and we'll know more."

"I did some work with Commercial Crime when I was with HQ," said Evanchuk. "It looks like some kind of identity theft thing, don't you think?"

"All will be revealed," said Windflower.

"Goodnight," said Jones as she bundled the cat up in her arms and left.

Tizzard and Evanchuk went to the storage area to start going through the evidence bag and Windflower went back to his office.

There were an amazing number of forms that had to be filled out when there was a suspicious death. That was doubled when it involved a murder investigation. Windflower was about halfway through that process when Sheila called.

"We're back from Marystown," she said.

"How was your big excursion?" asked Windflower.

"It was fine. Amelia Louise was nearly perfect. She fussed when we were at the supermarket, but once I changed and fed her, she was great. She has simple needs: to be clean, to be fed, to be held."

"Just like the rest of us. We sometimes chase after all this other stuff when all we need is to be loved and cared for."

"True," said Sheila. "I got all the supplies, and I also picked up some fresh shrimp and salmon from the fish truck. I was hoping that we could have salmon on the barbecue."

"Absolutely," said Windflower. "I've got to get out of here before I go crazy. I'll be home soon and get that organized."

"Great," said Sheila. "See you soon."

Windflower finished off his forms and was on his way to Betsy's desk to drop them off when Tizzard and Evanchuk came out of the back.

"Did you find something?" asked Windflower.

"There's not only expired documents in here," said Tizzard. "There's also some current ones and a stack of blank passports."

"Canadian?" asked Windflower.

"Canadian, American, European," said Evanchuk. "It's not easy to get these blanks. They're tightly controlled."

"Can you talk to Commercial?" asked Windflower, pointing to Evanchuk. "You've got some connections there. See what they think. We might need you here for a few days to sort this out."

"That's fine with me, sir," said Evanchuk. "But you'll need to talk to the inspector."

"I'll call him," said Windflower. "Tizzard, I want you to talk to the forensics tech person. Froude is her name. She's working on Crowder's computer. See what she's got."

Both Tizzard and Evanchuk looked excited about the possibility of working together on the case. They stayed there looking at him until he shooed them back to work.

"I'm going home," he said. "I've got a date with two beautiful girls and a barbecue. But I'll call the inspector."

Windflower could hear Evanchuk and Tizzard talking to each other loudly as they went to the back. He picked up the phone and called Marystown.

"Sergeant, how goes the battle?" asked Quigley.

"I am but 'a wretched soul, bruised with adversity'," said Windflower.

"That's good, but what exactly does that mean?"

"We've got the media on board to help us look for Crowder's vehicle, and it's starting to look like some form of identity theft operation. Forensics is still here, and their techie is going through Crowder's computer. But we're way in over our heads on some of the stuff we're finding. I need you to lend me Evanchuk for a few days. Maybe next week. She's got an in with Commercial Crime, and we'll need somebody to translate."

"Okay. Keep me posted. I'll be over tomorrow for Frost's party, and we can talk more then. And remember, 'Suit the action to the word, the word to the action.'"

"What?" asked Windflower, but Quigley had already hung up the phone. Smiling to himself, and before anything else could get in between him and his dinner, he turned off his lights and raced home.

Everybody was happy to see him. Amelia Louise was awake and lying on the couch next to her mother while Lady was curled up at her feet.

"All my girls together," said Windflower. "What a beautiful sight."

He kissed Sheila, patted an eager Lady, and touched Amelia Louise's cheek with his finger.

"The salmon is in the fridge. And we already took Lady around the block, even though she's pretending she hasn't been out all day," said Sheila.

Windflower laughed. "She can help me barbecue." He went to the kitchen to get everything ready. He took two large potatoes out of the bag, peeled and sliced them, brushed the slices with olive oil, and put them in tinfoil with a large scoop of butter on top. With Lady at his heels, he went to the backyard and lit the barbecue. He placed the potatoes on the grill and went back in with Lady close behind

He took the salmon from the fridge and put it on a plate, then brushed it with olive oil and sprinkled it with cayenne pepper and a dash of chili powder on each side. He got two handfuls of baby carrots and put them into another piece of tinfoil with a dollop of butter and a teaspoon of maple syrup. Then he chopped up half a head of broccoli into small pieces for another tinfoil packet. This one had a teaspoon of water and was sprinkled with garlic fragments.

Lady followed as he left to turn on the other burner of the barbecue and move the potatoes over. He placed the salmon on the barbecue and laid the carrots next to the potatoes. He played with Lady while the salmon and vegetables cooked. When the fish was done on one side he turned it over and laid the broccoli on as well.

Five minutes later he was coming into the house with two perfectly cooked salmon fillets and his vegetables on a tray. Lady made sure that if anything fell, she would be there to get it. He rewarded her for her vigilance with a Milk-Bone and called Sheila to the table. Sheila got them both a glass of water while Windflower laid their food on their plates.

"Oh, this is so good," said Sheila. "I love salmon on the barbecue. And these veggies." She murmured over the potatoes, cooed over the carrots, and sighed when she tasted the broccoli with garlic. Windflower, meanwhile, was lost in food heaven. He didn't know that she, or anything else, existed in the world until he was nearly finished his meal. When he raised his head, Sheila had stopped eating and was smiling at him.

"What?" he asked.

"I love you, Winston," she said.

"I love you too, Sheila. What's for dessert?"

"Well, the baby is sleeping."

Windflower did not have to be asked twice.

TWENTY

Windflower woke to the sun streaming in through the bedroom window. He hadn't heard a peep, even though he was pretty sure that Sheila had gotten up with the baby sometime during the night. Right now, she was sleeping solidly next to him, and when he glanced into the bassinet, Amelia Louise was doing the same.

Leaving both his angels in their peaceful repose, he slipped on his jeans and hoodie and crept downstairs. Lady was sleeping, too, but she roused herself quickly when she saw him enter the kitchen. He put on his running shoes and grabbed her leash. He led her outside and soon they were both moving at a rapid pace throughout the quiet morning streets of Grand Bank.

It was a glorious morning, and both man and dog were embracing the feelings of being alive and, at least for Windflower, of being extremely grateful. They wound their way down by the wharf and up to the highway. Normally, Windflower didn't take this route, but he wanted to try something new for a change. Lady didn't care a whit about where they were going.

But she was very pleased when they turned down a gravel road a few minutes up the highway. This route led down to the sea and connected back up to the path from Grand Bank to Fortune. There was a small, abandoned cemetery and one lone house, more of a cottage, near the footpath. Lady was excited for the new adventure and was soon off exploring her newly found territory while Windflower unfurled his smudging bowl and medicines.

With the sun in his face and the warm air floating in from the Atlantic, Windflower lit his bowl and sent the smoke all over his head and his body. He paused for a moment to smell the intensity of the sage and cedar and tobacco. Then he gave his prayers of thanks to Creator for his many blessings. He prayed for Sheila and Amelia Louise, the two main loves of his life. And when Lady came back from her explorations, he gave thanks for her, too.

He prayed for all the other people in his life and the ones that had come before him. He remembered his mother and father and his spiritual guide, his grandfather. As he was finishing up, a hawk flew overhead. He looked up, and it was as if the hawk dipped his wings to wave to him, a reminder that he needed to watch for the signs from Creator.

With Lady at his heels, he ran back up the gravel road, down the highway and in through the back of town to home. When they arrived, he filled Lady's bowls and put the coffee on to brew. He could hear Sheila and the baby stir upstairs. When the coffee was ready, he took two cups with him and went to see his beautiful wife and baby. What a way to start his day, he thought. I am one very lucky man.

He spent a very pleasant hour with Amelia Louise and Sheila, had some toast and peanut butter and a banana for breakfast, showered, and went to work while Sheila and the baby had a lie-in. He would rather have spent his morning in that same manner, but duty called.

It was quiet when he arrived at the detachment office, but that didn't last, and once it got busy, it didn't stop. Frost arrived a few minutes after Windflower, and he spent a few minutes chatting with him on his last day in Grand Bank. He said that a report had come in about an abandoned car that someone saw near the old dump.

"Can you go over and check it out?" asked Windflower.

"Yeah, I'm on my way over there right now," said Frost.

Windflower nodded, and Frost drained his coffee cup and left. Betsy was his next visitor. She had another series of forms to be completed now that officially transferred all of the evidence from forensics to their detachment, and more paperwork that he didn't even bother to read but just initialled or signed.

"You could slip a raise form in there for yourself any day you'd like, and I'd sign it," he said to Betsy.

"You already did, sir, last week," said Betsy. "My annual increment."

Windflower smiled but said nothing.

"I've also got some more information on the rental van that Corporal Tizzard was tracking. There are currently five vans still out on rental. All the rest were returned more than a week ago. Two were taken out of province according to the company. That only leaves three to check. I've put those details in Tizzard's basket."

"He has a basket?" asked Windflower.

"Well, a slot, actually, like everyone else," said Betsy. "He said he was back at work."

Windflower smiled and again held his tongue. But he made a mental note to talk to Tizzard when he arrived.

"I guess it's better to have him back than to see him wandering around like a ghost," said Betsy when Windflower didn't respond.

"Do you believe in ghosts?" he asked Betsy, finally finding his voice.

"I don't think it matters whether I believe or not. They either are, or they aren't, as my Bob likes to say. I know there's too many coincidences to believe that there's nothing else but us. My mother used to believe in fairies. She blamed them whenever anything went missing overnight. One lady said that last week when she was in to complain about her missing passport," said Betsy.

"We found a lot of missing passports and other stuff in Crowder's house," said Windflower. "I don't think that was the fairies or a ghost."

"Well, you may be right," said Betsy. "But I've seen the lady of the house moving around over at the B&B."

"You mean Diane Matthews," said Windflower. "Are you sure it wasn't Beulah?"

Betsy didn't get a chance to answer before they heard voices coming in through the front door. It was Richard Tizzard and Uncle Frank.

"Good morning, Sergeant," said Richard Tizzard.

"Good morning, Richard," said Windflower. He waited for his uncle to greet him, but Frank went immediately to Betsy. She greeted Uncle Frank warmly and the two embraced like long-lost relatives. When they untangled, Uncle Frank finally recognized his nephew, only to ask if there was any coffee.

"Let's go to the back," said Windflower.

"A snack would be good, too," said Uncle Frank. "Some of them Purity Cream Crackers and cheese."

Windflower looked back at his uncle and, for the third time this morning, stayed quiet.

He put on a fresh pot of coffee and laid out a plate of crackers and a chunk of old cheddar. The two older men buttered a couple of crackers each and laid thick slices of cheese on top. Windflower watched as they enjoyed their snack and each other's company. He was busy, but not ignorant, and he remembered how much he liked having his uncle around.

"So, we've been yarning about this mental health stuff," said Richard Tizzard.

"We talked to some of the men down at the wharf, too," said Uncle Frank.

"What's surprising is how many other men they know who've been having trouble," said Richard. "We counted up eight or nine men in the last few years who people know have tried to hurt themselves or died suspiciously."

"Why don't we know about it?" asked Windflower.

"Men don't like to talk about stuff like that," said Uncle Frank. "It's too embarrassing, and the family feels ashamed, too. But when you start asking questions, that's when people open up."

"We thought we should do a survey or something," said Richard Tizzard. "Something confidential that people can fill out at home, or maybe on their computer, and send back to us. We could then at least get a handle on how big the problem is. And the men won't feel so alone."

"Afterwards, it would be good to have a men's circle, a place where they could come and talk about their issues if they wanted and we would just listen. I told Richard I could help with that part," said Uncle Frank.

"We need to move this out into the open," said Richard. "Men are dying and no one's noticing."

Windflower was struck by how much love and caring he could

hear and see from the two men in front of him.

"I like your ideas a lot," he said. "Constable Jones is leading our initiative on this. She's been talking to the clinic and the Town. I'll make sure she speaks to you, too."

Uncle Frank smiled at Richard Tizzard, as if to say that he knew his nephew would come through. For his part, the other man stood and went to shake Windflower's hand. "Thank you, Sergeant," he said. "Come on," he said to Uncle Frank. "We've got to go talk to the guys down at the wharf and tell them about our plan."

Uncle Frank winked at Windflower as they were leaving. "See ya later," he shouted as they headed out the door.

Windflower didn't have much time to process all of that information before Betsy came on the intercom.

"It's Constable Frost on line two."

"Boss, I found the car, actually a van, at the back of the road out here. It might be the one we're looking for. I think there's a body in there, too."

TWENTY-ONE

I'll be right over," said Windflower. He grabbed his jacket and ran to his Jeep. As he was getting into his vehicle, he could feel a chill in the air. When he looked up, he could see the cause of the cooling. Fog, thick and penetrating, was swirling above him and, judging by the wind, heading directly for Grand Bank. By the time he reached the road to the dump, it had taken over completely. He could see Frost's cruiser, but only because Frost's warning lights were on.

The constable was standing beside a blue van with local license plates. Might be Crowder's, thought Windflower as he walked closer and wrote the number in his notebook. Frost pointed to the front where a body lay slumped in the driver's seat.

"Have you checked?" he asked.

"No pulse," said Frost. "A little ripe, too. I'm no expert, but I'd say he was shot, judging by the blood spatters."

Windflower took one quick look and then called Betsy.

"Betsy, we have a body in a van on the old dump road. Can you get the paramedics and call Doctor Sanjay?"

"I guess I know how I'm spending my last day in Grand Bank," said Frost.

The two Mounties stood around in the stunned silence, waiting to hear the sirens that inevitably follow such grisly discoveries. It was almost a relief when they finally heard noise and saw the lights of the ambulance as it came up the road through the thick fog.

Windflower greeted the paramedics and then left Frost to handle the scene. "Call me if you need me," he told Frost. "I'll send over relief as soon as I can."

Windflower drove back slowly and carefully as the fog settled down closer to the ground. Visibility went from bad to worse in the time it took to get back to the detachment. Eddie Tizzard was waiting for him when he returned.

"I hear we found the van," said Tizzard.

"And a body," said Windflower.

"Is it Crowder's van?"

"Here's the number, check it out."

"Great," said Tizzard, and he started to leave.

"But hang on a second," said Windflower. "Betsy said you told her you were back full-time."

"I didn't exactly say that."

"You're not, until we and you get clearance. I don't mind you helping out, but let's wait for the official word before making announcements. Okay?"

"Got it. That works out better because I can spend a bit more time with Carrie."

Tizzard decided it was time to change the subject, now that the mild reprimand was over. "My dad says that this fog means the capelin are coming in early this year, maybe even tonight when the tide comes in."

"I thought that happened later in the summer. Wasn't it early July last year?"

"It kind of changes a bit every year. And with climate change you never know anymore. It used to be one of the highlights for me and my family every year, seeing the capelin roll in on the beaches to spawn."

"I know. It's crazy when tens of thousands of those tiny fish swim in. You can go down to the beach and scoop them up in a bucket. Aren't they members of the smelt family?"

"They are indeed," said Tizzard, proud to be asked for information about the ocean's gifts. "I hear some other places have smelt runs, but only in Newfoundland will you see the capelin run. My dad always said that a good capelin run meant a good year for the cod fishery."

"Around St. John's they even have whales chasing them in," said Windflower. "I was in Middle Cove one year when a whole pod of humpbacks came in for a meal."

"If we get some tonight, I'll fry a few up for you."

"I'd like that. I think I've only had them dried and salted before."

"What was that?" asked Smithson who had arrived while Tizzard and Windflower were talking.

"Capelin," said Tizzard.

"Tell him all about everything while you're dropping him off to relieve Frost out at the dump," Windflower told Tizzard.

"What about the capelin?" asked Smithson, but Tizzard was tugging on his arm before Windflower had time to respond.

"You have a visitor," came Betsy's voice over the intercom.

Windflower walked wearily to the front. What now, he thought?

"This is Elizabeth Crowder, Sergeant," said Betsy.

She was not what Windflower had imagined. "I'm . . . I'm Winston Windflower," he said. "Pleased to meet you. I'm sorry again for your loss."

It was hard to place her age, but then again, he was never very good at that. She was stunningly beautiful, almost glowing at whatever age it was she was gracefully moving towards. She wore a tan blazer with a flowery scarf that Windflower guessed was silk and a lighter tan skirt. Her hair was light, not quite blond, with streaks that suggested a professional and pricey touch. She had high cheekbones, with just a hint of blush, and very little makeup, not even lipstick.

Elizabeth Crowder was used to that stunned look that often crosses men's faces upon being introduced to beautiful women. Windflower had that look, now, too. Betsy noticed her boss's dilemma and came to the rescue.

"Would you like a cup of tea?" she asked the other woman.

"That would be very nice," said Elizabeth Crowder. "With a splash of milk, please."

"Sergeant?" asked Betsy.

"No, not for me, thank you, Betsy," said Windflower, finally recovering his composure. "Would you like to come into my office?" he asked his visitor.

He could not help but notice the way she glided in front of him and took the chair opposite. He was smitten, despite himself, and watched closely as she laid her purse, expensive, of course, on the desk in front of him and crossed her legs. Windflower smiled and could have stayed there for hours, transfixed, but Betsy saved him again.

"Here's your tea," she said, passing the woman a cup and then going back to her post.

"When will I be able to see my son?" asked Crowder, breaking Windflower's daze and bringing him back to the rather unpleasant business at hand.

"I think that the coroner is finished with your son's body," said Windflower. "I can have him transported to the funeral home if you'd like."

"I'll have him cremated. There's no one left around here anymore."

"What about relatives on the mainland?"

"How long have you lived here? You're starting to talk like them."

Windflower laughed. "I'm sure there's a name for that. Maybe Stockholm Syndrome or something."

This time Elizabeth Crowder laughed. "That's good, Sergeant. But no, no one on the mainland would be interested in paying their respects to my son. Some of those who knew him would likely be happy to know that Jake Crowder is dead. His father isn't around anymore, and he was one of the last who still cared."

"Your son clearly had some troubles. We are thinking that he was murdered, likely by people he was associating with, maybe doing business with, too. Any ideas about who they might be?"

"They'd be the last people I'd know or would like to know. Jacob was my son and I did what I could. But, I never knew any of his associates. He kept them away from me. I'm at least grateful for that."

"What kind of business was your son involved with?" asked Windflower. "I know he was a computer expert of some sort, and I saw his arrest record."

Crowder didn't say anything. Instead she looked at the ceiling and then down at the floor, as if searching for imperfections. Windflower was determined to get as much information as he could from Jacob Crowder's mother.

"Something doesn't add up for me," he said. "It doesn't feel right. You obviously had, and have, some things going for you. But it looks like your son only had a downward trajectory."

TWENTY-TWO

Jacob was always a smart kid," said Elizabeth Crowder. "That came from his father. I couldn't add two plus two. He excelled in school and was planning to become a video game designer. But he got involved with drugs early and that put the kibosh on those plans. He was a whiz with computers and could easily find work when he was able to do it. Eventually, he became unemployable and set up his own business."

Elizabeth Crowder paused and sipped her tea. "His father set him up. His business, if you want to call it that, became advising companies about security issues with their technology. That lasted about six months until his initial cash flow ran out and his drug habit took over. Then he just drifted along, picking up a bit of work here and there—enough to survive, along with handouts from me and his father."

"Did he have any friends?" asked Windflower. "Anyone we can talk to about him?"

"He was the ultimate loner," said the woman. "Jacob connected with other people, even me, only when he needed something. I mean, there's been a few girls along the way, but none of them would stick around once he started to go down the tubes. You know the story, Sergeant. Arrests, overdoses, rehabs. Repeat. I may sound cynical, but I did everything I could. I reached the point where I had to let go."

"What about his father?"

"Bruce cared about Jacob, as best he could. He was always good about giving money, but he never really had the capacity to do anything more than that. After he died, I was all Jacob had. That's why he kept coming back to me."

"You said that he called you about a month ago. Can you tell me what that was about? What did he say he wanted the money for again?"

"Like I told you, he always had some scam. I didn't really pay attention. But he was rambling on about some new form of currency. Bimcoins or something like that?"

"Was it bitcoins?"

"Yeah, that was it. Jacob was saying that he could take my money and convert it over to this and then we could hide it away from the government and that it would be worth a lot of money real soon."

"What did you say to him?"

"I told him that I wasn't giving him any of my money so that he could convert it to anything—that I liked it just where it was, in the bank."

"We may have some more questions for you later," said Windflower, getting up from his desk. "Thank you for talking to me, and I am sorry for your loss."

"I am sorry, too," said Elizabeth Crowder. "But I knew this day was coming for a long time. Jacob has been lost to me and the rest of the world for a long time."

Windflower nodded. "I'll get Betsy to contact the coroner's office for you."

"Thank you, Sergeant."

Windflower walked to the front with Elizabeth Crowder and handed her over to the ever-competent Betsy to look after.

Harry Frost and Eddie Tizzard came in as Elizabeth Crowder was getting into the taxi that Betsy had called for her.

"Who was that?" asked Frost. "Is she a model or somebody famous?"

"Jacob Crowder's mother," said Windflower, rather nonchalantly, as if he hadn't been as impressed as the other two men clearly were.

"She is gorgeous," said Tizzard.

Windflower tried to pull them back to the task at hand. "How did it go out at the dump?"

"Smithson's got it in hand," said Frost. "He's still a bit shaky."

"He'll be okay," said Tizzard. "We all had to go through that.

It's a bit of PTSD. You forget because you're old," he said, pointing to Frost.

"I'm not that old," said Frost.

Both Windflower and Tizzard started laughing, and Frost soon joined in despite himself.

"The paras were waiting for Doc Sanjay when I left. The good news is that site is off the beaten track, so there's less likelihood of anybody tampering with the scene," said Frost.

"Great," said Windflower. "Can you run over and see Corporal Brown at the Crowder house? Maybe they can have a look out at the dump, too, before they leave town."

Frost left to go see the forensics guys. Tizzard went to get a fresh cup of coffee. He was sitting down with his feet up on the table, having a snack, when Windflower came back in for a refill.

"Oh good, you're still here," said Windflower. "Betsy left you a note in your basket about the rental cars. Can you check that out, along with the plate from the van?"

"I'm on my break right now," said Tizzard. "Can I do it later?"

"If you're not back at work, how can you be on a break?" asked Windflower.

Before Tizzard could answer, Windflower filled his coffee cup and left. He was sure he could hear Tizzard muttering something behind him but smiled to himself and carried on.

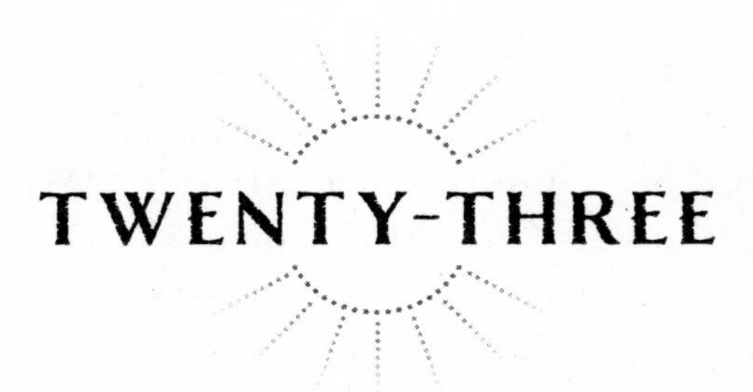

TWENTY-THREE

Windflower didn't have much time to enjoy his coffee. Frost was back with Brown and the female forensics technician, Froude.

"I met these guys on the way," said Frost.

"Morning, Sarge," said Brown. "Thought you might want to see some of this stuff." He handed Windflower over another clear plastic bag with several small baggies inside, along with a large quantity of what looked like marijuana. "We didn't test it," said Brown, "but I'm pretty sure we have weed and cocaine from the house."

"We also found this," said Froude, passing over another bag that was filled almost completely with American money, all of it in what looked like two denominations: Twenties and hundred-dollar bills.

"Wow," said Windflower. "That's a lot of money."

"It would be if it were real," said Froude. When Windflower raised an eyebrow at this, she continued. "I spent some time in Commercial on the counterfeiting file," she said. "It seems that people who like creating false identification also have an interest in counterfeiting. This is pretty high quality, though." She held up a hundred-dollar bill. "You'd have to be an expert to tell that it's fake."

"How do you tell?" asked Frost.

"I don't have a real one to show you," said Froude. "But they have a slight ridge on them, and there's a different texture with the genuine bills because they are made with a paper that is only available to the U.S. Mint. The easiest way to tell a counterfeit is by looking at the portrait on the bill. Look at Benjamin Franklin here. The picture is a bit dull, almost blurry. Real bills have a clear and crisp look to the portraits."

Windflower looked closely at the bill that Froude handed over. Sure enough, the picture of Ben Franklin was a little off.

"Good job," he said to Brown and Froude. "Were you able to find anything else from Crowder's computer?"

"Not yet," said Froude. "Still working my way through the security encryption, but I'm getting there. This looks like a pretty big operation."

"Did Frost tell you about our other problem?" Windflower asked Brown.

"He did, and after we get some lunch, I'm going to drop Froude back at Crowder's and we'll take the truck over to the dump. We came by to show you this, and to see if you wanted to join us. I've been telling her about the cheesecake."

Windflower almost drooled at the thought of lunch and cheesecake at the Mug-Up but had to decline. "Not today," he said. "Maybe Frost would like to join you, though, to help celebrate his last day here."

Frost looked very pleased at that suggestion, and soon Windflower was alone, and his office was quiet again. But he had a feeling that was not going to last. He was right.

His phone rang as he was contemplating his meagre lunch options.

"Good day, Sergeant Windflower. The sun may be gone, but it seems like 'hourly joys be still upon you'," said Quigley.

"'Tis torture and not mercy,' Ron. We've got another dead body, most likely shot by the looks of it."

"When did Grand Bank become the murder capital of Canada?"

"I know," said Windflower. "I have a feeling these are connected. We still have to check, but it looks like Crowder's missing van. I'll bet it was one of his associates—the unlucky one by the looks of it. And our evidence locker is getting filled up with old passports, maybe some new I.D.s, drugs, and a bag of counterfeit Yankee dollars."

"I'm on my way over. Anything I can bring you?"

"Three more officers?" asked Windflower hopefully. "But I'll settle for two more and Evanchuk for the week. She's got some background in Commercial Crime that might be helpful."

"I'll bring a box of doughnuts from Tim Hortons," the inspector said as he hung up.

That reminded Windflower again how he had missed lunch. He went to the break room to scrounge a snack when Jones showed up.

"Sarge," said Jones.

Windflower continued to search through the fridge, finding another small yogurt and a scrawny apple. "This looks like lunch."

"On a diet?" asked Jones.

Windflower almost scowled but grimaced instead. "What's up?" he asked as he found a spoon and started eating his yogurt.

"We've got everybody on board for the planning meeting on youth mental health," she said.

"That's great. Except we may have to expand the scope of the meeting." Windflower explained his earlier discussion with Richard Tizzard and Uncle Frank.

"No worries," said Jones. "I'll call everybody back and see if they're okay with letting them come to the meeting. I think it'll be fine."

"Okay," said Windflower, biting into his apple. "How's that cat of yours doing?"

"Molly is great. But I think you may be right. I'm going to bring her back to the SPCA after the weekend. I can't find anyone to take her, and I really can't keep her."

"Too bad," said Windflower before turning to more pressing problems and asking her to take a run up to the dump to relieve Smithson.

"Sure," said Jones. "He's working overnight and would probably like a break first."

"What time does the party start?"

"I think around seven."

"Still a couple of hours. Maybe I'll take a break too."

Jones went to see Smithson at the dump and Windflower waved goodbye to Betsy on his way out the door. A few minutes later he was greeted by a very happy Lady. He patted the collie and could hear Sheila singing softly upstairs. It sounded like she might be putting Amelia Louise back to sleep. He grabbed Lady's leash and, as quietly as he could, led them both outside.

It was a quick walk through the fog-shrouded streets of Grand Bank but Lady was grateful for the time with Windflower and the exercise. So was he. Both would have liked longer, but that would have to wait. They arrived back at the house as Sheila was plugging in the kettle.

"I'm glad that nobody stole the dog. I was a little surprised when I came downstairs. You were pretty quiet," said Sheila.

"How's the baby?"

"She's well. Cup of tea?"

"Sounds grand," said Windflower, and then he told her about finding another body that morning.

"I heard. Bad news always travels fast. What's going on, Winston?"

"Well, I'd say the two deaths are connected, and there's a whole lot more happening behind the scenes at Crowder's house than anyone could imagine," said Windflower.

Sheila poured them both a cup of tea and laid a small plate of gingersnaps on the table. "I know you can't tell me anything because it's an ongoing investigation, but people are already pretty shook up. I'm pretty shook up, too, if you want to know the truth of it."

Windflower took a couple of gingersnaps and thought for a moment about asking for something more substantial. But he wisely refrained and ate his crisp biscuit as quietly as possible.

"First there were all those break-ins, and then Levi Parsons shooting himself, and Jacob Crowder murdered. Now, there's another dead body. This is Grand Bank for God's sake," said Sheila.

'I know," said Windflower. "I think we're all struggling with this, even at the RCMP. But we'll figure it out."

"I hear that the mental health meeting is on. That's good news."

"Yeah. Richard Tizzard and Uncle Frank came to talk to me about mental health services for men, too. Did you know that 75 percent of all suicides are men?"

"I did know that," said Sheila. "I saw a study that showed that more middle-aged Canadian men die by suicide every year than by motor vehicle accidents, homicide, and HIV combined. Apparently, there's an increased risk starting in their forties that peaks at fifty and then gradually drops over time."

"Anyway, I've asked Jones to see if anyone minds if they take part in the meeting. Richard wants to organize some specific events for men. Uncle Frank is going to help him get it going."

"Well, if anyone can get things going, it's those two," said Sheila. "I'm glad Uncle Frank is here. We don't have nearly enough family around. I wish Auntie Marie was well enough to come."

Windflower nodded. "That would be nice. We might have to take a trip out to Pink Lake some time, you know. Let her see Amelia Louise."

"Maybe in the fall after we shut down the B&B for the year. I'm assuming you're going to Frost's party tonight."

"Only for an hour or two. Are you sure you don't want to come?"

"Too much for me and for the baby. I'll be out Saturday and Sunday nights. But you go and have fun. Maybe we can go for a short walk when you get back. It's foggy but still mild."

"Sounds great," said Windflower. He rose and held Sheila in a long and lingering embrace. It was hard for both of them to let go. Finally, he managed to leave and drove to the pub where the party for Harry Frost was just beginning.

The parking lot was crowded and, inside, the pub was nearly full. Harry Frost was near the small stage where many of his friends from the force and the community had gathered around him. There was a duo playing country songs, but most people were more focused on their Friday drinks or the buffet table. That was Windflower's first stop.

He loaded up a plate of wings and fries and took a few sandwiches from a tray at the end of the table. There was a beautiful cake with "Goodbye Harry" printed in icing on top. Windflower would have liked a piece of that, too, but had to wait until it was officially cut. He was walking to find a seat when he saw Ron Quigley. Quigley waved, and Windflower gestured to him with his full hands in return. Quigley gave him the thumbs up and went to the buffet.

Jones, Evanchuk, and Eddie Tizzard were sitting at a table with Richard Tizzard and Uncle Frank. They called Windflower over, and he sat beside Richard Tizzard. Jones was heading to the bar for a round and offered Windflower a drink.

"Ginger ale," said Windflower.

"Me too," said Jones, "I'm on call in case Smithson needs help." She left for the bar.

"I knew a girl named Ginger once," said Uncle Frank, whose ears were clearly working fine. Windflower cringed. It sounded like there was an Uncle Frank story about to be told and those could end up anywhere, but almost certainly nowhere good. Then Windflower saw the India Beer bottle in front of his uncle, and he pulled back at the sight.

"Are you sure you should be doing that?" he asked.

"No problem," said Uncle Frank. "Who are you, the police?"

Everybody laughed at Uncle Frank. Everybody always did. But, unlike his stories, Uncle Frank and alcohol almost never ended up in a good place together. He wasn't a mean drunk, but Uncle Frank had never been able to drink safely and sooner, rather than later, things would go the wrong way down a one-way street. Windflower thought about saying something else but decided that this subject might be better broached when his uncle was sober. Ron Quigley kind of saved the evening by coming to sit at their table. Uncle Frank liked the inspector and Windflower thought he might be afraid of him, too.

The pub was soon completely filled, and the place was getting warm and noisy. Windflower wasn't great at small talk, but he made sure to wander around and say hello to as many people as he could. Community relations, Sheila would call it. She was good at it, thought Windflower, and genuinely cared about what was going on in people's lives. If there was any way that she, the mayor, or town council could help improve the community, she wanted to hear about it.

He tried to approach Frost, but he was surrounded by well-wishers. Windflower took that as his cue to go outside to get a breath of fresh air. He was kind of surprised when he was joined on the back steps of the pub by Richard Tizzard.

"Evening, Sergeant," he said.

"How are you tonight?" asked Windflower.

"I'm good," said Richard Tizzard. "It's foggy but nice. You can almost smell the capelin coming."

"Will they come soon?"

"They're probably coming in right now with the tide," said the older man.

"Are you going down to get some?"

"Nah, Eddie said he was going down later. He'll get me a few. Years ago we'd get so many we'd have barrels of them pickled, and we'd all spread what was left over on our gardens," said Richard Tizzard.

"You're lucky to have Eddie," said Windflower.

"I know," said the other man. "You're lucky to have Uncle Frank visiting. He's a great guy."

"He is," said Windflower, suddenly growing quiet.

Richard Tizzard sensed his discomfort. "I know you're worried about his drinking. He promised me he'd only have a few."

"That's what he always says. It seldom works out that way."

"I'll keep an eye on him. He's had a hard time lately. He is really upset about your Auntie. I think he's just scared. It's good that he's here. We can look after him together."

"Thanks, Richard. You're a kind man."

Eddie Tizzard appeared at the door to the pub and called out. "Sarge, Dad, come on. They're ready for the speeches."

TWENTY-FOUR

Windflower walked to the front of the room where he was finally able to say hello to Frost. All the people from the detachment were there, even Smithson, as Jones had gone to relieve him for his break. Betsy and her husband, Bob, were also in attendance, along with most of the town council and other local dignitaries.

Some of the Mounties from Marystown had come over for the party, and Ron Quigley brought greetings and best wishes from his crew. Deputy Mayor Skinner gave Frost a plaque from the town of Grand Bank, and Windflower was the next to speak. He told a couple of funny anecdotes about times with Frost in Grand Bank, and then presented him with his card from his fellow officers and Betsy.

"I want to thank you for your service and your support," said Windflower. "But mostly, I want to thank you for your friendship. Please accept this gift on behalf of all of us. May your journeys be smooth and may you never have to paddle alone." He passed over the canoe paddle in a large, long box that had been expertly decorated by Betsy.

Frost opened up his gift and looked at Windflower in surprise.

"The main part of your gift is being shipped to Portage La Prairie from Peterborough. We didn't think you could take it as carry-on," said Windflower.

Frost shook his hand and turned towards the crowd.

"Thank you so much for your kind words and this great gift. I'll certainly be thinking about all you guys as I'm paddling down the Assiniboine. And to my friends in Grand Bank, I want to thank you for welcoming me into your homes and making me feel at home. This is the longest I've been anywhere since I left Manitoba, and I'm very grateful. I also wanted to particularly thank Sergeant Windflower. You have helped me to grow as an RCMP officer and as a man. If you ever need anything, just call."

Once again, the men shook hands and Frost was soon surrounded again by everybody in the room who wanted to personally say goodbye. First up was Betsy and her husband. Bob shook Frost's hand and wished him all the best. Betsy was more direct in her show of appreciation, and Frost had some difficulty extracting himself from her warm embrace.

Windflower thought this was as good a time as ever to make his exit, and before anyone noticed, he was out the door and on his way back home. Sheila and Amelia Louise were amusing each other when he got there. And it was hard to tell who was having more fun.

"You're home soon," said Sheila as Windflower sat beside her. "How was the party?"

"It was good," said Windflower. "Everybody was there, except you, of course. And Frost really liked his gift."

"But? I can tell that something's bothering you."

"Uncle Frank is drinking. Richard Tizzard says that he thinks he's depressed and worried about Auntie Marie."

"That's no excuse to get drunk," said Sheila, raising her voice a little more than she wanted to. "How's that going to help?"

There was no argument from Windflower on that. "It's not," he agreed. "Richard said he'd watch him tonight, and I'll talk to him tomorrow. But I don't have a good feeling about this."

Sheila patted him on the shoulder and rubbed his back. "I'm sorry," she said.

"Thanks," he said, giving Sheila a quick kiss and then deciding to talk about happier things. "Richard thinks the capelin might be in. Let's take a walk down to the beach and see."

"Moira called earlier and said there was a big crowd gathering down there. Let me get the human baby ready while you look after the other one."

Windflower petted Lady, who had been sitting impatiently waiting for her share of his attention. He let her out in the back to do her business and, when she came back, Sheila had Amelia Louise all bundled up and in the stroller. Windflower put Lady on her leash and let her lead the way. She almost knew where to go by the noise they could hear in the distance. They walked through town and down to the beach where there must have been a hundred people of all shapes, sizes, and ages lined up along the shoreline.

There were a couple of bonfires going, and many of the pickup truck drivers who had delivered their passengers left their lights on. That led to an eerie scene on the beach as everybody scrambled near the water's edge with the fog hovering above their heads. It looked and felt like a carnival. You couldn't see much more than a mass of people, but you could hear their shouts and squeals, especially from a distance.

As they got closer, Windflower held Lady tightly because she was pulling to get closer to the action. Finally, he got her to sit, very reluctantly, with Sheila while he went to take a look. It was easy to see the cause of the excitement and joy. Even the fog couldn't completely dull the silver tsunami that was swimming near the top of the water as tens of thousands of capelin tried to get in to spawn on the beach. As they came close, they were being scooped up by nets, buckets, and containers of all sizes.

Windflower laughed as a young boy of about six kept filling his toy bucket with the tiny fish only to have them squirm away soon afterwards. The boy couldn't care less, he was so caught up in his game. Alongside him, the rest of his family, including his mom and dad, were busy gathering up their quota. Windflower said hello to as many people as he could recognize in this mad scene and went back to give Sheila a quick report. She wasn't surprised or the least bit impressed as she handed him a large plastic bag that had been folded in the back of the baby stroller.

"Get us a few," she said. When he looked at her suspiciously, she added, "I've been doing it since I've been old enough to walk. Fill the bag with a couple of dozen, and I'll cook you some for breakfast in the morning."

That was enough to overcome his doubts, and soon Windflower was chasing the silvery fish with the enthusiasm of that little boy he had just witnessed. He watched an older woman next to him to get the technique down. She would wait until the wave had completely come in and then run out into the water with her fishing net low. As the water went back out, it carried the capelin right into her waiting net. She was good. Windflower could see her success as she filled a small cooler beside her almost to the top.

With some trial and error, mostly error, Windflower managed to get a few of the slippery fish into his bag and trotted back to show Sheila his prized catch. Sheila peeked in at the dozen squirming fish and pronounced herself satisfied. Windflower drained the water and carried the bag in one hand while fending off Lady, who was determined to get inside it, with the other. They managed to get home safely with their capelin intact. Windflower went to follow when Sheila pointed to the bag. "You caught 'em, you clean 'em," she said.

Windflower knew this fisherman's axiom all too well, so he let Lady in the house and went to the kitchen with his capelin and a small steel bowl. Ten minutes later he had a baker's dozen of fresh, clean capelin waiting in the fridge for his breakfast. A few minutes after that he was in the shower getting rid of the guck and slime and finally allowing himself to relax from the day. As he crawled in beside Sheila, who was reading a book, he thought about getting Wayne Johnston's *First Snow, Last Light* from the nightstand, but he just couldn't manage it. Before he knew it, he was solidly and peacefully asleep.

Unfortunately, it wasn't for long.

TWENTY-FIVE

He could feel himself falling. That was usually the first step, the precursor to a dream. He knew that if he allowed himself to collide with the ground, he would wake up, just like everybody else did when they had this kind of dream. He had learned this from Auntie Marie. But now he used his lessons to steel himself against the fall and will himself to stay asleep inside the dream world.

The other trick that his Auntie and Uncle Frank had taught him was to try to find his hands when he was dreaming. That was another great way to be fully alive while entering into this other realm. It was something that had been passed on within his family for generations, but Windflower had read about this technique from others who claimed to master the dream world, like Carlos Castaneda, the mystic who had written about his dream journeys under the influence of peyote in *The Teachings of Don Juan*.

But Windflower had no need of peyote or other substances to help his dreams become real. He struggled under the weight of his sleepiness to find his hands. Once he did, he felt a lightness and sense of control that came with this full entry into his dreams. It was as if his dreams changed from black and white to technicolour, which they actually did. The first thing he saw was that he was in a large, open meadow. He realized that this was the place from his last dream, the one with the lady in white.

But now the seasons had changed and it was full summer. He could hear birds singing and something rustling in the forest around him. He could also hear water running, like a brook, and walked towards that sound down a narrow path that led to the water. There, in the middle of the brook was a beautiful white swan. She floated on top of the water like a ballerina and, when Windflower looked closer, he could see something around her long, elegant neck. It was the blood-red amulet that he'd seen around the lady's neck in the previous dream.

This time he did not call out but sat down on the riverbank and watched the graceful swan glide across the brook towards him. The swan came right up to him and stared into his face.

"You are not listening," said the swan.

Windflower was surprised that the swan would speak, or could speak, but he'd had enough dream experiences to know that this was not unusual. Why couldn't swans speak?

"What do you mean?" he asked the swan.

The swan continued to stare at him, full face. "The signs and the messengers are here. They come every day, but you ignore them, pretend that you do not hear them or see them. Wisdom is not knowledge. It is experience. What have you learned from your Elders? What have you learned from your child? From me?"

With that the swan turned swiftly and slipped away down through the brook and around the bend. Windflower chased after her but could see that the brook flowed right into a large river down below where he was standing. There was no sign of the swan. Windflower stared longingly into the distance but only he and the water remained. He could feel that falling sensation again, and this time he allowed himself to wake up.

Sheila was sleeping quietly beside him and, when he looked over, he could see Amelia Louise's angelic, sleeping face. He thought about his dream for a few minutes, but his thinking was no match for sleep, and soon he was back into his restful repose. He heard the baby crying sometime in the night and got up to change her. She was a little fussy until he handed her over to Sheila, who looked after that by feeding her.

Afterwards, the parents took turns dozing and watching the baby until she tired them, and herself, out again. Then, all three fell fast asleep, and not one of them stirred until the morning light shone through their bedroom window.

Saturday morning was Sheila's time off. Windflower changed Amelia Louise's diaper and handed her to Sheila. Once she was fed, she was Windflower's responsibility for a few hours. He was quite happy with his responsibility. He would have gladly taken a few more baby shifts each week. He also had a plan and hoped that his little charge would cooperate.

He took the baby downstairs and put her into the stroller. Lady came to inspect. She wasn't quite sure what this creature was yet, but her smells fascinated the dog. "Come on girl," he said to Lady as he tied her leash to the stroller and headed outside. Despite his dreams and restless night, Windflower was in a good mood. Lady didn't need any excuse for her good humour and was quite content to travel along with Windflower and Amelia Louise.

Windflower was greeted by many boys who wanted to pet his dog, and by just about every woman in town because they wanted to see his child. He obliged them all which made for a very excited dog and an almost irritable baby. That meant he had to hurry their pace to get to his destination, the B&B. Beulah was already there. She was his assistant this morning as he got started on his dinner menu for the evening.

Beulah Janes was a long-time fixture in town. She had lost her husband early in life before having any children and, in place of her own family, she adopted others. She was a cook and cleaner for many families in Grand Bank over the years and of late had become the baker of choice for many more. She made Mug-Up's speciality cheesecakes, the ones that Windflower and others drooled over. Now, she had decided to come work for Sheila and Windflower at the B&B.

And she loved Amelia Louise, almost as much as Windflower and Sheila. That made Saturday mornings even more special. She got to see her adopted child, and Windflower got some time to prep his soup and sauce and get a start on chopping vegetables and readying other ingredients that would make up dinner later that day.

"Morning, Beulah," said Windflower as he came into the living room where Beulah was dusting.

"Good morning, and how is my beautiful baby this morning?" Beulah scooped up Amelia Louise, and almost immediately the baby's mood improved. Windflower imagined he could see a slight smile cross Amelia Louise's face as she reacted to the kind lady's touch and gentle voice. He smiled, too, as he took off Lady's leash and let her wander around. It was important that the dog feel comfortable here since the family would be spending a lot more time at the B&B when it opened full-time in a few weeks.

Once everybody was comfortable, Windflower went into the large and airy kitchen where he engaged in one of his life's great passions, beyond his family and the RCMP—cooking. He put on a hairnet and apron, washed his hands, and then checked the menu that Sheila had gotten printed off and conveniently left for him on the kitchen table. She knew he'd be looking for it. He checked the items and made sure he had all the ingredients ready for the shrimp, pasta, and chicken dishes, along with the salad and fish soup.

He noticed the last item on the menu called "Desserts by Beulah." There was a chocolate mousse cake, an upside-down pineapple bowl, and a coconut cream cheesecake. He hoped there would be leftovers of that last one. He took the shrimp, chicken, and fish he needed out of the freezer to thaw and then chopped, minced, and got his sauces ready. He put them on to boil and prepared his fish stock.

While he was waiting for all of that to come to a boil, he cleaned a few bulbs of garlic. He chopped up a couple of them and put them into the fridge for later. Then he took a handful of whole cloves, covered them with tinfoil, and put them in the oven for roasting. Once all of that got going, the aroma was overwhelming and even Lady, who had found her favourite resting place in the living room, came in to check on Windflower's progress.

"Everything's good in here, girl," he said to Lady as he quickly took her out of the room. He made a mental note that he would have to train her to stay out of the dining area and kitchen. That would be hard. Lady liked food even more than he did.

Windflower, with Lady in tow, went to check on Beulah and Amelia Louise. The woman reluctantly handed the baby over to him and went back to the kitchen to clean up. That was their arrangement and routine. She would also turn down the soup stock and put everything in the fridge for later.

Windflower took the baby upstairs and laid her on the bed while he changed her once again. She gurgled at him as he put on her clean sleeper and clung to his finger when he placed it in her tiny fist. He almost cried, he was so happy. In fact, a few tears ran down his cheek as he saw, and felt, the small life lying in front of him. After a few minutes of play time, he put her in his arms and walked around the room. Before long the baby was asleep, and he placed her in the extra bassinet they had stored in the master bedroom.

Windflower turned on the baby monitor, crept downstairs, and changed aprons and washed his hands again before double-checking his stock and sauces. He added a few more spices and left them to simmer while he chatted with Beulah.

"Thank you for all your help, Beulah. We couldn't make this happen without you. I certainly couldn't."

"Thank you, Winston. I'm happy to help. I loves that child to bits," said Beulah.

"Well, we're glad to have you, especially with the inn opening up full-time soon," said Windflower.

"I loves this old house, too. Even when she starts walking around upstairs, I don't mind. It's a bit of company."

"Who's walking around upstairs?"

"The Missus. Everybody knows she's still looking for a place to sleep. But maybe now that you're going to be here with your family, she'll get some rest. Anyway, I gotta go get my por' cakes and pea soup, if you're done with me."

"Sure, sure," said Windflower, a little dazed. "See you later, Beulah."

He was still thinking about the ghost when he went back to the kitchen and turned off the stove. He put his stock and sauces in the fridge. As he was finishing his clearing up, he heard sounds through baby monitor. His thinking about ghosts needed to wait. His baby was awake.

TWENTY-SIX

Windflower, Amelia Louise, and Lady scurried back home for lunch. Sheila was happy to see everyone and, after the baby was fed, she put her back in the stroller and all three of them headed to the café to join most of the other locals in a favourite Saturday tradition, por' cakes and pea soup.

Por' cakes, or pork cakes, had been a Grand Bank staple and delicacy for as long as anyone could remember. They were cheap and easy to make, with the only basic ingredients being minced pork, pork back fat, and potatoes along with some baking powder and flour to bind everything together. Baked in the oven and served hot with molasses and a bowl of pea soup, this was the traditional Saturday morning lunch in Grand Bank. And this is what Windflower hoped was awaiting him at the Mug-Up.

On their way, Windflower took a diversion to the RCMP office to check in, promising to join Sheila soon. That took longer than he planned because when he arrived, he got a bit of a surprise. Constable Jones was sitting at the front in Betsy's work station.

"Good morning, Sergeant. I was going to call you, but now that you're here."

"Now that I'm here, what?" asked Windflower.

"We have a guest in the back," said Jones. "But I think he's waking up."

Windflower walked to the cell area.

"Good morning, Winston," said a groggy and rough looking Uncle Frank.

"Uncle Frank, what are you doing here?" asked Windflower.

"I guess I had one too many last night."

"One is too many for you."

"Are you going to let me out now?" asked Uncle Frank, a little sheepishly.

Windflower didn't answer. He was spitting mad, but tried to control himself. He walked to the front.

"What happened?" asked Windflower.

"I don't really know," said Jones. "When I got here this morning, your uncle was in the back sleeping. All Smithson said was that it wasn't pretty. Something about a blackout and an altercation at the pub. He said he didn't think there were any charges, but he got called to pick up your uncle."

"Great." Windflower threw his hands up and did a 360 on his heels, not quite knowing what else to do.

"Should I let him go?" asked Jones.

"No. Leave him there. I'm going for lunch. I'll deal with him afterwards."

Windflower left and walked over to the Mug-Up, still fuming, but settled down enough by the time he got there to smile and sit down. Sheila had people coming to talk to her and see the baby, so he got a chance to cool down while he ate his lunch.

Sheila was busy with her visitors but could sense that something was wrong.

'What's going on?" she asked when she finally had a break from the well-wishers.

"Uncle Frank," said Windflower. "He's over at the shop."

"That can't be good."

"No. I'm not sure what happened yet, but you're right. Whatever it is, it isn't good. I'll go see him after lunch. Maybe we'll go for walk in the woods, find out what's going on with him."

Sheila squeezed his hand. "You can help him."

Windflower smiled. "We'll see."

The couple finished their lunch, had a short visit with Moira who came out of the kitchen long enough to say hello and get the baby in her arms for a cuddle. Then Windflower walked back home with Sheila and the baby, dropped them off, and drove back to the detachment.

He waved hello to Jones and walked to the cell where Uncle Frank was sitting on the side of the bed.

"Come on," said Windflower. "We're going for a walk."

Uncle Frank shuffled behind Windflower and got into his Jeep. Wordlessly, Windflower drove them up to the start of the trail near the brook and got out. The older man again shuffled behind him. Still without saying a word, Windflower led them off the main pathway to a side path that was quite overgrown but passable.

"This looks like a deer path," said Uncle Frank.

"More like a moose path," said Windflower. "Deer are pretty scarce around here. In fact, I don't think there are any even though we have a Deer Lake."

"But lots of moose. I know that because I studied up. Did you know that four moose were introduced here on the west coast of Newfoundland in 1904? Apparently, they were trying to develop the interior of the island both to feed the people and to attract big game hunters. Now dere's tousands of 'em b'y."

Windflower was in no mood for Uncle Frank's history lessons or attempts to sound like a Newfoundlander. "Thanks for the moose history," he said curtly. "But we're not here to talk about moose."

They came to an opening in the narrow path that led to an old tree stump. Windflower had sat here many times before, usually with Lady, contemplating some problem in his life. "Sit down and make yourself comfortable."

After a few moments of silence, Uncle Frank started to speak. "I'm sorry, Winston. I guess I thought I could handle it. Richard wanted me to go home with him. I should've gone. But I was having fun, and Frosty wanted me to stay around. He said I made him laugh." Uncle Frank put his head in his hands and started to cry softly.

Windflower softened, wanting to comfort his uncle. But he knew Uncle Frank had to fully feel his emotions right now because that might be the key to him making a change for the better. So, he let him cry for a few minutes.

"Do you remember what happened last night?" asked Windflower.

"Things were going along great, until they weren't," said Uncle Frank. "There's a blank in the middle that I don't remember. I was okay while I was drinking beer, but when they started buying me drinks of Screech and ginger, I was a goner."

"You could have said no. Nobody forced you to drink anything. It's not anybody else's fault but yours."

His uncle was about to protest when he saw the look on his nephew's face. It was a combination of pity and disgust. He stayed silent.

"You don't need to drink to have a good time," said Windflower. "Or to get people to like you. Everybody around here is crazy about you. Although I have no idea why." Uncle Frank allowed himself his first smile of the day at the last comment.

"I know things are hard right now," he continued. "But you are a strong, brave man, someone that I don't just love, but admire. Alcohol makes you dumb and do dumb things."

"I know, I know. It's just that, with your Auntie being sick, I kind of feel lost. I guess I'm afraid I'll lose her."

"She is still a strong and great woman. And she needs you. She sure wouldn't want to hear that you were making an ass out of yourself down here."

"You won't tell her, will you?"

"If you stop right now, I won't. Otherwise, I will call her up and tell her everything. Your choice."

"I can get Richard to help me. I've only been drinking a few days, so I can get back on the wagon. And he can drive me to the meetings. There's one in St. Lawrence and another over in Burin."

"Good," said Windflower. "You know that you'll be okay, no matter what. That's something you taught me."

"I guess life really does come around in circles," said Uncle Frank. "I'll tell you something else I've learned, Winston. Wisdom is not just what we learn from our successes. We learn much more from our failings and mistakes. Pain is a great teacher."

"Thank you, Uncle. I'll remember that, too. Now let's get you home and cleaned up."

Windflower and his uncle walked much more briskly down the pathway than they had on their way up. At the bottom, Uncle Frank stopped Windflower to give him a great hug. "Thank you, Winston. I won't let you down."

Windflower returned the hug and said, "I love you, Uncle."

TWENTY-SEVEN

He drove Uncle Frank to Richard Tizzard's house and swung back around to the RCMP offices.

Jones was still there, but she had been joined by another officer that Windflower hardly recognized out of her white coveralls. It was Froude from forensics.

"Afternoon, Sergeant," said Froude. "Corporal Brown and the team left early this morning, but they left a few things for you. And I'm going to stay to keep working on Crowder's computer. I'm making progress, but it's slow."

"What have you got?" asked Windflower.

"Not much more from the house. Although, we were able to scan some fingerprints besides Crowder's from there. We've identified two other people, a Jason Scott from Toronto and Freddie Tutlow from Halifax. Both have links to the Hells Angels," said Froude, reading from her notes. "Scott is the guy in the van," said Froude. She waited to see if Windflower had any comments or questions, but he nodded for her to go on.

"And we found this on him," she said, holding up a knife that she flicked open to reveal a six-inch blade.

"The murder weapon?" asked Jones.

"Probably," said Froude. "We've scraped it clean and sent it back to the lab.

"Where do you get a knife like that?" wondered Windflower. "They've been illegal for a long time."

"The bikers in Halifax had them," said Jones.

"True," said Windflower. "The ones I dealt with in Grand Falls had them, too."

"You can order almost anything you want online now," said

Froude. "Anyway, I'm going back to work. I'll give it another day or so, and then I may have to ship the computer back to HQ."

"Evanchuk knows something about identity theft," said Windflower. "Have you met her?"

"I saw her at the party last night. If she has time, I'd love to have her take a look at what I have so far."

"I'll send her over to see you, and thanks for your help," said Windflower as Froude walked back to the Crowder house.

"We're going to need some help, boss," said Jones. "I'm on today, and Smithson is on again tonight. But at some point, we'll burn out doing doubles."

"Well, we do have Evanchuk for the week. Maybe we can get her to cover off a couple of shifts, too," said Windflower. "I think she and Tizzard are coming to dinner tonight. I'll ask her when I see her."

"Great," said Jones. "That will help in the short term."

"I know, we'll need someone for the long term, too. I'll talk to the inspector again. Enjoy the rest of your shift," said Windflower. He drove back home where Sheila was curled up on the couch and Amelia Louise was sleeping in the bassinet beneath her. He kissed Sheila on the forehead and went upstairs. A short nap before dinner would be just the ticket.

Half an hour later, right on cue, he heard their alarm clock, Amelia Louise, looking for attention. After a few minutes with the baby and Sheila, Windflower left to go to the B&B to start his dinner preparations. It was a lot of extra work but truly a labour of love for him. He wasn't a gourmet chef by any stretch of the imagination, but he did want to try and fill a gap in the town's dining options, which mostly ranged from snacks to fast food. The Mug-Up served up a great lunch but didn't have the staff or capacity to offer many dinner choices. That's where Windflower and the B&B came in.

He was humming to himself as he walked along to his weekend task when his cell phone rang.

"Good afternoon, Sergeant. I hope you are getting my dinner ready. Repa and I have been looking forward to it all week. It's nice to have more selections to choose from than a hot turkey sandwich."

"I am on my way, Doc. I am very pleased that you and your lovely wife are coming. I hope you will enjoy our menu."

"I am confident in your abilities, my friend. I wanted to give you a call as well about my review of the latest homicide."

"That is a police definition, Doc. Are you sure?"

"Well, he was shot in the head, and there is no weapon nearby, so I think that is a safe assumption, even if I am trespassing on your jurisdiction. I am prepared to call it death by lead poisoning if that would be appropriate."

Windflower laughed. "That's fine, Doc. Did you recover any bullets from the deceased?"

"Yes," said Doctor Sanjay. "Two nine-millimeter caliber bullets were recovered. Is that helpful to you?"

"It will be if they match the bullet we found at the late Jacob Crowder's house," said Windflower. "I'll send someone over to pick them up."

"I will bring them with me tonight," said Sanjay. "I will pass them to you surreptitiously. We do not want to mix our business with the pleasure of our meal."

"Thank you, Doc. See you tonight."

Windflower soon came to the B&B and looked up at the beautiful old house. Then he saw what he thought was a shadow move across a window on the top floor, near their master bedroom. Must be Beulah tidying up, he thought. He was mildly surprised when he opened the door and found Beulah with her coat on heading out the door.

"We need a bit of fresh parsley," she said. "I'm running up to Warren's and I'll be right back."

Windflower paused for a moment, shook his head, and walked into the kitchen. Beulah had warmed up the soup stock and sauces and was already halfway through chopping the vegetables. Once he donned a new hairnet and freshly laundered apron, Windflower washed his hands and got to work.

First up, the soup. He added some more water and a cup of white wine to the stock, then put in a large portion of chopped cod and two handfuls of shrimp. He plopped in some diced tomatoes and celery and then brought the mixture to a boil. When it was done he tasted it, added a bit more garlic and another whole red chili. Perfect, he thought as he left it on a very low simmer.

Next was the salad. Beulah had shaved the bok choy, which Windflower assumed meant that there was no fennel in Marystown. No surprise there. She had also toasted and crushed the almonds as per his instructions. Windflower peeled and sliced the oranges and then put that aside. Just before the guests arrived, he would mix half of it together with some fresh mint and vinegar and oil and save the rest for later guests.

He browned the chicken and, when that was done, put the kale and tomatoes and chicken into a pan and put it in the oven on a one-hour timer. The shrimp could wait until the last minute, and he had already roasted the garlic for the pasta, so he had little left to do but to clean up and get ready for his guests.

Sheila arrived a half hour later, having dropped the baby off with Moira. She would have to do a quick feeding pitstop halfway through the night, but for now she and Windflower had a few quiet moments before the first people arrived. After that, the evening was a bit of a blur for Windflower. But he managed to talk to all of the guests, including Doctor Sanjay, who slipped him an envelope with the evidence that they'd talked about. And he visited briefly with Eddie and Carrie, even having time to ask her to work a couple of shifts for Jones and Smithson. She, of course, easily agreed.

At around 10 o'clock, the last of the straggling diners finished their coffee and left. There was still an hour left to clean up, but this was actually relaxing for Windflower as he and Sheila and Beulah went about their tasks. Sheila drove Beulah home, while Windflower went to Moira and Herb Stoodley's house to pick up Amelia Louise. It was a pleasant evening, but the fog had returned, maybe even thicker than before, if that were possible. He was about to knock on their door when Smithson pulled up in their driveway.

"What's going on?" asked Windflower.

"There's been an accident out on the highway, down towards Fortune," said Smithson.

TWENTY-EIGHT

Anybody hurt?" asked Windflower.

"It's Jeremiah Parsons," said Smithson. "The paramedics took him to the clinic. I think he's in bad shape."

"Okay. You go back and mark off the scene. Close the road until I get up there. I've got to drop off the baby, and then I'll meet you."

Smithson drove off, and Windflower found himself standing in front of Herb Stoodley.

"Sounds awful," said Stoodley. "Anything I can do?"

"Thanks, Herb. But I'll pick up the baby and go"

Moira came out moments later with the stroller and Amelia Louise fast asleep inside of it.

"Thanks, Moira. We really appreciate it," said Windflower. "I hope she wasn't too much bother."

"No problem," said Moira. "We love having her visit. Makes us feel young again."

"Plus, we feel like the grandparents, which is the best part of all," said Herb.

"Thanks, again," said Windflower, as he trundled off home in the fog. He looked behind him after a few seconds. But the Stoodley house had vanished, gone in the mist. Windflower shook his head. Only in Newfoundland, he thought.

Sheila was sitting on the couch drinking a cup of tea when he arrived. He handed her the baby, who had woken along the way.

"There's been an accident," he said. "Jeremiah Parsons. I have to head over to take a look."

"Oh dear," said Sheila. "I understand. We'll be fine. I have just what Amelia Louise wants. But your friend over there may not be as understanding." She pointed to Lady who was circling Windflower with her tail wagging.

"I'll put her out in the back before I go," he said. "It may be a while before I can get back here." He gave Sheila and the baby kisses on the forehead and led Lady to the kitchen. She looked confused and then more than a bit disappointed when she realized what was going on. But she went outside and dutifully came back in when called.

"Sorry, girl," Windflower said. "Not my idea of how I wanted to spend what's left of my Saturday night either."

He got in his Jeep and turned on the fog lamps. They were helpful but mostly in helping others see him rather than improving his visibility. Nothing really cut this type of dense fog. He drove slowly out to the highway and turned right. He could faintly see where Smithson's cruiser was only because of the flashing lights and red flares Smithson had put on one side of the highway. As Windflower got closer, he could see the constable standing in the middle of the road with a flashlight.

"That's not the safest place to be tonight," he said to Smithson.

"I know," said Smithson. "Even with the fog, people still drive too fast. I usually jump to the side and wave my flashlight until they slow down a little. And there's not too many people out this evening anyway."

"So, what have we got, Constable?" asked Windflower.

Smithson swung his large flashlight around and pointed it towards the side of the highway that he had cordoned off. There was Jeremiah Parson's truck lying sideways in the ditch.

"It's hard to tell in the dark. But maybe he lost control as he was driving along in the fog. He barely missed that telephone pole," said Smithson.

"I don't see any major skid marks," said Windflower, shining his own flashlight along the narrow shoulder of the highway. "There's not much indication he was braking."

"He could have been tired. Or drunk."

"I think he's a teetotaler. But he may have been tired. And it's not easy to see anything tonight. We can ask for a blood test anyway. I guess the best thing to do is to take as many pictures as you can tonight. Have a good look around inside the cab as well. We don't want to miss anything. Then get the van towed back to our yard and mark the scene as best you can. We'll have another look in the morning. I'm going over to the clinic."

Smithson took the camera out of his truck and was taking pictures when Windflower drove off. He watched as the red lights faded behind him. Luckily, he didn't discover Jeremiah Parsons in the vehicle. Somebody had called the paramedics first. That would have made his rough week a bit tougher. But then again, it didn't look like anybody in Grand Bank was having a great week.

Windflower parked in front near the ambulances and walked into the clinic waiting room. There was Charlene Parsons and, sitting beside her looking more than uncomfortable, was her son, Levi. He nodded to Levi and went over to the woman and took her hand. "How's he doing?" he asked.

"Not good," she said. "The doctor is working on him. He was out when they brought him in, and he's still out. But at least he's alive."

Windflower squeezed her hand and then let it go. "I'm so sorry," he said. "He's in good hands in the clinic anyway. And if they need to, we can get the helicopter here to take him to Burin at a moment's notice."

Charlene Parsons looked like she was ready to collapse. Windflower thought she might have already, if it wasn't for the young man beside her. She was trying to be strong for him.

"Is there anybody I can call?" asked Windflower.

"No, thanks," said the woman. "My sister, Shelley, is coming over."

"Okay," said Windflower. "I'm going to check in with the desk."

He walked over to reception and asked who the doctor was on duty.

"It's Doctor Gonzales," said the nurse. "I think she's still inside with our patient."

"I'll wait," said Windflower.

He went to the vending machine and got himself and Charlene Parsons a cup of tea. He brought them back to the waiting room.

"Did you want a Coke or something?" he asked Levi. The boy shook his head. Windflower and his mother sipped their tea in silence until a larger, older version of Charlene Parsons showed up.

"This is my sister, Shelley," she said. "Here is Sergeant Windflower." The older woman nodded to Windflower but gave her sister all her attention.

"Is there any news?" she asked. "Do you want me to take the boy home?"

"No," said Charlene. "We're going to see this out as a family. No matter how it goes. It's in God's hands now."

"And the doctor's," said her sister. "Who's on tonight?"

"Doctor Gonzales," said Windflower. "She's very good."

"Yes b'y," said Shelley. "My Abe was in here with his 'pendix, and she looked after him great."

While they were talking, a young doctor with her hair in a braided ponytail came out into the reception area. All four of them jumped. The doctor went right to Charlene Parsons.

"Your husband is in critical condition," she told Charlene. "We have him under sedation until the swelling goes down. He's lost a lot of blood, but that we can deal with. We do not know yet the extent of his head injuries or whether there is internal damage. We're going to monitor him all night, and we'll know more in the morning."

"Will he be okay?" asked Charlene.

The doctor looked sympathetically at the woman but did not offer much encouragement. "It's too early to tell. We don't know exactly what his injuries are yet. We just have to wait."

Charlene Parsons looked weak, but she pushed on. "Can I see him?"

"Come with me. Sergeant, did you want to accompany her?"

"Yes," said Windflower, a little stunned at first. Then he realized that the doctor didn't want Charlene to see her husband alone in his condition.

"Let's go," he said to Charlene, offering her his arm. "Your sister will look after Levi."

TWENTY-NINE

Charlene stood, took his arm, and walked unsteadily down the hall. The doctor gave them each a mask and opened the door to the clinic's emergency area. It looked like an all-in-one operating room, recovery area, and intensive care unit. Jeremiah Parsons was lying in one of three beds in the corner of the room. He was hooked up to a respirator and a heart monitor and had several tubes inserted into him. Windflower recognized one for pain medication and another as outflow.

Parsons was heavily bandaged around his head, and he lay almost perfectly still. If it had not been for the machines, the room would have been completely quiet. It was like Parsons was in suspended animation, which, of course, he was. Windflower led Charlene Parsons to her husband's bedside and, as they got closer, Windflower could see the bruising and swelling on Jeremiah's face. He was almost unrecognizable.

Charlene gasped when she saw her husband's face and instinctively reached for his hand. But the doctor intercepted her. "We have to be careful about germs and infections," she said softly as she pulled the woman's hand back. Charlene stared at her husband, clearly in shock, and then she knelt by the side of his bed, put her head down and started to pray. Windflower and Doctor Gonzales stayed as still as they could, like witnesses to her devotion.

When it looked like she was finished, Windflower helped her up and walked her out of the room and back down the hallway. He helped her sit next to her sister and her son and then went again to see the doctor.

Doctor Gonzales was standing at the desk outside the emergency area, taking notes. She looked up from the computer when

Windflower approached.

"What do you think?" he asked.

"It's not good," said the doctor. "He's barely hanging on and was nearly gone when he got here. Even if the internal damage is not too severe, I have no idea about brain injuries, and his heart is weak. He will need a miracle, maybe more than one. But all of that will be clearer in the morning."

"We might need a blood test."

"Do you have any cause?"

"We need to rule out alcohol or drugs. I can get someone to sign for it. But under the circumstances I think we'll wait."

"That's probably wise."

Windflower nodded silently. He thought about his own new life back at home as he left the doctor and walked back to reception. One life grows stronger and one grows weaker, he thought as he searched his mind for some quote to ground him. But all he found was a sense of dread that he knew meant that death might be near.

Windflower left the Parsons family to their sad vigil at the clinic and drove home in the darkness. He looked up at the sky and could see a glimmer of the moon. That meant the fog was starting to lift. Maybe it was too late for Jeremiah Parsons, but Windflower took it as a sign, an omen that things might start to get better in Grand Bank. It was hard to see how they could get much worse.

There was a single light left on in the upstairs bedroom, and even Lady didn't stir when Windflower got home. He slid quietly into bed behind Sheila and didn't move a muscle until he heard the baby cry a few hours later. He got up, changed her almost mindlessly, handed her off to Sheila, and fell back to sleep. When he woke again, it was light, and both baby and Sheila were gone. He got out of bed and padded downstairs. There was no sign of anybody, neither mother nor child nor dog. But there was a note.

"We're gone over to the bazaar at the church. There's a bowl of fruit in the fridge. I'll make you something special when I get back. Love, Sheila."

What a wonderful woman, thought Windflower as he put on a fresh pot of coffee and turned on the radio for *Weekend Arts Magazine*. Sunday morning was his time off. He lounged around in his pajamas and read the *Evening Telegram* while some very lively music played. He ate his bowl of fruit on the back porch with the sun beating down and the air around him filled with the sounds of people enjoying their lives. Maybe this is what retirement feels like. Whatever it was, he liked it a lot.

But at the same time, he was happy when his wandering family came home an hour later.

Sheila gave him the baby to watch while she went to the fridge and took out their capelin catch from Friday night that Windflower had cleaned and then promptly forgot about. She rolled the small fish in flower and fried them crispy brown on both sides. She put three on a plate for Windflower and made them some thick brown toast to go along with their fish. He ate his first three and asked for three more before she finished her first order.

"That, my dear, was simply delicious. We should have them again."

"Same time next year," said Sheila with a laugh. Then her mood softened.

"Isn't that awful about Jeremiah Parsons?" she asked. "That poor family. I wonder how Charlene is holding up."

"She was pretty shook up last night. What are people saying today?"

"They're saying it doesn't look good. Do you know anything else?"

"Nope. I'll find out more when I go to the detachment and maybe to the clinic later. I'll call you."

"Thanks," said Sheila, handing Amelia Louise over to Windflower. "This little stinky one needs a bath."

Windflower had a wonderful few minutes giving the baby a bath. When that was finished, he bundled her up in a blanket and passed her back to her mom. His next task was just as pleasant. He and Lady took a stroll all over town and back home again. The dog could have gone on forever, but Windflower had to go check in at work and then get ready for the Sunday edition of dinner at the B&B.

THIRTY

Sunday was a simpler version, roast beef with all the trimmings, plus the same soup and salad from Saturday's menu. Beulah would top up the desserts with another special treat. That reminded Windflower to check the fridge when he got over there to see if there was any of that coconut cream cheesecake left. But first he had to go to the detachment.

Jones was on duty when Windflower arrived, and he checked for any news about Jeremiah Parsons from the clinic.

"Nothing yet," said Jones. "I swung by early on this morning. The mother and her sister were there, and the boy was flaked out on the couch. They didn't have any more news. They were waiting for the doctor to come in. By the way, his truck is out back. I'd say it's a write-off."

"Did you go by the crash site?" asked Windflower. "Anything unusual?"

"I did," said Jones. "I know it was foggy last night, but there's no sign that the vehicle skidded off the shoulder, or that the driver braked when he felt it going."

"What do you think that means?"

"He could've fallen asleep or been drunk."

"I don't think he drank."

"Medications? Maybe he had a heart attack?"

"Maybe..." Windflower's voice trailed off.

"But you don't think so," said Jones, starting to get what her boss was thinking.

"I don't know anything for sure," said Windflower. "I'm going over to see if I can find any facts to go along with the theory."

He didn't get a chance to leave right away because Tizzard,

Evanchuk, and Uncle Frank showed up. There was also a cute little cat that almost jumped out of Evanchuk's arms when she saw Windflower.

"She likes you," said Evanchuk, seeming somewhat surprised.

"Everybody thinks I hate cats," said Windflower. "That's just not true," he said, almost sadly.

"That's okay, boss. I was afraid of cats one time, too," said Tizzard.

"I'm not afraid of cats," said Windflower, this time maybe too plaintively. "I don't think they particularly like me."

"That might be true. My dad told me that cats tolerate us but don't love us the way that a dog would. He says that they have old souls," said Tizzard.

"Old or new, she likes you," said Uncle Frank. "I think she is claiming you as her human."

All of the others agreed. "Let's not get too carried away," said Windflower. "I'll think about it and talk to my boss."

"Great," said Jones. "Maybe that could save me a trip to Marystown. I could use a break."

"I'm coming in for a shift tonight," said Evanchuk.

"That's super," said Windflower. "How'd you make out with Froude?"

"She's really good. She's able to weave her way into the dark web like nobody I've seen."

"What's the dark web anyway?" asked Windflower.

"That's a long story," said Evanchuk. "But I'll try and give you the short version as I understand it. Years ago, some U.S. government or Navy researchers found a way to hide their identity when they went online. They thought a system like that could help police catch bad guys more easily, and certainly they could use it for covert intelligence."

"But the bad guys figured out how to use it, too," said Tizzard.

"Very good, Eddie, you've been paying attention while the smart girls have been talking," Jones quipped.

"He's right," said Evanchuk. "Lots of people want to hide their identity when they go online. That's why we have anonymous comments and avatars. Usually it's because they want to do or say something that might not be quite correct."

"Or legal?" asked Windflower.

"Absolutely," replied Evanchuk. "So, the dark web started to become a haven for child prostitution, scammers and, of course, drug dealers. Most of the phishing, malware attacks, and ransom requests, along with identity theft operations, flow through the dark web. We keep shutting one site down and another pops up."

"But aren't all the identity theft and other scams run out of Nigeria and places like Slovenia or the old Soviet republics?" asked Tizzard.

Evanchuk shook her head. "We've had quite a bit of activity on identity theft in Canada," she said. "There was a famous drug dealer named Ross Ulbricht who ran the Silk Road operations for years. Made millions of dollars from it. He got caught, partially because he used his real name when ordering fake ID papers from a dark web site in Canada."

"Wow," said Windflower. "Do people in Canada buy illegal drugs online?"

"Some do, for sure," Evanchuk continued. "It may come as a surprise, but a lot of dark web activity originates from right here in Canada. On the drug dealing side, this country was once home to the highest number of dealers globally in one dark web market called AlphaBay. That was shut down a few years ago, but even today you can order any drug you want online and have it delivered to you anonymously by Canada Post."

"And Jacob Crowder was connected to this?" Windflower was amazed by how much Evanchuk had learned about the dark web.

"He was in some way," she said. "It looks like he was ordering drugs online and then paying for them through some kind of identity scheme. A bit too deep for me, sir. Froude can explain it better than me."

"I got something too," said Tizzard. "It's kinda low-tech."

"That would be you, Corporal," said Windflower. "Me, too." Everyone laughed.

"I found the van, the one we think may have been at Crowder's house. Well, I didn't exactly find it. But I know who it was rented to. And it hasn't been returned." Tizzard waited to be asked.

"So, who rented it?" asked Windflower, a little impatiently.

"It was registered to a Frederick Tutlow, and Jason Scott was the second driver. I've put a watch out on the vehicle."

"They're the guys that forensics got prints from at Crowder's house," said Windflower. "And the dead guy at the dump is Jason Scott." Then, turning to Jones, he said, "Put out Tutlow's name and picture all across the island and to airports and ferry terminals. Maybe he's still around the province somewhere. Good job, everybody."

"Yes, good work, everybody," said Uncle Frank. "Now are you taking me cod jigging or not?"

"Yes b'y," said Tizzard. "I told him last year we'd go out and get a fish, and he's never shut up about it since."

"Well, you can't be making promises and then breaking them now, can ya?" asked Uncle Frank. "Come on, before I tells yer da on ya."

"Oh, my God," said Windflower. "You just got here and you're talking like the locals."

"It's pretty good, eh b'y?" said Uncle Frank.

"Yes b'y," said Windflower as everybody laughed. "I hope you catch your supper. But if you don't, you and Richard are welcome over at the B&B later. We've got roast beef."

"We'll be there," said Uncle Frank. "We can save my fish for tomorrow."

Windflower laughed again and went to his Jeep for the short ride to the clinic. As he was turning into the parking lot, he noticed Lillian Saunders getting into the passenger side of an ambulance. He parked his Jeep and walked over as she rolled down her window.

"We're getting ready to take Jeremiah Parsons to Burin," she said.

"How is he?"

Saunders shook her head. "I don't think he's woken up yet, but they want to do a scan on him, and that's why we're going to Burin."

Windflower nodded and walked into the clinic. The reception area looked like a disaster zone. Charlene Parsons and her sister sat in stunned silence while Levi played a video game on his phone. There were remnants of last night's snacks and this morning's makeshift breakfast that someone had brought over. Windflower wished he'd thought about bringing some food over. Not that it would help them, but it might help him feel better about the difficult situation.

"They're taking him to Burin," said Charlene.

"I heard from the paramedics," said Windflower. "Do you want someone to drive you over?"

"No, Shelley is going to drive me. Levi wants to stay with a friend."

"What did they tell you?"

"They still don't know much. The doctor was here a while ago. She said that they were keeping him sedated. The swelling hadn't gone down enough. Now, they need to do a scan on him. But I don't know what any of that means. It can't be good." Charlene Parsons shivered as she spoke those last words, and her sister wrapped her arms around her. Windflower could tell that this wasn't their first cry of the night. But at least they had each other.

Doctor Gonzales came out of the back and walked towards them.

"He's ready to go now," she said. "Do you have a ride over?"

"Yes," mumbled Charlene as she stood to talk to the doctor. Her sister continued to hold her. "Is he going to die?" she asked.

The doctor looked at her and paused before she spoke. Windflower watched her intently as she struggled to find the right words. "He is relatively stable right now. That is all we can hope for. Once we get him over to Burin, they will see what the damage is, and then we'll know more."

Not bad, thought Windflower. No lies and a faint ray of hope. As they were processing this information, they could see the paramedics wheeling Jeremiah Parsons, still full of tubes and now hooked up to a portable monitor and respirator, into the waiting ambulance out front. Both women sighed and, if they hadn't been supporting each other, both may have fallen over.

All four adults watched the ambulance being loaded and slowly driving away.

THIRTY-ONE

I'll be going over later to check in with the doctors in Burin," said Doctor Gonzales.

"We're going to head over soon," said Shelley Parsons. "First, we're going home to get cleaned up and to help Charlene pack a bag. We've got cousins in Salt Pond we can stay with."

"I can give Levi a ride," said Windflower, trying to be helpful.

"That would be great," said Shelley. Charlene was trying, and not quite making it happen, to regain her voice. She squeezed Windflower's hand and smiled weakly at the doctor. In response, the doctor's maternal instinct kicked in, and she pulled the older woman into her embrace.

"I know it's hard, but I'll be with you," said the doctor. The two Parsons women were now openly sobbing.

Before he started bawling too, Windflower went to Levi Parsons and tapped his shoulder. The boy looked up at the Mountie in surprise, but after saying goodbye to his mother, followed Windflower out the clinic door. He was even more surprised when Windflower opened the passenger side door of his Jeep and invited him to jump in. With equal parts terror and excitement, Levi Parsons got in as Windflower shut the door behind him.

Windflower tried to make small talk with the teenager but to no avail. He crunched himself as small as he could in the seat and it looked to Windflower like he was trying to either levitate or disappear. Since neither was possible, Windflower asked him if he liked ice cream. The kid shrugged his shoulders. Windflower took that as a yes and decided to drive to the best place around to get an ice cream, the small store in Garnish.

They drove in silence. When they got there, Windflower simply asked the boy if he wanted chocolate or vanilla. Those were the two main soft-serve options. Once again Levi shrugged so Windflower decided to get them both a swirl, a combination of both flavours. He brought them back to the Jeep and passed one to the boy. He took it and Windflower drove off. They started back towards Grand Bank when Windflower pulled over at the lookout in Frenchman's Cove.

It was called a park, but there wasn't much there but a small wooden structure and some steps that led down to the beach. Whenever he was over this way, Windflower liked to stop and gaze out over the ocean. Today was one of those days. He got out of the Jeep and walked down toward the water. He peeked behind him, but it looked like Levi was still sitting in the passenger seat, although Windflower thought he could see the boy eating his ice cream cone. Progress, he hoped.

He walked along the beach for a few minutes and then returned to the Jeep. Levi Parsons had eaten his cone and put in his earbuds. Windflower tapped on the window of the Jeep. "We don't allow them in RCMP vehicles," he said.

Levi Parsons almost jumped out of his skin and quickly took his earbuds out.

"What kind of music do you listen to, anyway?" asked Windflower as he started up the Jeep and turned back towards Grand Bank.

"Dunno," replied Levi, in that universal language of teenagers that signified their wish to be left alone. But Windflower wasn't having any of that today. Whether Levi Parsons liked it or not he was going to be with him for at least 20 minutes. He could talk or listen. Preferably both. But Windflower was going to talk in any case.

"I'm not much for modern music," said Windflower. "I guess that makes me an old fogey." Levi had his head down while the Mountie was speaking, but Windflower could tell by his body language that was exactly what the boy was thinking. "I like classical music," said Windflower. "I wish I had learned to play an instrument. I hear you were in the band at school."

Windflower could see the boy's eyes light up a flicker and, just as quickly, go blank. He didn't speak, but since Windflower was interpreting teenager, he assumed that this reflected Levi's disappointment with the music program being cancelled. He switched gears. "No headphones, but we are allowed to have music."

Windflower pulled over to the side of the highway and plugged in his iPhone. He scanned for a minute to find what he was looking for. It was a group called the Joe Trio from Vancouver playing Queen's "Bohemian Rhapsody." Windflower had heard this group play a bit of a concert on CBC radio and was amazed by the combination of classically trained musicians performing a very modern classic rock song. The piano, violin, and strings mimicked the guitar and vocal solos that made the piece so memorable and entertaining. By the end, Levi Parsons was nodding his head along with the music. He was almost smiling when Windflower dropped him off at his friend's house a few minutes later.

Windflower watched as Levi Parsons trudged up the driveway and even though he did not speak or wave goodbye, Windflower felt that they had made some kind of connection. The power of music, he thought. He put the music back on and turned it up. He was still humming Queen when he walked into the B&B.

THIRTY-TWO

Beulah was singing in the kitchen as he came in. He paused for a moment and listened. It reminded him of his mother when he was small. She was almost always in the kitchen when he came in after school or from playing outside. He'd smell the aroma of venison stew or a pie being baked in the oven. And his mother would be singing, often along with the small radio that was always on in the kitchen. But at other times, she'd be singing a hymn or a spiritual verse she had heard at the local church. She wasn't particularly religious, but she loved the music.

Beulah was the same. She had long since given up going to church. Some falling out over the years. But she still loved to sing the hymns, and Windflower thought he recognized the words to one of his mother's favourites. It was "What a Friend I Have in Jesus." Windflower wasn't religious, either. But he loved to hear a woman's voice raised in praise.

"Hi Beulah," he said as softly as he could.

"Oh, hi Sergeant. I'm just fixin' to put the roast in the oven."

"That looks beautiful," said Windflower. "Do you have any desserts for tonight?"

"I bet you're wondering if there's any of that cheesecake left."

"You're reading my mind."

"I made two. So, I have a full one left for tonight. But I put aside a piece for you from the first one. I meant to give it to you last night, but I forgot. It's in the fridge."

"You are the best," said Windflower. He reached into the fridge and took out the cheesecake that had been plastic-wrapped and placed on the lower shelf, where nobody but Windflower would look.

"Thank you," he said as he took his first mouthful of the coconut cream cheesecake. "This is heaven on earth."

Beulah smiled and watched Windflower slowly and deliberately demolish the cheesecake.

"That was great," he said.

"I'm glad you enjoyed it. It's great to see a man with an appetite."

"Oh, he has an appetite, all right," said Sheila, who had just come into the foyer with Amelia Louise in the carriage and Lady's leash wrapped around her arm.

"She fell asleep on the way over," said Sheila as Beulah lifted her out of the stroller.

"I'll take her upstairs and get her straightened away," said Beulah.

Windflower patted Lady's head as Sheila took out her baby supplies and got organized. Lady would hang around in the living room for part of the evening, and then Windflower would put her upstairs in a spare room. She didn't particularly like it, but she would have a nap until they came to get her later.

"It doesn't look too good for Jeremiah Parsons," said Windflower. "They shipped him over to Burin for a scan, but his swelling hasn't gone down, and he's still out of it."

"What did the doctor say?" asked Sheila, walking into the kitchen to put the kettle on.

"She didn't really say anything. But her body language told me that she doesn't think there's much hope."

"Such a terrible accident."

"It may not have been an accident."

Sheila's eyes widened in surprise. "What do you mean?" she asked.

"Well, I don't know anything, but there's no skid marks or obvious signs that Jeremiah Parsons tried to slow down or avoid the accident. I've got no proof, only questions. And nobody to answer them."

"Do you think he tried to kill himself?" asked Sheila. Windflower didn't reply. She poured them both a cup of tea. "I guess this is the way it happens," she said.

"What do you mean?"

"Someone hurts themselves, kills themselves. Makes it look like an accident. The family knows but doesn't want to say anything. We know and we don't want to say anything. Who are we protecting? The man is nearly dead," said Sheila.

"I think you're right," said Windflower. "That's exactly how it goes. That's why we never hear about the problem. 'Cause nobody wants to talk about it."

"Talk about what?" asked Beulah.

"Jeremiah Parsons," said Sheila. "He's been taken over to the hospital in Burin."

"That can't be good. I hope he's okay," said Beulah. "He was a stern man, but nice underneath."

"Did you know him growing up?" asked Sheila.

"Yes b'y," said Beulah. "He was a bit younger than me. A quiet boy. His father was a hellfire and brimstone man. He fished by himself because some of the other men would cuss sometimes. I don't think Jeremiah had an easy life."

"Nor does his son," said Windflower.

"Levi's a good boy," said Beulah. "I knows some people calls him strange, but I likes him. He's calm and polite and a good worker, too."

"We were thinking about hiring him to help out over here during the summer," said Sheila. "What do you think?"

"I think it would be grand," said Beulah. "Now, I gotta go home for a few minutes before everything gets busy here. I'll be back to look after the baby in a little while."

Windflower and Sheila enjoyed their tea in the kitchen for a few more minutes until he had to start getting ready for dinner. He kissed Sheila on the forehead and went about recreating the soup and salad from yesterday. He checked the roast, and the smell nearly drove him crazy. It needed a bit more cooking, he decided, not too much but some. He put it back in the oven and set the timer. In an hour, he would take it out, cover it with tinfoil to keep it warm until the first guests arrived, at which point he would start carving for the first round of Sunday dinner.

THIRTY-THREE

He and Sheila prepared the vegetables together until she heard the familiar squeal of the baby monitor. She went upstairs to look after Amelia Louise while Windflower finished putting the final touches on the dinner. He loved Sunday nights most of all. It felt more like a big family dinner, the ones that you see on TV, the ones that Windflower never had growing up. But he could certainly have them now.

The first guests were Herb and Moira Stoodley, and Windflower was pleased to sit for a minute with them while he poured them each a glass of wine. Sheila and the baby joined them soon after, and she took over the hostess duties while he went back to the kitchen. Within half an hour, the dining room was full, the last arrivals being Richard Tizzard and Uncle Frank. Windflower made it around to visit everybody and to deliver their food and wine, but it was only after almost all the guests had left that he finally got to sit down himself.

Sheila helped the final diners settle up while Windflower got them both a plate of food, and they sat down at the table with his uncle and the elder Tizzard. They were drinking tea and chatting about Uncle Frank's trip out on the water.

"It was a grand day," said Uncle Frank. "Sunny, warm, not a cloud in the sky."

"Yes b'y," said Richard Tizzard. "You had a great day for it. I've been out days when you could hardly see with the fog. You had to navigate by smell."

"Did you get any fish?" asked Sheila. Windflower was too busy eating his roast beef dinner, rare with more than a touch of pink, garlic mashed potatoes swimming in gravy, some more of those maple-glazed carrots, and two of the last Yorkshire puddings, to do more than listen.

"I got a big whopper, and Eddie got one, too," said Uncle Frank. "I think him and Carrie are having some of theirs tonight. Richard is going to make us cod's head stew."

Windflower almost choked on his roast beef. "You're eating the cod's head?" he asked

"Yes b'y," said Richard Tizzard. "There's lots of fine fish still in the head, including the cheeks and the tongues, of course." Windflower nodded. "We fry 'em up lightly with some onions and celery and then add water and a few potatoes, milk if we got it, and that's it. It's sum good b'y."

"We don't eat the bones, though?" asked Uncle Frank, just to be on the safe side.

"No b'y," said Richard Tizzard. "But people all over the world cook and roast the whole fish after they've cleaned it. And they eat everything. Even the eyeballs. The fact is that these extras have a lot of vitamin A, omega-3 fatty acids, iron, zinc, and calcium. They eat fish head curry in Southeast Asia and all over Africa. It may be the next foodie trend."

Everybody laughed at that last remark. Windflower finished his meal and got a fresh pot of tea. He poured everybody a cup.

"It's awful about Jeremiah Parsons," said Richard Tizzard. He was waiting for Windflower to respond, but the Mountie stayed quiet and sipped his tea.

Sheila was the first one to reply. "Yes," she said. "I hope he's okay. It was such an awful accident."

Richard Tizzard looked at Uncle Frank as if to check with him first before speaking. Uncle Frank nodded. "We don't think it was an accident," said Richard Tizzard.

Now he had Windflower's full attention. "What do you mean?" asked Windflower.

"Well, he wasn't drunk. Unless he started drinking that night. He wouldn't even go to the convenience store when they started to sell beer. He would make his wife go in," said Richard Tizzard. "And he was a troubled man. None of us were close to him, but we've seen him driving around the wharf and down by the dock in

Fortune, mooning and watching the fishermen come and go. I'm no psychiatrist, that's for sure, but he was depressed. No doubt about that."

"Off the record, and very unofficially, I share your concerns," said Windflower. "I'm not even going to comment on what is an ongoing investigation. But Sheila and I have been talking, too. Whatever happened with Jeremiah Parsons, only the doctors can deal with that. But we have to make sure that nobody else has to suffer alone."

"We need to break this silence," said Sheila. "It's killing people, and it has to stop. I'm glad that you're talking about it openly. Maybe we can make a difference for other men and women in our community."

This discussion quieted everyone down and no one had the appetite for more dessert or tea. Richard Tizzard and Uncle Frank walked off into the dark, softly talking amongst themselves. Right after they left, Beulah came downstairs with Amelia Louise, who had woken and was now desperately seeking her mother.

Sheila fed the baby while Windflower and Beulah cleaned up. They scoured the pots and pans and loaded up the dishwasher. Beulah took all the tablecloths and napkins off the tables and washed the floor. Windflower took all the garbage out to their box out back. Anything left exposed was an invitation to the ever-present, ever-hungry seagulls that floated over town.

He came back in as Beulah was just finishing her chores. They both saw it at the same time as it saw them. At first, the mouse froze, like a rabbit pretending not to be there. When Beulah screamed, it ran and Beulah screamed again. Windflower tried to grab it, but the little creature scooted between his legs and out the door he had just entered. It disappeared into the grass in the backyard.

Sheila came running in with the baby. "What happened? Is everyone okay?"

"We're fine," said Windflower.

"It was a mouse," said Beulah.

"It's gone now," said Windflower, trying to reassure everybody, especially Beulah.

"Where there's one, there's many," said Beulah.

"She's right," said Sheila. "I'll call the pest control people tomorrow. It was on my list."

"That will get them out," said Beulah. "But I think you need a cat."

Windflower looked at Sheila. "There's something I have to talk to you about," he said.

Sheila raised her eyebrows and handed him the baby. "I'll go get the dog."

Beulah folded some linens while Windflower played with his daughter. Lady came down with Sheila, excited to be free and to see her people again. They closed up the B&B and wished Beulah a good night. The little family strolled home together.

"Are you talking about adopting that stray cat, Missy, or whatever?" asked Sheila.

"It's Molly," said Windflower. "And she's not a stray, she's an orphan. We'll talk when we get home."

But both he and Sheila knew that Molly the orphan was about to become a new member of their family. Hopefully she would take on the important role of head mouser at the B&B.

THIRTY-FOUR

Monday morning came too early for Windflower. Amelia Louise had been fussy and didn't settle down 'til late. Then she woke up and wouldn't go back to sleep until she had exhausted both her parents. Such was the life of a family with a newborn, thought Windflower, dragging himself out of bed to change anzby up before passing her on to an equally tired Sheila.

He jumped in the shower and let the hot water lull him half back to sleep. Then he shook himself awake, shaved, and dressed for the day. He could hear Sheila trying to coax the baby back to sleep, but that didn't sound promising. He went downstairs, put the coffee on, and headed out for his morning walk with Lady.

The day was dawning gloriously. The wind was moderate and mild, and the sun was already taking the chill out of the air. It was mornings like this that Windflower knew what people were talking about when they called this island God's Paradise. It was enough to make you forget the long, dreary, and snowy winters, and the endless summer days and nights of RDF—rain, drizzle, and fog—that would sometimes go on for a month.

But today was perfect, thought Windflower. It seemed like Lady agreed. After a brief but brisk walk they got back home. He brought a cup of coffee up to Sheila and commiserated with her about their sleepless night.

"I'll have a nap as soon as she drops off," said Sheila. "I'm going to try and get over to the meeting at the clinic this afternoon."

"Oh yeah," said Windflower. "That's on today. What are you going to do with her?"

"I'm taking her with me," said Sheila. "If I'm going to be a working mom, she's going to have to get used to that. Plus, if she gets fussy, any of the women in the room would love to have a cuddle."

Windflower laughed. "I'm going to try to get over there, but if not, Jones will represent us well. Anyway, I gotta run. Duty calls. Goodbye my loves," he said as he kissed baby and mother on their foreheads. He grabbed a banana from the top of the fridge on his way out and drove to work.

When Windflower arrived, Betsy and Jones were sitting together in the lunchroom. Molly the cat was in a cage beneath them.

"Where are you taking her?" he asked Jones.

"Smithson is going to take her over to the SPCA later today," she said. "We couldn't find a home for her."

"That is so sad," said Betsy. "I'd take her, but Bob's not partial to cats."

"Well, why don't you put her in the cell for today?" said Windflower. "We might have a plan for her."

"You're going to keep her?" asked Jones. "That is great news."

Betsy rose to give him one of her special hugs, but Windflower was too fast this morning. "Put her in the cell, for now. We'll talk about this later," he said as he grabbed a cup of coffee and escaped to his office.

He could hear them chattering to themselves and cooing to the cat to give her the good news. That made him smile. It also made him smile when Betsy walked by his office and nodded, giving him one of her "you did good" looks. This might turn out to be a good day.

Jones came in shortly afterwards, cat-less, but holding up an envelope with his name on it. "Smithson said that Froude from forensics dropped this off last night. She came by in Matthews Taxi and said she was leaving."

Windflower opened the envelope.

"Dear Sergeant, sorry for the short notice, but HQ wanted me back in Halifax and to bring Crowder's computer hard drive with me. I'm gone to Gander and they're sending a chopper to bring me over. Evanchuk has an idea what this is about. She can fill you in."

"Is she gone?" asked Jones.

"Gone to Gander and then Halifax. Took some of Crowder's

computer stuff with her. Can you go over to the house and take one more look around? We should be able to release it as a crime scene now."

"No worries," said Jones. "I'll go by there this morning. I'm at the meeting at the clinic this afternoon."

"Thanks," said Windflower.

Jones left and he had a few minutes to eat his banana and drink his coffee. Breakfast, or some brief facsimile, he thought. He didn't have much time to think before Eddie Tizzard showed up at his office.

"Good morning, Sergeant. What a grand day. We had a beautiful feed of fried capelin for breakfast."

"Yeah, they're sum good b'y."

"I've got news on our rental car and Freddie Tutlow," said Tizzard.

"Spill the beans, Corporal."

"It looks like he tried to make a run for it but got spotted at the airport when he brought the van back. He was booked on a flight but never showed. Our guys at the airport said they saw him on the tapes looking worried. They think he's still in St. John's."

"Okay. Talk to the constabulary in St. John's. Maybe look up that guy we worked with before. Langmead?"

"Yeah, that was his name. A good guy. I'll give him a call."

"Good," said Windflower. He noticed that Tizzard didn't move. "Something else?" he asked.

"Well, we were wondering, Carrie and me, if we could talk to you for a few minutes later."

"Sure. Is something wrong?"

"No, no. Everything's great. It's just that we have some decisions to make, and we wanted your advice."

"Absolutely. Come back later and we can go for a coffee. Better yet, let's go over to the B&B. It's quieter there. Maybe around five o'clock."

"That would be great. Thank you, boss."

Tizzard went away looking both pleased and relieved. Windflower smiled again to himself. Three people happy with me. Maybe I'm on a roll. He spent a few quiet moments in the office feeling pleased with himself, although he was aware that self-praise was faint indeed. But this morning, he'd take it.

"Doctor Sanjay on line one," came Betsy's voice through the intercom.

Windflower punched the button and said good morning.

THIRTY-FIVE

"And a fine Newfoundland morning to you, my friend," said Sanjay. "I heard a new one last night. Stay where you're to 'til I comes where you're at."

"What does that mean?" asked Windflower.

"I think it means to stay put," said Sanjay. "But the fellow said it so fast, I had to have him repeat it three times before I understood a word he said. And I still had to have him explain it to me."

"That's a good one, Doc. I'll have to see if I can find a way to use that with the inspector. He would be impressed. So, what's on your mind this morning?"

"I've got some preliminary tox results on Jacob Crowder that I wanted to share. Not the full results. That takes time. But I asked them to test for street drugs."

"And?"

"THC, cocaine, and opioids, several strains including fentanyl," said the doctor. "High enough presence to suggest regular, if not habitual, use. Probably the only reason he stayed alive as long as he did is because it looks like he didn't take it intravenously. No needle marks."

"Another piece to the puzzle. It looks like he was ordering drugs online."

"Anyway, thought I should let you know. I am releasing the body to his mother this morning. She said she's going to have a small service at the funeral home before cremation. I think I'm going to go over. I don't think people should have to do this alone."

"That's nice of you, Doc. 'When beggars die there are no comets seen.'"

"True enough, my friend. Yet in the religion of my youth, death is simply part of the transition from one world to another, the samsara or the eternal cycle of birth, life, and death. So, we are never really alone. We just think that we are sometimes."

"That is very interesting. In my traditions we are moving from one world to another all the time. My Auntie says that only a fool would believe that all we can see with our eyes is all that there is."

"Hmm, interesting, as always, to chat with you, my friend," said Sanjay. Windflower and Sanjay enjoyed sharing their stories with each other about their traditions growing up in very different parts of the world. "We simply must have our time to talk longer," said Sanjay. "Oh, and to enjoy that beautiful Scotch that is waiting for us. Do you have any time this week?"

"Let me check with my superior officer at home. I will let you know. I would very much like that, too."

Windflower went to the back to get a cup of coffee when Betsy came running in behind him.

"Sergeant, it's Charlene Parsons on the phone. She's laughing and crying, and I can't make any sense out of what she's saying other than it's a miracle," said Betsy.

"What's a miracle?" asked Windflower.

"You better talk to her yourself."

"You won't believe what happened," said Charlene Parsons, and Windflower had a hard time following along as she kept speeding up the more excited she got. "Jeremiah woke up and he's talking and he says he's sorry and that he was all wrong and that he wants to talk to Levi."

"It sounds like great news," said Windflower, when he was finally able to get a few words in. "What would you like me to do?"

"I know it's a lot to ask, but could you get someone to bring Levi over? My sister is the only one with a car, and our truck is beat up. He really wants to see him."

Windflower thought about it for a moment. But just a moment. "Of course, we can," he said. "I'll drive him over myself."

"That is so kind of you," said Charlene. "He told me that you were nice to him when you dropped him off. He's not used to having people be nice to him."

"No worries. Is he still at his friend's house?"

"Yes, he's still there. Thank you, Sergeant. Thank you so much. Jeremiah will be so happy when I tell him."

Windflower had little time to process all of this before Betsy was standing in front of him with at least one, and possibly 100, questions visible on her face.

"Jeremiah Parsons is out of his coma and talking," he said.

"Thank God," said Betsy. "It's a miracle."

Windflower thought about saying that this was probably more medical than spiritual, but he wisely declined. It might well be a miracle that the man wanted to talk to his son. And who was he to get in the way of the story that would soon be known as the Jeremiah Parsons Miracle?

"I'm going over to the hospital. I have to drive his son over," said Windflower.

"That's very kind of you," said Betsy. "Seeing how busy you are and all."

Now Windflower was really feeling his pride at doing good. And rather than risk losing that good feeling by saying anything else, he grabbed his hat and drove over to pick up Levi Parsons.

The teenager was sitting on the porch with his friend, although Windflower noticed that neither of them paid any attention to the other. Both had music on and were playing games on their phones. He parked the car in the driveway, and when Levi noticed him, he walked up to the Jeep. Windflower could tell that the kid was trying to act cool but was also more than a bit proud to be chauffeured around in an RCMP vehicle. He nodded briefly in the direction of his friend, who didn't hide his surprise at Levi's ride for the day.

Once in the vehicle, Levi went into his protective shell and pretended that nothing or nobody, including Windflower, existed. That was okay with Windflower. He could use a little peace in his life. But riding along the highway, he changed his mind. Windflower reached into the console in the middle of the Jeep and pulled out a CD case. He rummaged very quickly through it until he found what he wanted. He plugged the CD in and turned up the volume a notch.

Levi Parsons tried to ignore the music at first but then started paying attention. "What's that called?" the boy asked.

"It's "Spring." Vivaldi. It's part of a set called the *Four Seasons*. You like it?"

"Dunno," said Levi, and he went back to zombie mode.

When the music was over, Windflower let the air stay silent. He peeked over at Levi. Levi saw him and said, "Do ya want to hear some of my music?"

"You're not going to blow my head off, are you?" asked Windflower, only half jokingly.

Levi Parsons smiled for the first time that day. "Nah," he said. "Dis is cool."

The teenager put his CD into the player.

What Windflower heard next was amazing. The music was loud, but it was melodic and, while there was the usual guitar, drums, and bass he associated with rock music, he could also make out strings like a violin or viola, maybe both, along with keyboards. And was that a French horn in there somewhere, too? But the lyrics were what blew him away. He heard "Somethin' filled up, My heart with nothin', Someone told me not to cry." Then he heard, "Children wake up, Hold your mistake up, Before they turn the summer into dust."

The song began as a dirge and picked up tempo until finally at the end there was a chorus of voices singing in unison. As far as Windflower could tell, they were asking the new generation to "wake up" and take action before it was too late. It was a joyous celebration in the face of everything.

"Wow," was all he said after the song was over and Levi had pulled the CD out of the player. "That was amazing," he added, once he recovered his voice. "Who was that?"

"Arcade Fire," said Levi. "Do you like it?"

"I think it's pretty cool," said Windflower. "Put it back in so we can listen to the rest on the way to the hospital." Levi Parsons had a second smile that morning and put the CD back in. Before they knew it, the pair had gone all the way through the CD and were pulling up in front of the Burin hospital.

THIRTY-SIX

Windflower parked near the emergency vehicles and walked into the hospital with Levi Parsons trudging behind him. The reception nurse directed them to a room in the recovery area outside of the intensive care unit. Windflower pushed open the door and was quite surprised to see Jeremiah Parsons hooked up to various machines but alert and talking to his wife in an animated manner. When he saw them, the father called his son over.

Charlene Parsons moved out of the chair to give Levi a seat. She smiled at Windflower and moved to stand behind her son.

"I know that I have been a bit strict," said the father. "I thought I was trying to guide you, but now I realize I was trying to control you. That wasn't right, and I can do better. I'm sorry, son. I hope you can forgive me."

Levi didn't know what to do. He looked behind at his mother who gave him an encouraging nudge towards his father. He moved closer, and the older man reached out his hand. Levi took it, and his father pulled him close. Soon, both embraced and one, maybe both of them, started to softly cry. Charlene Parsons didn't pretend to hide her open tears.

Windflower almost started to cry himself. Maybe it really is a miracle, he thought as he watched this splintered and troubled family come together in front of his eyes. Then, Jeremiah Parsons surprised Windflower again by turning to his wife and asking her to leave while he talked to the Sergeant.

"I think my wife told you I had a dream," said Parsons. "I don't know how it happened or why, but you were in my dream. I saw you talking to that woman."

"Which woman?" asked Windflower, although he was starting

to get a sense of where Jeremiah Parsons might be going.

"The lady with the red amulet," said Parsons. "Who is she?"

"I don't know," said Windflower, thinking that this was one of the weirdest situations he had ever found himself in. "But yes, she was in my dream. And she came as a white swan, too." He couldn't believe he was talking to another man, a relative stranger, about his dreams. But, here he was. And so was Jeremiah Parsons.

"The swan came too, later on," said Parsons. "I don't remember much of what happened over the last few days. It was like I was hovering above all of this, watching. I could see my wife and the doctors, but I couldn't wake up. First came the lady, then the swan. They started talking to me about my life and how much my wife loved me and how much trouble my son was in. They asked me if I would do better if I had another chance."

The man paused now, almost overcome with emotion as he tried to go on. He found his voice again. "I promised I would in every aspect of my life," said Parsons. Especially with Levi. They told me that he had lessons to teach me. I never knew that. Now I'm ready to learn and just love him. Will he be okay?"

"He already is," said Windflower quietly. "He's teaching me things right now. But he needs you. He needs his dad."

As they were speaking, a doctor came into the room. She said hello to Windflower. He recognized her, Doctor Frances Larkin, from a previous visit.

"That's enough for one day," she said to Parsons. "You need your rest." She did a quick examination of the tubes and checked the monitors. Jeremiah Parsons smiled at her and winked at Windflower as he dozed and then drifted off to sleep.

"Is this a miracle?" he asked the doctor as they were leaving the room.

Doctor Larkin thought about it for a minute. "I'm sure there are those who could give a perfectly logical medical explanation. But I'm not one of them. Sometimes we get lucky. And yes, sometimes there are miracles." She went to give Charlene Parsons an update while Windflower thought about her response.

He was still thinking about that after he had said his goodbyes to the rest of the Parsons family and was driving back to Grand

Bank. He looked over on the passenger side and saw something on the seat. It was the Arcade Fire CD. Levi Parsons must have left it. He put it in the player and settled back in. Of course, the first song was "Wake Up." How appropriate was that? For Levi, for Jeremiah Parsons, and for Windflower himself.

He was making great time along the highway when his cell phone rang. He pulled over to the side of the road just past the turnoff to Molliers.

"Hi boss, it's me," said Jones. "I'm on my way to the meeting at the clinic. But I wanted to tell you that when I got to the Crowder house, his mother was there."

"Maybe she wanted to say goodbye."

"Maybe. But I think she was looking for something. The drawers in the bedroom were all thrown about and that's not how forensics leaves things. I asked her what she was doing there, and she got all defensive. Kind of told me to mind my own business. I told her it was still a crime scene and escorted her out."

"What was she looking for?" asked Windflower.

"I don't know, sir," said Jones. "But I have a feeling something's not right about this."

"Well, they do teach us to trust our intuition," said Windflower. "I'm on my way back. I'll run over there and take another look around. In the meantime, can you get our locksmith to put a security alarm in? It needs to be kept secure."

Jones indicated that she would look after that, and Windflower continued his journey home. A woman's intuition was not to be ignored, or ignored at your peril. He would drop by the Crowder house. But first things first. A sandwich and a cup of tea at the Mug-Up were in order.

Windflower got to the café right at the tail end of lunch. Most of the tables were stacked with dirty dishes and the harried waitress, Marie, was busy lugging them to the kitchen one table at a time.

"A cup of English Breakfast and a turkey with dressing sandwich on whole wheat," he said when she finally came to take his order.

He was enjoying the peace and quiet of the near-empty café when he noticed a visibly upset Elizabeth Crowder come in the front door. She scanned the place quickly and found what she was looking for. Him. She strode towards him, her fancy purse dangling from her arm.

"I was looking for you. Who do you think you are, keeping me out of my own son's house?"

"We're keeping everyone out until we complete our investigation," said Windflower. "Perhaps I can help you if there's something in particular you are looking for."

"You don't know who you're messing with," said the woman. "I want access to my son's house, unrestricted and by the end of the day. Or my lawyers will be talking to you." Then, Elizabeth Crowder huffed, puffed, and marched out of the café without saying another word, the only sound being her high heels clicking on the hardwood floor.

Herb Stoodley had witnessed the scene as he was bringing Windflower his cup of tea. "Beautiful lady," he said as he arrived at the table. "But clearly not happy with the service she's getting from the local gendarmes."

"I guess so," said Windflower. "But her threats, 'they pass me like an idle wind.' Did you know her growing up?"

"Just a little. But Moira was more her age. I'll check with her later and let you know."

"Thanks," said Windflower as Marie brought him his sandwich. "I was having such a good day up to that point."

"Well, it's never too late to start your day over," said Stoodley. "After I finish washing up all these dishes, I'm going trout fishing. That always works for me."

"Well, good luck with that," said Windflower, taking time to eat his sandwich.

"Ah, to paraphrase an old Roman, our fate is not in luck or in the stars, but in ourselves. Have a great day, Sergeant," said Stoodley.

Windflower smiled and, after he wiped up the last of the crumbs on his plate, paid his bill and drove over to the Crowder house.

Jones was right, he thought, as soon as he entered the place. Forensics might strip a house down and take it apart, but they always put it back together. The person who had been here after them did not have the same visiting etiquette. Papers had been scattered everywhere, and it looked like Crowder's remaining computer equipment had been subjected to a physical pounding by a hammer or some other blunt object.

Windflower thought that was really strange since he knew that Froude had taken the hard drive out. But maybe the person who had done this wasn't aware of that. It could have been Elizabeth Crowder, but what was she looking for? Maybe there was something else here that forensics had missed. He didn't have time today, but this was getting more interesting all the time. One thing was clear, they had to keep this house under surveillance until they could do another, and more complete, search.

Forensics would have done a good job in capturing all of the evidence in plain sight, but what if something important was hidden? And how could they keep an eye on the place until Windflower could organize that search? All his cops were tied up on regular duty, but he didn't really need a police officer. He needed a night watchman. Uncle Frank, he thought. He'd be perfect.

Windflower closed up the Crowder house and replaced the police tape out in front that had been shredded by the wind and likely Elizabeth Crowder, if not others. He drove back to the detachment where Jones was also arriving. In the back of her car were Richard Tizzard and the man he was looking for, Uncle Frank.

Windflower said hello to Betsy, who was on the phone, but followed him into his office a bit later to get an update on Jeremiah Parsons. The other three went to the back to get coffee and talk about the meeting that had just finished. Windflower would get his briefing later. First, he had to give Betsy Molloy sustenance for her information network.

"Is it true? Did he really come back from the dead? Was it a miracle?" she asked.

Windflower thought about it for a second and, with all he had seen, the word miracle qualified. "That's way above my pay grade to define," he started. "But the fact that he's alive and that it looks like that family is going to be okay, that's a miracle, at least in my books."

"We heard he asked for his son," said Betsy. "Did you see them meet? What was that like?"

Windflower thought again. "It looked like more than one of them had woken up," he said. That left Betsy muttering prayers aloud to herself and Windflower smiling as he watched her tear down the hallway to pass along the good news. That must be nine smiles today already, he thought. This is a very good day.

THIRTY-SEVEN

He walked to the back and could hear the laughter and good cheer all the way down the hall. He joined Jones, Richard Tizzard, and Uncle Frank and grabbed a couple of Purity Jam Jams from a half-eaten package. He poured a cup of coffee and listened as Richard Tizzard talked about what he and some of the older men planned to do as a follow-up to the meeting.

"We need to do a survey. But we can't send it by e-mail," said the elder Tizzard. "People don't trust it."

"We could hand deliver it," said Frank. "Walk it around and get some of the boys down at the wharf to help us."

"But how will you ensure confidentiality?" asked Jones.

"Put all the answers in a plain brown envelope," said Richard Tizzard. "They can drop it in the mail and send it back to us."

"Have it sent back to the new mental health person at the clinic," said Jones.

"There's a mental health person at the clinic?" asked Windflower.

"Not yet, but there will be," said Uncle Frank. "The mayor is going to look after getting that for us."

"And we're planning a big community meeting for next month, so we've got to get busy," said Richard Tizzard. "Let's go Frank. We'll start on the survey tonight."

"That reminds me," said Windflower. "I need Frank for tonight. I have a special assignment."

"Me? Working with the RCMP? That'll be a first," said Uncle Frank.

"Well, come over and have some supper first," said Richard Tizzard. "I was going to fry up a nice piece of cod that somebody dropped off."

"Can I have my dinner first, boss?" asked Uncle Frank.

"You can," said Windflower as Richard Tizzard said his goodbyes. "I need you to keep an eye on a property for us."

"Like a stakeout?" asked Uncle Frank.

"Kind of." Windflower explained the task to his uncle and told Jones about his interaction with Elizabeth Crowder. "I want you to stay inside and out of sight," he told Uncle Frank. "If anybody comes near or tries to get in, call us. Okay?"

"That's pretty easy. Do I get a badge?" asked Uncle Frank.

"Go have your dinner," said Windflower with a laugh. "And no drinking, right?"

"I'm dry as a bone," said Frank. "A bit thirsty, but I'll take a thermos of tea with me to keep me going."

"Can you get him set up before you leave and tell Smithson to check in on him a few times overnight?" he asked Jones after his uncle had left. "Just to be on the safe side."

"Are you worried about Elizabeth Crowder?"

"Not particularly. I'm more worried about Uncle Frank." This time, Jones laughed. "Now I've got to go see the younger Tizzard and Evanchuk," said Windflower. "Do you know what's going on with them?"

Jones shrugged her shoulders. "Not for me to say, boss."

As Windflower walked to the front to leave the building, Betsy was leaving, too, so he walked her out the door to the parking lot. "Good night, Sergeant," said Betsy. "This was a good day. We don't get a miracle every day."

"It was a good day," said Windflower. "But maybe there are more miracles than we think. We just don't see them."

Betsy nodded, and Windflower got in his Jeep and drove to the B&B. Tizzard and Evanchuk were sitting on the front porch talking when he pulled up.

"Hey boss," said Tizzard.

"Sergeant," said Evanchuk.

"It's a grand day," said Windflower in return. "I just saw your dad. He and Uncle Frank are really excited about the mental health work."

"Yeah," said Tizzard. "That's all they're talking about. I hear the meeting went well."

"Sounds like it," said Windflower as he unlocked the door and ushered the pair in front of him. "Let's go to the parlour."

"You've got a house guest," said Evanchuk, who pointed to a tiny mouse skittering across the floor and escaping into a hole in the wall.

"More than one, apparently," said Windflower. "But I've got a solution."

"Pest control?" asked Tizzard.

"Yes, of sorts," said Windflower.

"The cat. Molly the cat," said Evanchuk. "That's brilliant."

"I don't often have great ideas. But when I do . . . ," said Windflower, leaving that line hang in the air. Tizzard and Evanchuk laughed.

"So, what did you want to talk to me about?" he asked.

Tizzard looked at Evanchuk, and she indicated that he should go first.

"Well, Carrie and I are going to get married," said Tizzard. "Well, engaged first and then married."

"That is great news," said Windflower. He gave Evanchuk a warm embrace and started to shake Tizzard's hand. But he quickly realized that wasn't right and hugged Tizzard too.

"I'm very happy for you both."

Evanchuk beamed and Tizzard smiled. Clearly, there was more going on here than that initial news. Windflower waited for Tizzard to go on.

"But the thing is," said Tizzard, looking at Evanchuk for support, "I'm not sure I want to stay in the Force. It's not that I don't like it and all. I love being a Mountie. I always have. It's only that after getting shot, and now planning a future with Carrie, I'm not sure I want the lifestyle."

"That's completely understandable," said Windflower. "It's a difficult life, especially when you start a family. What are you thinking about doing?"

"I think he should go to law school, and so does his dad," said Evanchuk. "He'd be a great lawyer."

"What do you think?" Windflower asked Tizzard.

"I'd love to go to school. Not just because my dad wants me to. I always thought I would, too. Then I got the Mountie bug, and that was the end of the school idea. I'm not afraid, you know," said Tizzard.

"I don't think anyone would ever accuse you of that, Eddie," said Windflower. "Foolhardy, reckless, driving too fast, for sure. But never being a coward. You are a hero to many people around here."

Tizzard blushed, and Evanchuk reached over to put her hand in his. "Think about it as a new adventure," she said to him. "And I'll be with you."

"You know, you might be able to do both," said Windflower. "There's a training program you can apply for that allows you to stay on the Force while going to school. There might even be some funding for it. If you're okay with it, why don't you get Betsy to find the info? Another option to consider."

"That might work," said Tizzard. "I'm really torn about this. I feel like I'm being pulled in two directions. But one thing I'm not torn about is having a life with Carrie." Now, it was Evanchuk's turn to blush. "I need to borrow her for a day to go to St. John's to pick out a ring. Hope that'll be okay."

"No worries," said Windflower. "I'm used to staying up all night with the baby, anyway. I'll look after an overnighter for you."

"Thanks, boss," said Tizzard, and he stood to shake Windflower's hand. To Tizzard's surprise, Windflower pulled him in for a man hug. Evanchuk got one of her own. "Go and enjoy your evening," he said. "I've got one more small task to look after here."

He watched as the pair walked down the steps, hand-in-hand, totally in love and not caring a whit who knew it. He thought of the play *As You Like It* and the lines: "No sooner met but they looked, no sooner looked but they loved, no sooner loved but they sighed, no sooner sighed but they asked one another the reason, no sooner knew the reason but they sought the remedy; and in these degrees have they made a pair of stairs to marriage..."

Ah, he thought, young love. And, for him, more domestic duties. Windflower got a couple of mousetraps out of the cupboard under the sink and baited them with peanut butter. "Sorry about this, but you're not welcome to be my guests anymore," he said aloud as he placed them strategically around the kitchen and pantry. Then he closed up the B&B and walked out to his Jeep. He took a quick peek back at the inn before he drove off. He caught a glimpse of something moving in the window. Maybe a curtain blowing in the wind. Better close that window when I come back, he thought.

THIRTY-EIGHT

Windflower arrived to a house that was excited to see him. The baby howled, the dog yipped, and Sheila ran to greet him in hopes that he would take one, if not both, off her hands. He was happy to oblige. He bundled Amelia Louise up, put her in the stroller, and put Lady on her leash. A quick peck on the cheek to Sheila, who waved goodbye, and they were off.

The baby stopped crying as soon as the stroller wheels hit the pavement. And Lady was happy, well, just to be Lady. They had a long walk all over town, a much-needed nap for Amelia Louise, and an even more-welcomed break for Sheila, who had found something in her freezer that filled the whole house with an aroma so delicious that Windflower got weak at the knees when he came into the house.

He took the baby out and, as he cradled her in his arms, danced around to show all of them how happy he was to be home. Lady, of course, joined in the festivities.

"Did you eat anything today?" asked Sheila. "Besides coffee and dessert?"

"Ah, you know me well," said Windflower. "But I managed to get a turkey sandwich at the Mug-Up on the way back from Burin. But pray, tell me, kind lady, what exactly is in that pot on the stove?"

"I found a container of moose stew. If you make us up a green salad, I think it'll do."

"Super." Windflower didn't need any more encouragement. He put the baby into the bassinet and put her on top of the table so he could see her while he put the salad together. She didn't do much, but he made faces and tried to entertain her anyway. She may not have been too amused, but Lady was very interested in his activities, and Sheila broke up laughing at his antics.

"So, I have big news. But it's secret," said Windflower.

"Talk, Sergeant," said Sheila, holding up the knife she was using to cut their bread. "Or I'll have to torture you."

"Tizzard and Evanchuk are getting engaged. I saw them over at the B&B."

"That's no secret. They can't keep their eyes or their hands off each other."

"Well, how about this, and you have to promise to hold onto this one tightly?"

"I solemnly swear. Tell me."

"Eddie's thinking about getting out and going to school."

"Wow. But you know I'm not really surprised. After what's happened to him, I think you're all a little different. Has he got a plan?"

"Not really. He's talking about law school, but that's a long path to follow. I suggested he check out what support might be available from the Force."

"That's good. And I thought I'd have all the news from the big meeting."

"I have more, too. But I refuse to provide any more information until I get fed. Geneva Convention or something."

"Sit down and I'll dish it up. Wouldn't be nice to see a grown man crying for his supper in front of his child." But Amelia Louise had nodded off, and Windflower was prepared to do whatever was necessary to get some of that stew.

Sheila ladled him up a bowl of steaming hot stew and, as soon as it cooled down a notch, Windflower was lost in moose stew heaven. Sheila used the opportunity to tell him all about the mental health meeting.

"That's so great," said Windflower when he finally came up for a refill on his moose stew. "Jones and Richard Tizzard and Uncle Frank were pretty excited, too."

"Well, it would be a minor miracle if we got a mental health worker, but if it's the last thing I do as mayor, I'm determined."

Windflower waited for his stew to cool. "Speaking of miracles," he said, "did you hear about Jeremiah Parsons?"

"I did. How'd he look when you saw him?"

"He was pretty broken up, but he's a changed man. Apparently, he had a dream that suggested he should be a better father and husband, and he's going to try."

"That meets my definition of a miracle," agreed Sheila, who decided it was time to catch up on news from their other home. "Was everything okay at the B&B?" she asked. "I called the pest-control guys, but they can't come until Thursday."

"We had another uninvited guest. I put down some traps. I hate doing that. At least we'll have the cat soon. Oh my, I forgot the cat at the detachment."

"I was thinking about the cat."

"Are you having second thoughts?"

"No, but how do you think Lady will react to having another pet to share you and everything else with?"

"Good point." Windflower realized they were going to have to think about this a bit more. "I'll help you clean up, then go back and get Molly. She can stay tonight, and we'll see how it goes."

Windflower thought Sheila looked a bit skeptical about that plan, but at least he had one. Now, if only all the people and all the animals could learn to coöperate and get along. Windflower washed while Sheila dried, and she put on the kettle as he drove back to get Molly.

Jones was still there, so he got her to help bring Molly and her cage out to his Jeep, along with all her food and supplies.

"First sleepover at her new home," said Jones.

"Technically, she will be living at the B&B," said Windflower. "Don't forget to check on Uncle Frank."

He drove slowly home, and Molly seemed calm and cool about her new adventure. That lasted thirty seconds after she saw Lady. For her part, the dog went completely out of her mind. Windflower ended up locking the dog in the kitchen and putting Molly in her cage on the back porch.

"That went well," he said to Sheila.

"Have a cup of tea and a date square," said Sheila. "You look like you could use it."

Windflower took two squares and sighed. "I have a feeling that the best part of my day is over," he said.

Sheila smiled and patted his arm. "That may be too rash, too unadvised, too sudden."

Windflower smiled back. "You may be right, Sheila Hillier. You may be right."

THIRTY-NINE

As long as the potential combatants were kept in separate rooms, Windflower was able to maintain the fragile animal peace in his household. But as soon as one got a whiff that the other would be entering their territory, the war was back on. Windflower had never seen Lady behave in this manner, and his knowledge of cats was minimal. So, for the evening, the dog ruled the kitchen while Molly had the back porch to herself.

He took Lady out the front door for her evening walk and, upon her return, she growled at the door leading to the back porch. She could certainly smell the cat and wanted to let Molly know that she was not welcome in her domain. The cat was also acting strangely. When Windflower cleaned her cage and refilled her bowls, she spat at him. It was as if she wanted him to know that she was not happy with his decision to bring her into such an obviously unsafe area. She hissed at the door as he was leaving. He realized that one wasn't for him. It was for the enemy on the other side of the wall.

"How'd it go?" asked Sheila, who was propped up in bed with Amelia Louise beside her.

"It feels like a peace-keeping mission where neither side wants you to intervene."

"I think we need to take it slow. The cat's likely been through a lot and is traumatized from losing her owner, and she probably didn't have a great life over at that house."

"And Lady has been the queen and the special one ever since we got her. I've got the late shift tomorrow night, so I'll bring them both over with me. I'll keep them separate, but they'll get used to being around each other."

"Somebody once told me that you can do that by petting one

and then the other. So, they learn the other's scent. But don't do it together," said Sheila with a laugh.

"No kidding. Even at the detachment we're not equipped for an outbreak of that type of hostility." Windflower was laughing now, too. "We'll take it slow. It'll be okay."

"Someone has already adapted to her new pet," said Sheila, pointing to the baby who had fallen fast asleep beside them. She picked up the baby and put her in the bassinet.

"Good night, my love," she said as she turned out the light.

"Good night, Sheila," said Windflower, exhausted from his day but grateful for his life.

He woke once during the night to change and play with Amelia Louise after Sheila had fed her. Then he quickly fell back into a deep sleep that took him all the way to the first light of morning.

He turned over when the sun came through the window and gazed down into the bassinet. Amelia Louise was lying there with her eyes wide open. She stared back at him, and he fell in love all over again.

He picked up the baby and carried her to the spare room where he changed her. Then he brought her back to Sheila for breakfast. After she'd eaten, he took her again and walked her until she burped. He carried her downstairs where a sleepy Lady woke and brushed herself up against him. He almost made the mistake of letting Lady out into the backyard, but some furious mewing convinced him otherwise. Instead, he wrapped Amelia Louise in a thick blanket and put the leash on the dog. Lady started to yap at the door that held back her new mortal enemy but soon decided to follow Windflower's lead out the front door.

They didn't stay long, but it was enough to deal with Lady's pressing needs and not so long that the baby would fuss. I can manage this multi-tasking, thought Windflower. That was until he opened the door and let Lady off her leash. She made a run for the back door and starting howling at the cat. The cat started screeching in return, sure that the demon dog was about to come through the door and eat her. And the baby joined in at a decibel level Windflower had never heard before in his life.

Sheila appeared at the top of the stairs. "What in heaven's name is going on down there?" she asked.

Windflower simply walked to the stairs and handed the baby over.

"This is going to take some time," he said. Sheila smiled and went upstairs with Amelia Louise who was now pretending that nothing had happened. Lady, too, decided to stop barking. Only the cat continued to roar, although Windflower sensed that was short term and would subside, too, as soon as he took Lady out again.

"Come on, Lady. Let's go."

He grabbed the dog's leash, which was still wrapped around her and stepped outside. Lady was her old, happy self in a flash. He thought about scolding her but realized that was futile and just started off on their morning walk. They both needed some semblance of normality this morning. By the time they got back to the house, Lady was completely back to normal. All that started to change the moment she got inside and saw Sheila petting the cat with the baby in the bassinet at her feet.

The dog began to buck and pull against Windflower, and it was all he could do to hold her back. But he did, and eventually got her to sit and stop barking. "Stay," he ordered in a calm but strict voice. Lady really didn't want to, but she obeyed.

"Now we switch," said Sheila as she moved towards Lady and handed Windflower the cat. "We have to get them used to each other."

Windflower took the cat. Sheila quickly reached for Lady and grabbed her leash. Good thing, too, because Lady had definitely decided she must save her master from the terrible cat. But she calmed a bit when Sheila started stroking her, although she sniffed the air to determine what that awful odour of cat was. Molly had tried to squirm out of Windflower's arms, but he had a tight grip. She, too, settled down when Windflower began rubbing her neck.

Finally, both animals were subdued and relatively content. That's when Amelia Louise decided she was the one left out. She howled for attention as loudly as any of the pets. Sheila put Lady in the back hall and went to the baby. Lady wasn't very happy about that and started to bark her disapproval. Windflower managed to shush her, while Sheila gave the baby exactly what she was looking for. Molly sat on the floor looking like she had won the war, which for the moment she probably had.

Windflower and Sheila looked at each other and burst out laughing.

"It's a beginning," said Sheila.

"I'll put some coffee on," said Windflower. "I could use a cup after that. How about an omelet?"

"I could use both," said Sheila, as she put the baby on her shoulder to burp. "By the time it's ready, she'll be back asleep."

Windflower mixed up the eggs for one large omelette between them, sliced a melon. and found a few pre-cut slices of bologna in the fridge. He whipped the eggs and fried them and the bologna. Along with the melon slices and a few pieces of home-made toast, this made for the perfect breakfast.

"Let's switch them up," said Sheila. She took Molly in her arms and when Windflower let Lady out, she quickly placed Molly behind the door. Neither animal was happy, and they could hear Lady growl and Molly kind of whimper and hiss. But Sheila and Windflower couldn't care less. Eventually, Molly quieted down, and Lady found her usual spot underneath the kitchen table. They thoroughly enjoyed their breakfast, and Sheila cleaned up while Windflower showered and dressed.

"It's going to be okay," said Sheila.

"It already is," said Windflower. He patted Lady on the head and went out to the back porch to give Molly a rub, too.

"Call me," said Sheila as he walked down the driveway.

"I love you," Windflower called back. And the baby and the dog and the cat. And my life. I am a lucky man.

FORTY

Windflower drove past the Crowder house on Tim's Lane, but there was no sign of life. Maybe Uncle Frank was still sleeping. He'd check with the office when he got in to see if there were any reports. He parked his Jeep outside and walked into the detachment. Betsy was in the back making her first pot of coffee for the morning, and Jones was waiting for a cup.

"Morning, Betsy, Yvette," said Windflower.

Both women said good morning. Betsy poured them all a cup of coffee and went to her station in the front. Windflower stayed for a few minutes to chat with Jones. He told her the Molly and Lady story. She thought it was hilarious as he recounted with mock horror when the animals started fighting with each other.

"No pet was really harmed in the making of this story," he said at the end, laughing along with Jones. As he walked back to his office, he realized that this was completely true. And that despite Lady's loud barking and Molly's vicious hissing, they were actually like two little kids, maybe a bit afraid, trying to protect what they had from an intruder that was a bit different. Sheila was right. They just needed a bit of time. They would get some of that tonight in the safety of a police station. How perfect was that?

Then he remembered he'd forgotten to ask about Uncle Frank. He went back to the coffee room.

"How did Uncle Frank make out last night?" Windflower asked Jones

"He was all set up over there when I left last night. He had a sleeping bag, a thermos of tea, and a bag of cookies. He said that Richard Tizzard was coming over later on for a game of cards."

"Did he seem okay when you left him?" asked Windflower.

"He wasn't drinking, Sarge, if that's what you mean. I would have smelled it if he had been. I am a police officer. And he poured a cup of tea when I was there—asked me if I wanted one."

Windflower almost said that he wasn't asking about Uncle Frank's drinking, then realized that was exactly what he was doing. "Thanks," he said, feeling a bit sheepish yet relieved

"Oh, and the locksmith is coming, but not 'til tomorrow," said Jones as Windflower was leaving. He waved his thanks and went down the hall to pick up messages from his slot.

A couple of calls from the media looking for an update, which he ignored, one from Ron Quigley, and a short note from Smithson reporting that he'd seen Uncle Frank around midnight and everything was okay. Should have read that first, he thought, as he went into his office to phone Quigley in Marystown.

"Good morning, Inspector. Reporting in for duty," said Windflower. "Hope you have some good news on the relief front."

"True hope is swift, and flies with swallow's wings," said Quigley.

"Is that good news or bad? After all, 'the miserable have no medicine but only hope.'"

"Are you miserable? Surely not with a beautiful wife and brand-new baby."

"It's because I want to spend time with them that I'm asking."

"Well, I do have some good news. I've got approval for Tizzard to go back to work on a three-quarter basis."

"That's good, but how does that help me, if you take him back to work with you?"

"I need somebody full-time. So I've suggested, and HQ agrees, that I keep Evanchuk for the rest of the year and Tizzard can be re-assigned for that period to work with you in Grand Bank. You are getting a three-quarter relief until Christmas."

Windflower thought about his discussion with Tizzard. He realized he couldn't tell Quigley about that chat and Tizzard's idea of going back to school—at least not yet. It was up to Eddie to talk to his boss. Instead, he thanked Quigley and hung up soon after. He was still mulling this whole conversation over in his head when the phone rang again.

"Good morning, Sarge," said Tizzard.

"I was just talking about you. You still in St. John's?"

"Sure am. Say, I hope you were saying only good things about me."

"Mostly good, Corporal, like you. How'd your ring shopping go?"

"That went well. I got all the diamond that an RCMP officer could afford."

"This is simply the beginning, my friend. But you didn't call to tell me about the ring sale at Peoples."

"No. I called you about Tutlow."

"The other guy at Crowder's?"

"The same. Langmead has a lead on a house up in the Battery area where he might be hanging out. I'm going to stay in St. John's for a bit to find out what happens. Carrie is on her way back to Grand Bank with my vehicle. Hope that's okay?"

"That's good. But Eddie, don't go with them to check this out. You are not officially back at work." Windflower paused. "And I don't want anything happening to you."

"Thanks, boss. Langmead already told me to keep my nose out of Constab business," said Tizzard with a laugh.

"Okay. Keep me updated." Windflower had just hung up when he heard, "Forensics on line one."

"Good morning, Sergeant. We found something else that might be of interest to you. There's a woman's fingerprints all over the house in Grand Bank," said Brown.

"Girlfriend?" asked Windflower.

"Might be. But might be something else going on. The woman is Elizabeth Ryan. We don't have a lot on her, just a couple of fraud charges that got withdrawn. But her name is associated with some sort of cryptocurrency scam."

"Like the one that Jacob Crowder was involved with? You know, that might be his mother. Her maiden name was Ryan. Do you have a picture?"

"Good-looking woman. She could be a model or something. I'll send the picture over."

"Send it to Betsy. I'd never find it on my computer."

"I know what you mean. I don't understand technology at all," said Brown, adding that he asked Froude to do more digging on the case."

"That great," said Windflower. "That'll really help. So, does this mean that Elizabeth Ryan or Crowder was here before Crowder was killed?"

"Or just after. Probably more than once. Her fingerprints are everywhere."

"Thanks again."

Windflower walked to the front where Jones, who had just completed her morning highway round, was talking to Betsy.

"I need to talk to Elizabeth Crowder. Will you pick her up?" Windflower asked Jones.

"She was staying at the efficiency unit over the convenience store," said the always well-informed Betsy.

"Is this a request or a demand?" asked Jones.

"It's a request, but an insistent one," said Windflower. "She may have been here before."

"Before Crowder was killed?" asked Jones.

"Maybe. That's what I want to talk to her about."

"I'll go over right now."

"Betsy, can you check the files for anything on Elizabeth Crowder or Elizabeth Ryan," said Windflower. "Any investigations in the past or anything current."

"Will do," said Betsy. "If she was here before, why didn't anyone see her?"

"I hope to find that out, too."

Betsy had a lot more questions she wanted to ask, but Windflower walked away and back to his office. He had some reports to fill out and other questions on his mind right now. He worked away for a while on the paperwork and then called Sheila.

FORTY-ONE

"I was wondering if you had time for a picnic," said Windflower.

"I have time for just about anything," said Sheila. "What are you offering?"

"I was thinking about a chicken and baguette down by the brook."

"Perfect. Amelia Louise and I accept. I'll make a small salad and you pick up the rest. I guess we'll have to leave one of the babies home, though."

"Let's take Lady. She'll love to be outside. I'll take Molly over to the office with me later."

Windflower waved goodbye to Betsy, who was in full search mode clicking away on her computer and fully engaged in a conversation on the phone at the same time. The matter of getting more information on Elizabeth Crowder, or Elizabeth Ryan, was in good hands.

Windflower drove to Sobeys and picked up a full chicken, a fresh baguette, some Boursin cheese, and a large bottle of Perrier. Soon he was loading Amelia Louise into her car seat and letting Lady into the back. Sheila jumped into the front seat with the baby stuff, the salad, and picnic gear. Moments later all of them were sitting or lying in the sunshine next to the brook.

Sheila sliced up half of the chicken and put helpings on both their plates with a serving of salad. Windflower broke the bread into chunks and gave them each a bunch of grapes. Lady watched expectantly as each crumb dropped, and the baby drifted off to sleep in the sunshine.

"What a beautiful day," said Sheila.

"Perfect." Windflower couldn't have agreed more. He tucked

another piece of chicken on his plate and added a piece of bread, spread thick with the Boursin cheese.

"We should do something to celebrate Eddie and Carrie," said Sheila.

"They haven't even told everybody yet. They barely got a ring."

"Technicalities. It's a good excuse for a party. We'll do it at the B&B. Get the Mug-Up to provide some sandwiches so you don't have to cook, and get Beulah to make a nice cake."

"You've thought of everything."

"I do have lots of time on my hands. Plus, they're such a nice couple. So, can I go ahead with the planning?"

"'In the springtime, the only pretty ring time, When birds do sing, hey ding a ding; Sweet lovers love the spring.'"

"I'll take that as a yes. Now, help me wrap all of this up. I can make you a sandwich for your snack tonight."

"You're the best, Sheila Hillier," said Windflower. "And you're pretty good, too," he said to Lady, who had snuggled up close to the pair. "Now, if only you'll get along with your new little friend."

Sheila laughed and put the baby back in the car while Windflower led Lady in from the other side. He dropped them off at the house and saw everybody safely inside. He drove back to work. Jones was waiting for him at the door.

"Elizabeth Crowder's gone," said Jones. "Took the early morning taxi. Betsy tracked down the driver. Said he dropped her off downtown."

"Get hold of Tizzard," said Windflower. "He's in St. John's. Ask him to contact our guys at the airport and the Constabulary to tell them we're looking for her."

"I have a picture I can send to St. John's," said Betsy.

"Put it up on the wire, and make sure the guys at the airport there get it, too," said Windflower. "Did you find anything else about Elizabeth Crowder?" he asked Betsy.

"Quite a bit," she said. "Not much on Elizabeth Crowder. But on Elizabeth Ryan there's three separate investigations. Two involving fraud over $5,000 and one money laundering case. But for Elizabeth Crowder, there's the question of her husband's death."

"What about her husband?" asked Windflower.

"Bruce Crowder died under suspicious circumstances," Betsy read from the paper in her hand. "Drug overdose, it seems. But the reason it was suspicious was that he was not a known drug user. There was some suggestion that he may have been poisoned. That's what his side of the family claimed. Elizabeth Crowder was questioned and released."

"That is interesting," said Windflower. "Thank you, Betsy. Good work. Can you do one more thing? Can you find out who the investigator was on the husband's death? I'd like to talk to him, if he's still around."

"Absolutely," she said. "I'll get right on it."

"Jones, I know it's your night off, but can you come over with me and Smithson to do another search of the Crowder house? Maybe around eight o'clock. It's not ideal to do it that late, but I think we should have one more look around."

"No problem," said Jones.

FORTY-TWO

While Jones and Betsy were busy with their tasks, Windflower had a visitor.

"Uncle Frank, how are ya b'y?" he asked his uncle.

"Well, if I were any better, I'd be dead," said Uncle Frank. "Smithson relieved me at my post. I'm prepared to do another assignment, although I have to admit my last job was a bit boring. I was hoping for a bit more excitement."

"Sorry to disappoint you," said Windflower. "But your services are no longer required by the RCMP. I'm going over afterwards to check out the house and let Smithson go, too. I think the danger is over. But, thanks for your help."

"What, laid off already. I'll have to go on the pogey now," Uncle Frank quipped.

"You're in good spirits," said Windflower.

"I think I'm back on track. There's something about this place that helps me get back to my roots. Brings me down to earth."

"I know what you mean. Even though this is so different from where I grew up, it feels like home."

"I have great sleeps here. I love the way it cools down at night."

"Me too, except when I have those dreams."

"Yes, I can sense there's a lot going on in your dream world. I lost a bit of connection when I was drinking, but it's coming back now."

"I was hoping for that. You and Auntie Marie can sometimes know what's going on with me, even when I can't. But have you ever heard of somebody you didn't know having the same dream?"

"You mean Jeremiah Parsons."

Windflower looked at his uncle, laughed, and shook his head. "I don't know why I'm surprised, but I am. How did you know?"

"Dreams are funny things," explained Uncle Frank. "They feel so personal, individualized, and for the most part they are. They are part of us, part of the connection that we make with the other world, the spirit world. But we're not the only ones with a key to the entrance. That's universal."

"Wow. We can see each other's dreams?"

"Only when we are open and connected to somebody else. That's why me and your Auntie can see yours. You could see ours, too, if you really wanted to."

"I have enough trouble managing my own. How would a stranger like Jeremiah Parsons get access to my dream?"

"First of all, you don't own the dreams. You are merely the channel through which they flow, through which your subconscious can communicate with the other side. But even more importantly, the messages are not only for you. They are for everybody, for anybody who chooses to access them."

"How did Jeremiah Parsons get in there?"

"I don't know. But I know that for me, when I am most emotional, I am also most spiritual. I come as close to Creator when I feel deep sadness as when I am elated or full of joy. There is a doorway to the spirit world at both ends of that spectrum."

"What do I do now?"

"Keep living your life. Learn your own lessons. Experience is knowledge. What did you learn from Jeremiah Parsons? You think that somehow you are here to teach him, give him a gift?" Uncle Frank laughed. "You are here to learn from him. Think about it."

Uncle Frank smiled and left Windflower's office. Windflower thought he could hear his uncle cackling to himself as he left the building. Windflower started to think about everything his uncle told him but, as usual, his thinking time was limited.

"Hey Sarge," said Evanchuk. "Eddie, umm, Corporal Tizzard called. They've got Tutlow."

"Can you get him on the line?" asked Windflower.

Evanchuk called Tizzard and put him on speaker.

"Tizzard, what's up?" asked Windflower.

"We got Tutlow," said Tizzard. "At least, the Constabulary's got him. He's in the lock-up right now. They don't really have anything on him, just some outstanding warrants. I can talk to him about Jacob Crowder, but I'm thinking it would be better to bring him to Grand Bank so you can do it. But I can't seem to convince the powers that be to let me have him."

"Let me talk to the Crown here, and we'll see if we can't move it along. I think we'll try to get him transferred to Marystown and interview him over there. It's a bit more secure than here."

"Okay, let me know. I'm going to hang around the jail until I hear back."

Windflower thank Tizzard for his work, then hung up. He pushed the intercom. "Betsy, can you come see me?"

Betsy showed up seconds later with her trusty pad and paper. "Can you call over and see who's on at the Crown today? I have a prisoner transfer request to process."

Betsy left, and Windflower motioned Evanchuk to sit down. "St. John's was good?" he asked.

"Yes, sir, it was fine. We did our shopping and went to Leo's for fish and chips. Eddie, I mean Corporal Tizzard, told me he never goes to town without dropping in there."

"Did you like it?"

"Oh my God. It was the best fish and chips I've had in my life."

"Yeah, I love that place. So, Froude from forensics left a note saying she was called back to HQ. She said you could fill me in with some more information."

"I don't know how much I can provide. Most of this stuff is way over my head. But as I understand it, the basic plan that Crowder had was to create a forum to buy and sell bitcoins. That was the front. Behind that he was trying to replicate the old Silk Road network."

"That was the one you were talking about before, the one that got shutdown."

"Yeah. The guy behind it, Ross Ulbright, is still a hero to all those dark web nerds, even as he serves out a life sentence. Froude told me that every few months Interpol puts out a new attempt to restart the old network. And it looks like Crowder made that list. That's when the alarm bells went off at HQ and why they wanted her at HQ so quickly."

"Were there any other people connected to this new plan?

"That wasn't really clear from what I saw. But like I said, I'm really a novice at this stuff. There was a code name that popped up though. Scorpion. But I'm not sure what that means."

Betsy came back in over the intercom. "Assistant Crown Attorney Lauren Bartlett is on line two."

FORTY-THREE

"Good afternoon, Lauren. How are you today?" asked Windflower.

"I'm well, thank you, Sergeant. I hear you want someone transferred."

"Freddie Tutlow," said Windflower. "He's being held in St. John's. We want to talk to him about the Jacob Crowder murder investigation."

"What's he being held on in St. John's?" the assistant Crown attorney asked.

"I think he might have some outstanding warrants, but nothing serious. We'd like to have him sent to Marystown and interview him there."

"Let me make a call. I'll get back to you."

"Thank you."

He nodded to Evanchuk. "The Crown will see what they can do," he said. "Can you come over tonight to the Crowder house. We're doing one last property search. Eight o'clock?"

"Yes, sir," said Evanchuk. She left his office and went to talk with Jones who was finishing up her shift. Betsy took Evanchuk's place in front of Windflower.

"I've got the name of the investigator in the Bruce Crowder case. Detective Barry Sherman, OPP. He was in Peel Region. Now he's in Orillia. I've got his number," said Betsy.

Windflower called the number on the paper from Betsy.

"Sherman," answered the man at the other end of the line.

"Detective, my name is Sergeant Winston Windflower, RCMP. I'm calling from Grand Bank, Newfoundland. I'm calling about a case you worked on a few years ago. Bruce Crowder."

"Crowder. Yeah, I remember that," said Sherman. "What do you want to know?"

"I'm interested in his wife, Elizabeth Crowder. She also goes by the name of Elizabeth Ryan. Did you talk to her?"

"Yeah, nice-looking woman. But a little cold, if I remember. We eventually closed the case, but something wasn't right about it. The guy overdosed. No question about that. But he had no record of using hard drugs. No tracks or anything. And this was before the opioid crisis. As a matter of fact, I think that was the first time any of us had seen a fentanyl death," said Sherman. "Today, it's everywhere. But back then it was rare."

"How did he get the drugs?" asked Windflower.

"That was another weird thing. We found an envelope at his house that had a few traces of the drug on it. And we had the lady's fingerprints on it, too. But it was like a regular Canada Post bubble envelope that looked like it came through the mail. That's what she said, too."

"That it came in the mail, and she must have picked it up inadvertently?"

"Exactly. She didn't seem too upset about him being dead, either. Although that's none of our business. Neither was the fact that she collected two million from the life insurance. It didn't look good, but we had nothing else to go on, so the case got shut down."

"What do you think?" Windflower wanted to know what this detective gut was saying to him.

"I always say, follow the money. Follow the money."

"Thanks for your help." Windflower sat back and took in a deep breath. More stuff to think about. His head hurt from so much thinking. But there was a good remedy for that. Go see a dog. Maybe a cat, too.

"I'll see you tomorrow," said Windflower to Betsy on his way out. "I'll be back in later."

He left his Jeep and walked home. It wasn't far, and he needed the air and the space. It felt good to have the wind blowing in his face, and he stopped for a moment at one of his favourite spots overlooking the ocean. Even though it was far from Pink Lake and what he had been used to growing up, there was something about the ocean that calmed his soul. He could sit and watch it roll on forever.

Today, there were a couple of small boats cruising along. They looked so tiny and powerless against the vastness that they floated upon. Kind of like people on the earth, thought Windflower. Powerless, alone, but once we connected to the land or the water, we were made more and became powerful, just like them. A nice thought to replace all those dark and dreary thoughts from work. Taking a deep breath, he let all those bad thoughts go and let in some clean, fresh ones, direct from the Atlantic Ocean. "That feels better," he said to himself.

"What feels better?" asked a voice behind him.

"I guess I was talking to myself," said Windflower, feeling a little embarrassed.

"No worries by me," said Herb Stoodley. "I do it all the time. Moira says that people who talk to themselves are either crazy or have money. I tell her I'm giving myself financial advice."

"That's good, Herb. Out for a stroll?"

"I'm on my way back," said Stoodley. "Got time for a cup of tea? I think Moira is there by now. I asked her about Elizabeth Crowder. Elizabeth Ryan, she called her."

"Sure, I can stop by for a minute. It is official police business."

They walked together the short distance to Stoodley's house overlooking the ocean. Stoodley had been painting landscapes since his retirement as a Crown attorney and he was happy to show Windflower his latest piece. "Not quite finished, but getting there," he said.

Windflower admired the painting. It was a winter scene, a view from Stoodley's back window. The waves were crashing into the rocks below, and the ocean mist was rising up to coat everything in a brilliant white sheen.

"Wow," said Windflower. "We really have to get you to do one for the B&B. Would you consider that?"

"Absolutely. Which season would you like?"

"I love the fall right after the berries are picked and just before the snow."

"You got it. I'm glad you didn't ask for spring. We only get a short one every few years." Both men laughed.

"What's so funny?" asked Moira. "At least you're not laughing by yourself again," she said to her husband.

"Winston dropped by for a cup of tea," said Herb. "I'm going to put the kettle on. I told him you'd tell him about Elizabeth Crowder."

FORTY-FOUR

Oh yes, Elizabeth," said Moira. "She and I went to school together. We were friends, not best friends, because we lived on the other side of the brook. And people didn't mix as much then."

"Like the other side of the tracks?" asked Windflower. "Although, in my case it was who lived in town and who lived on the rez."

"Something like that," said Moira. "None of that exists now, of course, but back then it was a big deal. You simply didn't hang around with those who didn't live on the same side as you."

"What was she like?"

"The best way to describe her might be driven. She was the girl who was determined to succeed, to get ahead. She was nice, but you didn't get in her way. If there was a prize or a reward, she wanted it. She was also determined to get out of Grand Bank. She told everybody she wanted to see the world. I'm not sure where she got all that. We were all too busy playing with dolls and then dressing up and trying out makeup to think about anything else."

"She was a dreamer, I remember that," said Herb Stoodley as he returned with a pot of tea and a plate of cookies and squares. He poured them all a cup and passed the cookies around. Windflower took a date square and sipped on his hot tea.

"She left here young, didn't she?" asked Windflower.

"Yes, she couldn't wait to get out of here," said Moira. "She worked at the grocery store long enough to save a few dollars, and she was gone on the taxi to St. John's. Her sisters were still here, and they would share pictures that she would send home, not just from St. John's—because that wasn't big enough for her—but from Toronto and even New York. She got a modelling job and was involved with a series of men, all of whom she claimed were rich."

"Then she married one, right?" asked Herb.

"Bruce Crowder," said Moira as she passed the cookies to Windflower again. This time he took a lemon square. "He was a banker, I think. Money trader or something like that. The pictures from the wedding in Brampton seemed unreal, especially for us here in Grand Bank."

"When was the last time you saw her before this past week?" Windflower asked Moira.

"She came back for a visit, maybe five years ago. It was after her husband's death. I saw her at the Mug-Up. She didn't recognize me, but I knew her as soon as I saw her. She was always pretty, but now she had the clothes and the hairstyle to match. She looked famous, like an actress."

"Did you talk?"

"We did. I introduced myself and we talked about some of the people we grew up with. But she wasn't much for small talk. The only thing I really remember is that she talked about getting the house fixed up. I asked her if she was planning to sell it, which is what most people do. But she said no, she wasn't planning on selling. When I asked if she was moving back, she laughed. She really laughed at that."

"What about her husband? Did she talk about him at all?" asked Windflower, finally managing to summon up enough self-control to resist a third cookie.

"I said I was sorry for her loss," said Moira. "She just smiled. I won't say she looked happy. But she certainly didn't look too broken up about it."

"Thanks," said Windflower. "That's very helpful. And thank you for the tea and snacks."

Herb Stoodley stood up to walk Windflower to the door. "I'm guessing your interest in Elizabeth Crowder is more professional than personal," he said when they reached the porch.

"There's some questions surrounding the death of her husband," said Windflower. "And right now she isn't available to answer a few more questions. Not exactly a fugitive from justice, but certainly evasive."

"Interesting," said Stoodley. "I'm no great judge of character, to be sure. But there's something else going on with that woman," he continued. "'By plucking her petals, you do not gather the beauty of the flower.'"

"I know that, Doc Sanjay told me. It's Tagore," said Windflower.

"Correct, Sergeant. Rabindranath Tagore, the great Bengali poet and Nobel Laureate."

"See you soon," said Windflower, taking his leave. More things to think about, but not right now. He had a date with a dog and a cat and, maybe, if he was lucky, a beautiful baby, too.

He walked into the kitchen and was met by a bounding Lady. He petted her while he listened for noise from upstairs. It sounded quiet on that front. He left Lady for a minute and went to the back porch. Molly was glad to see him, too. She rubbed up against his leg, and he spent a few minutes stroking her back. She purred while he was sure he could hear Lady grumbling from behind the door. He left the cat, grabbed Lady and her leash and went outside.

"Let's go down to the brook," said Windflower. Lady was more than happy to oblige. They strolled through the late afternoon at a great pace and only paused when they neared the wharf. Windflower spotted Uncle Frank and Richard Tizzard among the small gaggle of men who stood around the apron of the wharf in the harbour.

Even though improvements were being made to the area, including some replacement beams for the aging waterfront and new lighting, the older men still gathered around in their usual location, as if nothing had happened or would happen. They'd been doing this all their lives, and some fancy new light posts were not going to take that away from them. Council had wisely decided to let their old benches and seats remain while the renovations were being carried out.

Richard Tizzard was at the centre of some intense discussion that could have as easily been about hockey as some deep political debate. Windflower didn't want to intrude or slow his walk down, so he and Lady stopped only for a moment to say hi and for Lady to get her usual attention. Then, the pair continued westward towards the brook where Lady gave the passel of ducks her usual attention.

The birds, so domesticated and used to being fed by passers-by, raced towards Windflower. They swiftly turned and swam the other way when they realized that he had 'that dog' with him. They hated Lady as much as she enjoyed chasing them from the shoreline. Eventually, they realized that her bark was the only threat she posed, and they started yelling back in duck language. Windflower wasn't conversant in that tongue, but he was pretty sure it was in the style of "go away you loser dog." Lady pretended she didn't even hear them.

Windflower had to pull her back from the water line to go home, but she pranced along next to him, convinced that she had won the battle again. Windflower smiled as he glanced back over his shoulder at the ducks who were coming back to the shore as quickly as Lady was departing. Maybe there was something to be learned from that, he thought. Yelling is not effective for getting what you want, and life goes on despite your anxieties and fears. It wasn't the first time he had learned something by watching nature at work.

FORTY-FIVE

When they got home, Windflower could hear that the regular routine was underway upstairs. He could hear Sheila preparing the baby bath for their little princess. He left Lady to guard the back door against any possible intrusion by the cat and went to check things out.

When he got there, he was very pleased to see Amelia Louise and her mom lying on the bed. And he was more than pleased to join them.

"How was the rest of your day?" she asked.

"Hectic," said Windflower. "But good. It looks like Elizabeth Crowder has left, which is too bad because we'd like to talk to her. How was your afternoon?"

"It was good. I know I grumble about being home all the time. But it hit me today that this is my time to do that, to be at home with our little girl. She will never be this age again, and I'm supposed to take the time to enjoy the gifts she's giving me."

Windflower nodded. "You know, we never slow down enough to really see what's going on right in front of us. I'm glad you're doing that. There's lots of time for work and other activities later."

"Oh, my God," said Sheila. "I've got so many ideas circulating through my head these days. It's like the baby has re-opened my creative juices. I was going to ask Herb Stoodley to give me a few pointers about painting. You know, painting has been in the back of my mind forever. I just couldn't figure out how to do it."

"Wow, that is amazing. I saw Herb and Moira on the way home. I asked him to do a painting for the B&B. Maybe I should have asked you."

"Stick with Herb for now. But it's like you say. When we slow down, we realize what's really important. I had the same experience after my accident. It's almost like we are forced to go at a slower pace in order to get the lessons that are being offered."

Windflower smiled. "Can I do the honours?" he asked, holding out his arms for the baby.

"Be my guest," said Sheila as she passed the baby to her father. Windflower took Amelia Louise in his arms and into the bathroom. There he spent the most wonderful few minutes of his day. After the bath, he bundled her up in a large towel and took her downstairs.

"Did you want something to eat?" asked Sheila. "I made sandwiches for your lunch. They're in the fridge."

"Thank you so much," said Windflower, handing the baby over to Sheila. "I had a couple of squares at the Stoodleys, and this will get me through the night," he said as he took a plastic bag out of the fridge. "Now I have to separate the potential combatants."

He went to the back porch and put Molly into her cage. He walked out into the kitchen where Lady was ready and started to bark. He got her to sit, even as she shook with a combination of what looked like fear and anger. Then he laid the cat's cage on the floor between them. Molly immediately put her back up and hissed her loudest at the dog. But suddenly, and almost miraculously, both animals stopped making any noise at all. Neither moved, nor made any concession to the other. They simply stopped moving or barking or hissing.

Amelia Louise broke the silence with a long and loud burp, and both Windflower and Sheila burst out laughing. The two animals recognized that this must be a good thing and almost relaxed.

"A temporary ceasefire," said Windflower. "But we'll take it." He put the cat in the cage and walked back to the detachment to get his Jeep. He put the cat into the front seat and drove home.

"Have a great evening," said Sheila when he came back to get the dog. She held the baby up so that he could give her a kiss. He gave them both one and took Lady out with him. "I'll call you later," he yelled back over his shoulder.

He drove to the detachment, which was now quiet, and brought the cat in first. He put her in her usual cell and closed the door.

Then he went back and got Lady. Once inside, the dog did her usual inspection tour, looking for any scraps that might be available. After finding nothing she returned to Windflower's side. But instead of taking her usual place beneath his desk, she left his office. When Windflower went to check on her, he found Lady lying on the floor in front of the cat's temporary home.

It wasn't clear if Lady was trying to keep the cat in, guard her against intruders, or wanting some company. Whatever it was, Windflower decided he would take it as progress in the cohabitation process. It beat all the hissing and howling. He went to the front and picked up the messages in his slot. There was one from Lauren Bartlett to call her at home.

"Lauren, it's Winston Windflower. Sorry to bother you at home."

"No problem," said Bartlett. "I've talked to St. John's. They are doing the paperwork and Tutlow is going to be transferred to temporary RCMP custody in the morning. Do you have someone to pick him up?"

"Corporal Tizzard is in town," said Windflower.

"Great. The prisoner should be ready for transport to Marystown," said Bartlett. "You'll only have 48 hours to charge or release him," she added. "Unless you have something, he's going back to Nova Scotia on his breach."

"Thanks. That'll be perfect. I'll let Tizzard know."

Before Windflower had a chance to phone Tizzard, his cell phone rang.

"I'm picking up Tutlow in the morning," said Tizzard. "They're releasing him to our custody."

"I know. I just got off the phone with the Crown."

"Oh, so you did it. I thought it was my usual, charming personality."

"You are a charmer all right. You heard about Elizabeth Crowder?"

"Yeah, Jones told me. Do you think she's taking a runner?"

"She left in a hurry, that's for sure. There's something not right about her. First of all, she was at the house, clearly looking for something. And it looks like she may have been in Grand Bank before, maybe even around the time of her son's death. Can you go to the airport and get them to take a look at the security tapes? Look for a couple of days before his death. Focus on flights from Toronto and maybe Halifax."

"I can ask. But they may not be happy about it. They're understaffed, too."

"What are you doing this evening?"

"I knew you were going there," said Tizzard with a half-hearted sigh.

"I thought you wanted to get back to work."

"I was hoping for a more glamourous assignment than watching grainy videos in the airport security room. But I'll take it."

"You're the second complaint I've had today about boring work. Duly noted."

"And filed away appropriately, I'm sure. I'm on my way."

Windflower laughed to himself at his younger friend's approach to life. He was still smiling when Jones and Evanchuk came in for the search party at the Crowder house.

FORTY-SIX

Windflower picked up a couple of heavy-duty flashlights from the supply room and drove over to the house. Smithson was inside the kitchen playing solitaire when he came in. The younger cop jumped up when he saw his boss.

"Sit down," said Windflower. "We're here to do the search. Evanchuk and Jones are right behind me. You can go home if you want."

"I'd like to be part of it if I could," said Smithson.

"Okay," said Windflower. "Why don't you start upstairs in the bathroom? Make sure to check inside everything. Toilet tank, all the cupboards, any ceiling tiles if this place has them. See if any of the floorboards are loose and check underneath everything."

"Great," said Smithson, happy to be part of what he thought was a grand adventure.

He gave Jones and Evanchuk the main floor, with similar instructions as he had given Smithson. Check in, under, and above everything. "We have no idea what we're looking for. Forensics would have gotten everything in plain sight, but I think there's still something left in here."

"Something that Elizabeth Crowder was looking for?" asked Jones.

"Maybe," said Windflower. "I'm going to do the bedrooms."

He walked upstairs and could hear Smithson moving things around in the bathroom. That was probably the least likely place for anybody to hide things, but it still needed to be checked. He went through the three bedrooms, closely and carefully. But nothing seemed to be out of the ordinary. There were clothes, but not a lot, a few sets of bedding, and some relics from the past, like an old radio with a frayed cord and a small black-and-white TV that didn't turn on when he plugged it in.

He checked under the beds and under the mattresses and in the closets and on the top shelves above the clothes. He found nothing but dust, dirt, and a supply of last year's dead insects. Smithson joined him for the last bedroom, but even together they couldn't find much more than a pile of dirty laundry. When they got downstairs, their female colleagues reported similar and unrewarding results.

"I think forensics dug up the backyard," said Windflower. "That only leaves downstairs. You can leave if you want," he said to Jones and Evanchuk. "Smithson and I will check that out."

After they had left, he handed Smithson a flashlight and turned his on as they walked slowly down the narrow, creaking stairs to the basement. There was an overhead light that Windflower turned on by pulling a cord hanging in front of him. The glare from the bare lightbulb was bright and harsh. Both men blinked.

There was a furnace in one section, and the washer, dryer, and water heater took up another corner. Various pieces of old furniture and equipment lay strewn around the floor. There was a suitcase that Windflower directed Smithson towards, but that quickly proved empty. He rummaged through a few boxes of books, and Smithson leafed through a couple of crates of old LPs. He absent-mindedly leaned against a bookshelf that was up against the wall when he noticed something.

"Hey, boss. I think this bookcase has been moved recently." He pointed his flashlight towards the ground where you could clearly see the dust marks from before and a clean spot now. Windflower walked towards it as Smithson started taking some books off the middle shelf. "There's something behind this."

Windflower and Smithson hurriedly took many of the books off the shelves and pulled the bookcase away from the wall. When Windflower shone his light, they could see that the concrete wall had been hollowed out, and there really was something behind the bookcase.

"It's a safe of some kind," said Windflower, moving in closer with his flashlight. "Built right into the wall." It was a new, almost shiny, black steel safe with a computer pad on the front. There was also a slot of some sort on the front of the safe. He pulled on the handle, but nothing happened.

"This is a special, computerized safe," said Smithson. When Windflower looked at him strangely, he added, "I watch a lot of tech stuff on Netflix."

"How does it work?"

"The safe is locked, but it can be opened if you put your finger in that slot right there."

Windflower tried that, but nothing happened.

"It's biometric. Somebody's fingerprint has been pre-programmed into the system. Only that fingerprint will allow the safe to be opened, unless you know the code."

Windflower looked dazed. Technology often did that to him. Then he had another look at the safe. "It's still only a safe. A locksmith could break it open, right?"

"Absolutely. They would likely drill a hole in it and open it that way, even if they didn't know the code. But it would ruin the safe."

"Not our problem. And it looks like the owner is not around to complain. I'll need you to stay the night until our guy gets here in the morning. Can you do that?"

"Sure," said Smithson. "I'll go home and get my stuff and my computer, and I'm good to go."

"Why do you need your computer? Oh yeah, Netflix. I'll stay here 'til you get back."

Smithson went home to get his stuff, and Windflower did one more walkabout. You never know what you might see, he thought. But all he saw was a tiny mouse skittering across the kitchen floor when he came upstairs. He laughed. "I bet you wouldn't be doing that if Molly was still here," he said to the mouse's back. He sat at the kitchen table and then realized he was sitting in the dead man's seat. A chill passed over him as he got up and paced around the kitchen.

Smithson came back soon, and Windflower headed back over to the office. He checked on the animals. Both seemed relatively happy. Lady was curled up outside the cat's cell and Molly was lying there in her little bed. Windflower thought she was asleep too, but when he went closer, she blinked at him. He smiled and went to get his dinner out of the fridge.

He was finishing off the last of his sandwich and carrot sticks when the phone rang.

"How are you, my little rabbit?" came a soft voice at the end of the line.

"Auntie Marie, I am well. How are you?" asked Windflower.

"I am still weak, but my spirits are high," said his aunt. "How is my baby? Frank has sent some pictures. He wanted to post them on Facebook. But I said no. I don't believe we should share other people's stories. Let her tell her own when she gets bigger. And my, how she is growing. Tell me all about her."

"She is truly a joy and a blessing, Auntie. I look at her and can't believe she is here with us sometimes. Sheila is such an adoring mother, too. I am sure Amelia Louise is starting to smile. I could cry when I see her."

"You have been given a great gift," said Auntie Marie. "Remember to learn from her. She is bringing you wisdom, if only you watch and listen."

"Like in my dream."

"Yes. Tell me, how is Frank?"

"He is well, Auntie."

"I know he has been drinking, Winston. He told me."

"Well, he seems to be working on that. I am just glad that he is here with us. I wish you could be here."

"I wish that, too. But I feel that my traveling days may be over."

"We may come visit. I talked to Sheila about coming in the fall after the B&B is closed for the year."

"That would be so nice. I'll make all of you some bannock and venison stew. I can still cook, you know."

"I'll look forward to that, Auntie. I can't wait for you to see her, to see if she reminds you of anybody."

"I think she looks like your mother. Your mother came to me in a dream."

"What did she say?"

"She did not speak. But she and I communicate in our own ways. She is proud of you and the man you have become."

"Thank you for sharing that, Auntie. I have learned so much from you, about my family and the dream world."

"It's part of the connection to the other side. We have to work to stay open, even if we don't understand, or don't believe in, some things sometimes, like in ghosts for example."

"I do have some trouble with that one. What do you know about ghosts, Auntie?"

"It's not what I know, but what I have experienced. There was someone in my life who could not live comfortably on the other side. They kept coming back to visit."

"What did you do?"

"I sat and listened and made tea. They didn't drink it, but it made them feel welcome. And when they were ready, they moved on. It sounds like there might be someone in your life like that, too."

Windflower stayed silent for a moment. "Maybe," he finally said. "Thank you, Auntie. I love you."

"I love you, too, Winston. Give Sheila my love and hug that little baby girl to your chest for me."

"Hopefully, we'll see you in the fall. Goodnight, Auntie."

FORTY-SEVEN

Soon after his call with Auntie Marie, Windflower took Lady out for a short spin around the building. When he came back in, the dog walked directly to the cat's cage and stared in. Then, she kind of stared back at Windflower. "You want me to let her out?" asked Windflower, incredulously. "Okay."

He opened the cell and let Molly out. The two animals circled each other, Lady sniffing and Molly with her back arched and tense. But they made it through that initial inspection without any disaster. Then, Lady again laid down in front of the cell while Molly went for a spin around the office. Windflower watched as she did her tour and then calmly came back and laid down in the open cell, directly opposite the dog.

"Wow," said Windflower to no one in particular. "I've got to phone Sheila." He called her cell phone. If she or the baby was sleeping, she had it on mute. But not right now.

"You'll never believe what's going on here," said Windflower. "The war is over."

"They're not trying to kill each other?' asked Sheila.

"Both asleep on the floor across from each other. No signs of immediate or pending hostilities. It's amazing. I don't know if it's permanent, but for now they have agreed to co-exist."

"Good job, Sergeant. How's the rest of your night going?"

"I talked to Auntie Marie. She sounded good. We have to go out for sure. She's dying to see the baby."

"In the fall, for sure. Have a great night. If I end up being awake for long later, I'll call. But I'm hoping our bundle of joy will sleep a bit longer."

"In that case, I hope I don't hear from you. Good night."

The overnight shift passed quietly and peacefully. Windflower got through a large mound of paperwork and read almost all the periodicals and articles in his inbox. His eyes were getting bleary, so he made another pot of coffee before taking his trip around town and then out onto the highway. He thought about leaving Lady and Molly alone to guard the detachment but, on second thought, he called Lady to follow him.

"Next time, it'll be your turn," he said to the cat. Molly gave him what he took to be a skeptical look, as if to say she knew he couldn't really be trusted. And he was sure that Lady had a smirk on her face as she pranced past the cat. Molly gave a mild hiss back. There might be a forced peace, but that didn't mean they had to like each other, thought Windflower.

He put Lady into the back seat of the Jeep and drove off. It was a beautiful night with a moon hanging on the horizon of the ocean at the edge of Grand Bank. It wasn't quite full yet, but in Windflower's Cree culture, the full moon of June was the Strawberry Moon, the time when strawberries would come into season back home. It might be later in Newfoundland, but it was a great reminder of old times with family when they ate more strawberries than they brought home and had their hands and faces covered in juice.

They strolled all over town and saw little activity, except for a few stray cats that were competing with sea gulls for a wandering bag of garbage. Lady was quite interested and would have gladly stayed longer to watch this activity and maybe join in, but Windflower drove on after a minute. He went to the outskirts of town and the first entrance to the highway.

His was the only vehicle on the road, and he liked the feeling of being almost alone with the universe. He headed down towards Fortune and circled around at the ferry terminal that took people across the water to the small French islands of St. Pierre and Miquelon. Still French territories after years of war between the English and French in the 1700s and 1800s, the small islands attracted tourists from all over Canada for a day or an afternoon in France.

But there were no ferries or tourists at this time of night, or early morning as Windflower realized when he checked the time. It was after 4:00 a.m. and nearing the end of his shift. He went back up on the highway and drove to Creston, near Marystown and at the end of his territory. On the way back home, he saw a pair of eyes glinting at him in the darkness and slowed. It was almost at the Garnish turnoff where he'd stopped a few days ago with Levi Parsons.

There, in a ditch at the side of the road was a large female moose. And then he saw the others. Two younger moose, most likely male, waiting for their mother's cue to cross the highway. Windflower turned off his lights and watched as the female gingerly walked across and disappeared into the thick brush on the other side. The other two followed shortly afterwards. Once they had safely passed, Windflower turned his lights on and continued on his journey.

That was a blessing, he thought, or maybe more than one. First, he was thankful he had seen the immense creatures before they came up onto the highway. Many drivers had learned to their shock and horror the damage that moose could wreak on a vehicle and the people inside. But even more importantly, Mother Nature was sending him a sign. Windflower thought about that as the moonlight streamed into his vehicle moving along the barren highway. Certainly, part of the message was to always listen to your Elders and follow them. But perhaps it was also a sign to him that younger people, like his more youthful officers, kids like Levi Parsons, and even his little child, were watching him and looking to him for direction. He thanked Grandmother Moon for the teaching and drove slowly back to the detachment.

He gave both Lady and Molly a treat when he got back and made sure to spend some special alone time with the cat, even as he heard Lady whimpering outside his office door. They would have to learn to share everything, including his time. After that he had another cup of coffee and managed to get through even more printed material, which he placed on Betsy's desk. She would be pleased, he thought.

He had a smile on his face when Evanchuk came in for the morning shift.

"You're in a good mood after being here all night," she said as she wished him a good morning.

"It's a good morning to be alive," he said. "'I bear a charmed life.'"

Evanchuk laughed and Windflower waved goodbye as he gathered up his animals and drove home. I truly do have a charmed life, he said to himself and then again to Lady and Molly. It appeared they did not understand, but Windflower knew better. They had a charmed life, too.

FORTY-EIGHT

He crept into the house and tried to shush the pets, but there was no need. Sheila was sitting on the couch with the baby on her shoulder.

"Just finished her breakfast. And we slept through the night," she said.

"Another miracle," said Windflower. "She's full, but I'm famished. Want some breakfast? I was going to do a fry-up."

"That sounds great. I'll make us some fruit."

Windflower got some sausages and bacon from the fridge and put them on to cook while he cut up some tomatoes and mixed eggs in a steel bowl. Soon, the kitchen was full of the beautiful aromas of breakfast. He sliced the last of the baguette into two pieces and put them under the broiler to toast.

Amelia Louise seemed content with all the activity as she lay in the bassinet that Sheila had placed on the table beside them. Both Molly and Lady had already made one loop around the kitchen in hopes of a few scraps, but they were disappointed, at least so far. Sheila and Windflower were not. They devoured their breakfast and talked about everything from the menu for the B&B and what needed to still be done before the official opening, to their Pink Lake visit in the fall.

They were finishing up when Windflower's cell phone rang. He apologized to Sheila. "It's Tizzard, from St. John's."

"Go ahead," said Sheila. "I'll clean up."

"What's up, Eddie?" asked Windflower.

"Morning, Sarge. Hope I didn't wake you."

"I was on the overnight. Haven't been to bed yet."

"Good. I spent most of the night at the airport. I started looking through security tapes until I thought my eyes would freeze. Then, I took another tack. I got HQ to get me access to the passenger lists for the last two weeks."

"What did you find?"

"Elizabeth Crowder was only here once according to the passenger manifests. That was when she came a few days ago." He paused and waited for his boss to react.

"There's more, right?" asked Windflower

"Correct. After I did that, I remembered somebody talking about Elizabeth Ryan as her maiden name. So, I ran that through the system. And she was booked on a flight from Toronto to St. John's. I saw her on the security tapes coming through on the day before Jacob Crowder died."

"Okay."

"That's not all, boss. She was in Newfoundland at least three times in the past year, according to the passenger records. How is it possible that she was here and nobody saw her?"

"We weren't really looking for her. I'd be surprised if no one saw her. We'll need to ask around. But at least we know for sure that she was in St. John's. We know she was in Grand Bank before her son died. Now we need to figure out what else she was doing here and who saw her."

"Great. I'm going to pick up Tutlow. Langmead's arranged an escort to Marystown."

"I'm going to have a nap. Call me when you get there, and I'll come meet you."

"Everything okay?" asked Sheila after Windflower ended the call.

"Perfect," he said. "Now if you give me that sleepy baby, we have a date with the bedroom."

Sheila laughed. "I'll be on laundry detail, Sergeant."

Windflower brought the baby upstairs and put her in the bassinet beside the bed. Amelia Louise gave one more great yawn and was soon gone. So was Windflower.

Amelia Louise woke first and Windflower half-heard Sheila pick her up and take her to the other room. A while later, he heard her filling the baby bath and then nothing until his cell phone rang again.

"Hi Sarge, it's Smithson. The locksmith, Ben Rossiter, is here and he wants to be sure that it's okay to drill a hole in the safe."

"Let me talk to him," said Windflower.

"Morning, Sergeant. I wants to make sure that I's got the green light to break this open. It's worth tousands of dollars," said Rossiter. "I know because I put it in fer the feller who lived here. The dead guy."

"Go ahead," said Windflower. "Unless you know how to get the code, break it open."

"No b'y, that come from the factory and you'd need a password to get into it. I'll go ahead and drill it open."

"Can you hang on a few minutes afterwards?" asked Windflower. "I got a couple of questions for you."

"No worries. I'm chargin' you fer the morning anyways. Special call-out rate."

"See you then," said Windflower. "Tell my guy to hang tight, too."

Windflower jumped in the shower and cleaned himself up. He dressed and went downstairs. Only Molly the cat greeted him. She purred and rubbed against his leg, and he patted her while he read the note on the table. It was from Sheila. "Hi Winston. Hope you had a good sleep. We're out for a walk. If I don't see you before you leave, give me a call. Love, Sheila."

Windflower made a heart on the back of the paper, wrote "I love you" inside and left it on the table. He drove to the Crowder house where a red panel van with big bright letters announcing "Rossiter and Son, Locksmith" was parked in the driveway. Inside the house, Smithson and the locksmith were sitting in the kitchen having a cup of tea.

Rossiter rose and shook Windflower's hand. "Ben Rossiter," he said.

"Thanks for waiting," said Windflower as Smithson handed him a cup of tea. "I'm assuming the safe is open."

"Ready for your inspection, sir," said Smithson.

"You said you installed this safe," said Windflower, sipping on his tea. "When was that?"

"About six months ago," said Rossiter. "First I got an e-mail from this guy and a number to call. When I called him up, he was very specific 'bout when I could come and install the safe. I could only come on a Wednesday between four and eight in the evening. I was to come alone and park my car down by the wharf and walk up with me tools. He said he'd pay me double. I sed, fine by me."

"So, you came and installed it. What was the guy like and was there anybody else here?" asked Windflower.

"Nar soul, but himself. He led me in, after checking to make sure I was alone, and peeked out afterwards to see if anyone had followed me. When he was convinced it was safe, we went downstairs. I did my job. He had the hole dug out already. I just had to install it and hook it up."

"Did he say anything while you were here about why he wanted the safe?" asked Windflower.

"No b'y. I tried to make small talk, like ya would, but he weren't interested. Did my job and went home. Fine by me b'y. Made a few extra bucks. Did you still want me to set up the silent alarm?"

"Please," said Windflower. "Will it take you long?"

"Half an hour. I'm getting to be an expert at it. Must have done 20 houses since all those break-ins. Mine is one of the few businesses where crime really does pay."

Smithson started laughing, and Windflower shot him a look. "Let's go downstairs." He and Smithson went down into the basement while Rossiter started setting up the house alarm.

"Quiet overnight?" he asked Smithson. "Get some sleep?"

"Pretty good, sir," said Smithson.

"Did you look inside the safe?" he asked the younger officer.

"Had a peek, sir. Looks like some cash and a couple of files and envelopes. But I didn't touch anything."

"Good," said Windflower. "Let's take a closer look, shall we?" He shone his flashlight directly inside the now-open safe.

FORTY-NINE

Windflower put on his latex gloves and reached into the safe. As Smithson had said, there was a stack of bills, Canadian and American. And there were four passports, two Canadian and two American, with Jacob Crowder's picture and various names. There were also some manila folders with papers inside and a large white envelope. Underneath all of that was a clear plastic bag with a variety of patches and pills. After Windflower took all of that out, he shone his flashlight one more time.

"There's something else in there," said Smithson. "I saw a glint of metal."

Windflower reached his gloved hand inside and rooted around. He found it, a thick, gold-coloured key, a little chunkier than a regular house key. When Windflower turned it over, he saw that it had the initials FG on the back. He put the key into a small plastic bag and handed it to Smithson, along with the money, the files and the envelope. He took one more look inside the safe and, satisfied it was finally empty, he closed the door and turned off his flashlight.

They went upstairs where the locksmith was testing the alarm. "Stay here 'til he's finished and then you can go home and have a break. I'll take all this stuff back and get it recorded. Good job here," said Windflower.

Smithson smiled at his boss's praise and went to take a look at Rossiter's work. Windflower put his package of materials from the safe on the front seat of his Jeep and drove to the office.

He handed the documents and money over to Jones who was working the day shift. He kept the plastic bag with the key on his desk. He wanted to take a closer look at it. He didn't get much of a chance to do that before he heard Betsy's voice on the intercom.

"Corporal Tizzard on line one."

"Are you in Marystown?" asked Windflower.

"I've got good news and bad news," said Tizzard.

"What's the bad news?"

"I'm still in St. John's."

"Have you got Tutlow?"

"Yes. But you didn't ask what the good news was."

"You're starting to bug me, Eddie. What's the good news?"

"We've got Elizabeth Crowder, too. She was trying to leave at the airport when our guys spotted her. They're holding her in the detention centre. Just waiting for transport. I guess we could've brought them together with me, but I was thinking we wanted them kept separate."

"Good thinking. What time do you think you'll get into Marystown?"

"Once I get confirmation that she's leaving, I'm on my way. Hoping to be there by suppertime."

"I'll call Quigley and ask him to get a room ready for our guests. Good job, Corporal."

"Thanks, boss. Isn't it good that you have me back on board?" asked Tizzard mischievously.

"It is, Corporal," said Windflower honestly. "But if you play that good news, bad news game again with me, I might have to kill you. Or better yet, do you remember how much pain you were in when you got shot?"

"Got it. I'll call when I have more info."

Windflower hung up from Tizzard and called Marystown.

"Good day, Sergeant. How is beautiful Grand Bank today?" asked Quigley.

"It is grand, Inspector. I'm calling to make a reservation at your fine Marystown facility. Two rooms, actually. One male and one female."

"We can accommodate that request. I'm guessing one is that guy Tutlow. I got calls from St. John's and the Crown about him. But who's the woman?"

"Elizabeth Crowder. Sometimes known as Elizabeth Ryan. Apparently, she uses her maiden name when she needs to."

"It sounds like Tutlow's at least a wingman in this operation. Where does the woman fit in?"

"That's not clear yet, and that's part of what I want to talk to her about," said Windflower. "She's been in Grand Bank at least once before her son's death and likely a few more times as well. She hasn't been telling me the truth, or at best she's omitting pieces that might be inconvenient for her. Maybe I haven't been asking the right questions."

"What time should we expect your guests?"

"Tizzard said he should be there with Tutlow by dinnertime, and we're waiting on confirmation of the woman's ETD from the airport in St. John's. I think everyone should be there by tonight. Can you set up an interview room for me in the morning? I'd like both our guests to stew overnight, especially Elizabeth Crowder."

"No worries. The woman is likely going to start screaming for a lawyer."

"Probably. My apologies to your people who may have to listen to that, but we haven't charged her with anything. We only want to talk to her. We believe she may be in danger. We're holding her for her own protection."

"That will buy us a few hours. Good enough for me. You are a wise man, Sergeant Windflower."

"Thanks Ron. I'm glad that you said it 'cause a man who thinks himself to be wise is a fool."

"And 'a wise man knows himself to be a fool'," said Quigley.

"And 'better a witty fool than a foolish wit.'" Windflower could almost hear Quigley's brain turning, trying to think up a clever riposte. But he hung up the phone before Quigley could get there.

Feeling a little smug and more than content, he went to see if Betsy had anything for him.

FIFTY

Anybody else looking for me?" Windflower asked.

"There's a couple of media calls, including a guy from the *Southern Gazette* who wanted to talk to you about the last death," said Betsy. "They've got a picture up on their website with a headline you might want to see. She swung her computer around so he could see her screen. There was a picture of Crowder's van out by the dump. The headline read 'Grand Bank: Murder Capital of Newfoundland and Labrador?'

"Yikes," said Windflower when he saw that. As he scrolled down, the story didn't get any better. If anything, it became shriller and even less flattering to the RCMP. If Quigley had seen it, he would have certainly mentioned it to Windflower. The article said that the local police had no suspects and no leads. It also brought up again the rash of break-ins in the community that had gone unsolved. All of this might be true, but it could be a bigger problem if there was no response.

"Let's get him over for a chat," said Windflower.

Betsy, who almost never offered advice, said, "I think that's a wise decision, Sergeant."

This time Windflower said nothing about being either wise or a fool. He might even end up being both on the same day. Instead, he called Sheila. She would love him regardless of his level of wisdom. She was just happy to hear from him.

"How are you, Winston?" asked Sheila. "Amelia Louise and I and our growing menagerie of animals are sitting in the backyard, enjoying the sun."

"That sounds grand. I'm thinking this would be a great day for a barbecue."

"Perfect. I'll take a run up to Warrens to see what they've got. Any preference?"

"As long as I have meat to burn, I'll be happy."

Sheila laughed. "I'll see what I can find."

"See you later, my love."

After his call with Sheila, Betsy came by to tell him that Paul Mitchell from the newspaper would be by in an hour or so. Jones came by to show him what she had learned by reviewing the material from the Crowder house.

"The money was three thousand Canadian and about two American," said Jones.

"We'll have to get all that checked for prints and maybe even for counterfeiting," said Windflower. "What was in the files?"

"In one file were stocks from a numbered company registered in Ontario. Signed by President and CEO Bruce Crowder. The other had a certificate of ownership of bitcoins registered to a bank in Switzerland, Forzano Group," said Jones.

"How many bitcoins?" asked Windflower.

"Two hundred and forty," said Jones. "Doesn't sound like very much."

"Two hundred and forty bitcoins is a lot of money," said Evanchuk, who had walked into their discussion. "I hope I'm not interrupting."

"Not at all," said Windflower. "How much is a bitcoin worth?"

"Maybe $10,000 American," said Evanchuk.

"Each?" asked Jones. "That would make it $240,000."

"American," added Evanchuk for emphasis.

Even Windflower gasped at that number. "What was in the envelope?" he asked, recovering from the shock.

"It looks like letters from Bruce Crowder to his son," said Jones.

"That's interesting. Leave the letters with me. I want to take another look before I go see Elizabeth Crowder," said Windflower.

"We got her?" asked Jones.

"They got her at the airport in St. John's. They're bringing her back to Marystown. I'm going over to see her in the morning. Along with Tutlow."

"That's great," said Evanchuk. "Is Eddie, I mean Corporal

Tizzard, bringing him back?"

"He's on his way," said Windflower. "Jones, I need to start asking around if anyone has seen Elizabeth Crowder here in Grand Bank before the last week or so. Maybe in the last year. Betsy has a picture. Start at the stores and the café. We think she may have been here a few times. If she was, maybe somebody saw her."

"Okay," said Jones. "I'll get on it right away."

She left, and Windflower started to look through the files. Evanchuk started to leave and then stopped. She noticed the key on his desk.

"Is that key from Crowder's house, too?" she asked.

"Yes," said Windflower. "Why?"

"It looks like a safety deposit box key," she said. "Can I see it?"

Windflower passed the bag over to Evanchuk.

"FG," she said. "That's the name of the bank.

"Forzano Group. That Swiss bank that is noted in the files."

"Can you take it out, sir, and turn it over?" asked Evanchuk. "You may need a magnifying glass, but most banks put the account number in very small fonts somewhere on the back. Learned that in Commercial Crime."

Windflower put on a pair of latex gloves, took out the key and got a magnifying glass from his desk drawer. There was a number on the back in minute detail. "It's 701724," he read aloud. "The account number?"

"I'll see if I can find out." Evanchuk wrote the number down and went off to investigate.

Windflower read through the files a few more times and managed to move quite a bit of paper from one side of his desk to the other. His paper shuffling was interrupted by Betsy's voice on the intercom telling him that he had a visitor.

Windflower had met Paul Mitchell many times in the course of his time in Grand Bank. He had found him to be fair and fairly reasonable in his dealings, and although they didn't know each other well, they seemed to have a connection. Mitchell and his newspaper had been particularly helpful to Windflower and the RCMP during the case of a missing Grand Bank girl last year.

"Afternoon, Sergeant," said Mitchell.

"Hi Paul. How's it going today?" asked Windflower.

"It's going well. I came over to check out the mental health story. But it looks like you've been busy," said Mitchell as a way of opening up the interview. "Two murders and a whack of unsolved break-ins."

"That's true," said Windflower. "But we're hardly the murder capital of the province."

"I don't write the headlines," said the reporter. "But it has a certain ring to it. I'm assuming you called me over because you have some information to provide."

"I guess I would start by saying that it appears the rash of break-ins that the community has experienced is over. The RCMP won't take all the credit for that, but we have been working with families and the community to make our neighbourhoods safer."

"I did notice that you had a series of meetings around town. Can you tell me about them and how they went?"

"They were well attended and allowed people to ask questions and for us to provide information about keeping their homes and community safer. While the imminent risk has subsided, it's important that we continue to improve our overall safety in Grand Bank. It's good to be protected and prepared."

"Nice line, Sergeant. But people seem to be really concerned about the two violent deaths in such a small community. What can you tell us about these, and your investigations?"

"The investigations are ongoing, and I can't give you too much detail, except to say that we have a person of interest in custody and on his way back to this area from St. John's."

"Are the two murders connected?"

"We want to talk to that person of interest about both deaths. But we can't say anymore until we interview him."

"Is he a suspect?"

"We don't know yet."

"I don't suppose you can give me his name?" Reporters, Windflower had learned over the years, were always hopeful.

"No," said Windflower with a laugh. "But give me your card. If we charge him with anything, I'll get Betsy to give it to you first."

"Thank you, Sergeant. A pleasure as always," said Mitchell,

folding up his notebook and putting it his bag. Windflower watched him leave and stop by Betsy's desk on the way out.

"Another satisfied customer," said Betsy.

"Keep your friends close and your enemies closer," said Windflower

"Is that Shakespeare?" asked Betsy.

"Michael Corleone from *The Godfather*, I think," said Windflower.

When Betsy reacted in mild horror, he added, "I take 'em where I get 'em, Betsy. Have a great night."

Windflower was smiling again to himself as he got in his Jeep to drive home. He was pleased about that last interaction, but he was really smiling because he remembered that he was barbecuing meat for dinner. What kind he didn't know yet. But whatever it was, it was going to be sum good b'y. That last thought brought his smile into a full laugh. He hoped nobody noticed how happy he was leaving work. Maybe he'd have to give some of his salary back.

FIFTY-ONE

The package from Warrens was on the counter, wrapped in brown paper. It sure smelled like meat. Lady thought so too as she came to inspect both Windflower and the package. Molly, his new shadow, was close behind.

"Pork chops," said Sheila as she came in with Amelia Louise in her arms. "Do you have any of that nice rub left?"

"I think I do," said Windflower. He rummaged around the cupboard and found what he was looking for, a slender silver canister. Inside was a plastic bag that, when he opened it, filled the room with scents of several kinds of pepper, garlic, and a special sweet paprika. He took the pork chops, beautiful and pink, and coated each one in a layer of the dry rub. Then he put them in a plastic bag and in the fridge.

He washed his hands and took the baby from Sheila. "We'll leave them for an hour," he said. "Everybody ready for a stroll?"

"You go ahead," said Sheila. "I've got a couple of calls to return, one from Eastern Health and another from the Ministry. Still trying to get our mental health worker."

"Good luck with that. Molly will stay and keep you company."

Windflower put the baby in the stroller and Lady on her leash. It was another beautiful evening for a walk, and he was happy to take advantage of the fine weather. He was walking along the side of the narrow road down near the rocky beach when a car pulled up alongside them. The passenger rolled down her window.

"Afternoon, Sergeant," said Charlene Parsons. Her sister, Shelley, was driving.

"Afternoon, ladies," said Windflower. Then he saw Levi Parsons in the back and waved to him. The teenager almost smiled, then caught himself. But he managed a brief wave back. That probably means he likes me, thought Windflower.

"How's your husband?" he asked.

"He's got a long period of rehabilitation ahead, but he is in fine spirits and happy. It truly is a miracle. He'd like to see you again, he told me."

"We'll see what we can do," said Windflower. He waved as they drove away. He thought he saw Levi wave back again. Now, that would be a miracle. Lady was pulling at her leash, and Amelia Louise was starting to fuss, so he put the stroller in motion and turned for home.

He walked around the kitchen with the baby on his shoulder while he took out the ingredients for a salad and two large potatoes from the cupboard. He scrubbed the two potatoes and put them in the oven to bake. When Amelia Louise started to doze, he placed her in the bassinet and spent a few minutes playing with his other baby, Molly. Sheila had gotten the cat some toys, including a contraption with a feather on one end and a ball on the other that fascinated Molly. She could play with that by herself for hours. But it was even more fun when Windflower joined in.

She wasn't as happy, though, when Lady tried to play along. Some things were just not to be shared. She hissed and growled whenever the dog came close. Lady finally gave up and went to sleep on the floor beneath the baby's bed on the couch. "Good girl," said Windflower. "Somebody's got to guard the baby."

Sheila laughed when she came out and saw Lady on sentry duty and Windflower playing with the cat. "I got her a new toy today." She pulled a furry stuffed mouse out of her purse. She placed it on the floor in front of the cat. Molly looked at it with really wide eyes and then crept closer as if it were real. Then she pounced, grabbing the mouse between her teeth and dashing off to her bed.

"I'm not sure if she's a mouse hunter or if she's adopted a new pet," said Windflower as they watched the cat hold the stuffed mouse in her mouth.

"I'll put the baby upstairs," said Sheila. "I really hope she's a mouser."

"Me, too," said Windflower as he rinsed the lettuce and chopped celery, carrots, and half a red pepper for their salad. He found a loaf of foil-wrapped garlic bread in the fridge and put that on the counter. He took the pork chops out of the fridge and laid them on a cutting board to breathe.

He went outside with Lady close behind and fired up the grill. He cleaned it one more time as it started to heat up. He always cleaned it right after use, but it never hurt to give it another scrape before cooking again. When the heat was about medium, he sprayed the grill lightly with oil and went back inside to get the meat. He put the pork chops on the barbecue, letting them cook on each side for four or five minutes. Then he turned them over and rotated them a half turn in order to get nice criss-cross grill marks. He flipped them twice on each side and the pork chops were done.

When he came back in, Sheila was sitting at the table. She had placed baked potatoes dressed with butter and sour cream on their plates and held her plate up to receive a pork chop. Windflower put one on his plate as well and took the salad as Sheila passed it over. He poured them both a glass of sparkling water and proposed a toast. "May we always be as happy as we are today."

"Amen," said Sheila as she cut into her pork chop, perfectly browned on the outside with a touch of pink in the middle. "Perfect. Purrrrfect."

"I'm glad you're enjoying it. Hmmmm, that is very nice meat." Windflower focused in on his meal but managed to still pay attention to Sheila's description of her many dealings with the health bureaucracy. "You are more patient than me," he said at one point.

"That's just the way the system works," said Sheila. "The patient bird gets the worm."

"'How poor are they that not have patience,'" said Windflower, happy to squeeze the Bard in beside them at the dinner table.

Sheila smiled and continued, "The good news is that they're going to send someone out to meet with us later this week. I think if we can convince them of our need, we can get some help, at least on a temporary basis. I was thinking about bringing Richard Tizzard to the meeting with me, along with your constable, Jones. What do you think?"

"I think that's a great idea, Mayor Hillier. It sounds like you have a great plan, as usual." He ate one more piece of garlic bread. "Another great meal," he pronounced. "Now, what's for dessert?"

FIFTY-TWO

Sheila went to the fridge, and Windflower could smell the strawberries before he could see them. He was delighted when he saw that his serving was in an extra large bowl.

"These are gorgeous," said Windflower. "Not local, though. I can tell by the size. They're enormous and so sweet and tasty."

"Ontario, I think, said Sheila. "Ours aren't out yet, and we don't have the warmth of the sun that they get on the mainland. There's always a few up near the brook, just not as plentiful as you get other places. But they're tasty, too."

"Yeah, but nothing like this." As he finished his ice cream, he could feel Molly rubbing up against one leg under the table and Lady nudging the other. "I'm being attacked on both sides," he said.

"Come on, guys, let's go close up the barbecue." Both pets followed him closely out the door to the backyard. He turned on the barbecue to heat up the grill and cleaned it as best as he could from the afternoon's event. Then, he turned it off and wiped everything down. He closed up the barbecue and replaced the cover. When he looked around, he saw the two animals sitting on the ground staring at him.

"Either you wanted to show me how much you loved me or you are looking for a treat," said Windflower. All three went back inside. Windflower got Lady a Milk-Bone and Molly a few of her special catnip treats. They went away to enjoy their snacks separately, and Windflower joined Sheila in the living room where she was pouring them a cup of tea.

"You know, these are the days I love the best," he said. "Even though I am crazy busy at work, I get to come home and spend time with you and my family. My extended family," he added as first

Lady, and then Molly, followed him into the room.

"I know," said Sheila. "For me, having a child has changed everything. What she needs is the most important thing, not all those things I thought I wanted."

"They really are here to teach us, just like our four-legged friends. Speaking of which, I'm happy that they decided to get along. I'm not sure they like each other, but maybe that's the point. We have to get along with those we don't like or don't agree with."

"If you keep that up you might have to go into politics."

Windflower laughed. "I don't think I have the required diplomacy and tact."

"Maybe. But remember, 'We know what we are but know not what we may be.'"

"Exactly. 'A fool thinks himself to be wise, but a wise man knows himself to be a fool.' I'd be a fool in the political world."

"But in this world, you're just perfect. Now, pass me the remote. Let's see what's on the old movie channel tonight."

The couple found one of Windflower's all-time favourites, Sheila's too, *The Bridge on the River Kwai*. Set in a prisoner of war camp in Burma in 1943, the prisoners, under the command of a British colonel played by Alec Guinness, are forced to build a bridge to aid the Japanese war effort. The film won many Academy Awards, including Best Picture of the Year. Windflower loved all parts of the movie, including the song that the men whistled as they worked.

Halfway through the movie Amelia Louise woke, and Windflower changed her and brought her to Sheila for her evening meal. She was propped up in the bassinet next to Sheila in the living room when he left. Molly was curled up next to the baby.

The night was calm, and the moon was now near full when he took Lady out for her last walk. The Strawberry Moon hung over Grand Bank like a hot-air balloon. The stars were so plentiful out over the ocean that they were almost blinding as Windflower and his dog walked along. The only blemish to the perfect evening was the cool breeze coming in off the water. That meant the fog was close and would likely be paying them a visit before too long. He pulled the collar of his jacket up around his neck and turned for home. Just before he arrived, his cell phone rang.

"Boss, it's me," said Tizzard. "I've delivered Tutlow to Marystown. Elizabeth Crowder is on her way. Carrie is coming over to get me. Once I have confirmation that Crowder is here, we'll head back."

"Thanks, Eddie. What kind of shape is Tutlow in? Did you talk on the way over?" asked Windflower.

"He's okay. Not the chatty type. He's not what you'd expect, either. At least, not what I was expecting."

"What do you mean?"

"I was expecting a more hard-core criminal, biker-gang type. Instead, he's clean cut, almost preppy."

"Interesting. Okay, that's great. I'm going over in the morning to see them both. Come by early tomorrow, and we can talk before I go."

"Great. I'll see you then."

Windflower closed the phone and went inside. Sheila was rocking the baby on her shoulder. She looked like she was nearly gone. When Sheila was sure, she passed her to Windflower who carried her upstairs. He came back down and sat with Sheila who was watching the news.

"Who were you talking to?" she asked.

"Tizzard," said Windflower. "He brought a prisoner back to Marystown. He's waiting for another, Elizabeth Crowder."

Sheila raised an eyebrow at that news. "Anything you can tell me about that?" she asked.

"Not for public consumption, but it appears she may have been in Grand Bank before her latest visit. We want to talk to her about that."

"Interesting. I don't recall anyone saying that they saw her. And she's pretty distinctive. So, she was here in Grand Bank, like what, a spy or something?"

"More like a ghost."

Shella paused at that last comment. "This is crazy, but you know people have been talking about a ghost lady wandering around town."

"I heard that, too. But I was only joking about Elizabeth

Crowder being a ghost."

"Keep an open mind, and don't rule out any possibilities. I think I've heard that more than once around here."

"Let's go upstairs before you start telling me that the world is more than we can see with our eyes."

Sheila smiled, and her eyes twinkled. "That would be true, too, as related to me by one Sergeant Winston Windflower. Let's go to bed. You turn the lights out."

Windflower went through the downstairs, turning off lights and saying goodnight to Lady and Molly. Each had a corner of the kitchen that was theirs. It wasn't exactly off-bounds to the other, but any intrusion across the imaginary line was met with a fierce stare. He petted them each for about the same amount of time. They seemed to notice when he didn't. Then he turned off the last light and followed Sheila upstairs.

She was propped in bed with her book and reading glasses on. Windflower slid in next to her and took his book off his nightstand. He started reading, but his eyes grew heavy very quickly. He laid his book down and snuggled into Sheila. He didn't hear a peep until the morning sun came in through the bedroom window and Amelia Louise started to stir beside the bed.

FIFTY-THREE

The baby and Windflower both woke in a great a mood after a long night's sleep. He picked her up and changed her and brought her back to bed. He put her in between himself and Sheila, and she stretched and yawned herself awake. Sheila fed her while Windflower went downstairs to check on the pets. Both were still sleeping, but Lady roused herself when she saw him. She followed as he put on his RCMP hoodie and grabbed his smudging materials from the cupboard. Molly blinked one eye at them, sleepily.

The wind hit Windflower in the face as soon as he opened the door. It wasn't a mild summerish wind but rather a cold foggy blast, and both the dog and human shivered involuntarily at its bite. The fog was everywhere. In fact, it felt like there was more fog than air. Cool, damp air. Windflower shrugged at Lady, and she went to do her business.

Windflower started the morning with a prayer of thanks for the air, the earth, and the water, even the fog. It was life, real life all around him. He gave thanks for his family, two-legged and four-legged members, and for his friends, allies, and those he shared the community with. They were all fellow travellers on the same road. They all needed love and support.

Then he mixed up his sacred medicines and lit his smudge bowl. When the first wisps of smoke started rising, he passed them over his head and brain so that his thoughts would be pure and his thinking straight. He let the smoke go all over his body, pausing at his heart to cleanse it from previous hurts and harm and to open it to the universe. He let the smoke drift all over his body and ended with passing the feather and the smoke under the soles of his feet to protect him on this journey and guide him safely back home.

Finally, he spent a few moments in quiet meditation amidst the near silence of the morning, letting the sacred smoke linger in his hair and all around him, thinking about his day and seeking guidance to follow a true and honest path. Young Levi Parsons came to his mind. Windflower thought about the boy and how he could be helpful in his life. He was still thinking about that when his solitude was interrupted by Lady. She had started digging in her section of the garden. She's probably remembering something she had buried there, thought Windflower.

"Come on, girl. Time for breakfast," he said.

Lady bounded in before him, and he had to grab her quickly to wipe off the morning wetness. He filled her bowls and went to Molly. The cat was more awake now and went up to him for some attention, and Windflower gladly obliged. She would have been happy for him to continue that indefinitely, but after a few minutes, he put the coffee on. He played with both pets until the coffee had perked. Then, he got a cup for himself and another for Sheila and went upstairs.

"Good morning to the most beautiful people in my life," he said as he passed Sheila a cup. He laid his down and started playing with a wide-awake Amelia Louise.

"I was thinking about Levi Parsons this morning," said Windflower.

"What about him?" asked Sheila.

"I dunno. It feels like he's in my life, or I'm in his for a reason."

"Maybe you're supposed to teach him something. His dad hasn't been that helpful."

"I have a feeling that will turn around. No, I think he's supposed to teach me something. Anyway, I'll think about that some more on the drive over to Marystown."

"Why don't you take him with you? See if he wants to visit his dad in Burin, and you could pick him up on the way home."

"That's a great idea. I'll give Charlene a call and see what she thinks. You are a very smart woman, Sheila Hillier."

"That's why they pay me the big bucks," she said. Then she noticed Amelia Louise drifting off to sleep even as her tiny fingers were still clutching one of Windflower's. "Looks like our little lady is ready for naptime," said Sheila.

Windflower picked the baby up and laid her in the bassinet.

"Why don't you clean up while I make us some oatmeal?" said Sheila.

Windflower kissed her on the cheek and went to the bathroom. A few minutes later the pair was sitting at the kitchen table drinking their coffee and enjoying breakfast. Windflower put a large tablespoon of brown sugar on his hot oatmeal and stirred it. He sipped his coffee, but it was too hot, so he chatted with Sheila about everyday life while he waited for it to cool. After breakfast, he gave her a hug and a promise to call and check in later. He waved goodbye and headed over to work.

FIFTY-FOUR

Constable Eddie Tizzard was sitting in the back room with Constable Carrie Evanchuk when Windflower arrived.

"Good to see the troops all set for work," he said.

"I'm just finishing up," said Evanchuk. "But I realized how much I liked working the night shift. It's so quiet and peaceful. And you can get so much done."

"I like it, too," said Windflower. "No phone calls, no e-mails, no crying babies. Actually, I don't mind the crying babies, at least not mine. Did Elizabeth Crowder get delivered safely?"

"About an hour after I got there," said Tizzard. "But she was really upset. Screaming for a lawyer. I got out as fast as I could. When are you going over to Marystown?"

"Later on this morning. Can you call over and make sure that they have two interview rooms set up?" Tizzard nodded and went to make the call.

"I did some online research last night about Swiss banks and the new cryptocurrency market," said Evanchuk.

"Like bitcoins?" asked Windflower.

"That's the best-known one, but since its rapid increase in price there's more coming online everyday. People want to cash in on the craze, and the banks are figuring out that there's money to be made," said Evanchuk.

"So, the banks are interested?"

"Exactly. Swiss banks, in particular, have been jumping on the cryptocurrency bandwagon. Forzano Group is one of the lead ones in this regard."

"That's where the key from Crowder's house came from."

"It looks like it. They will confirm that they have an account with that number but won't say anything else. In order to get into the box, you have to meet their requirements. We certainly couldn't do it by e-mail or over the phone."

"Can the RCMP or somebody over there get into the safety deposit box?"

"I e-mailed HQ last night with the bank info and Crowder's name. I got a reply back almost right away, which is unusual since it was the middle of the night. I talked to somebody in Commercial Crime. They want all the info and will take it over from here. They asked me to courier the key to them. I wanted to check with you first."

"Absolutely," agreed Windflower. "This sounds bigger than us."

"The HQ guy said it was part of Project Scorpion. That's the name I saw earlier. But that's all he could tell me. Is the mother really involved in all this? She looked so stylish and classy."

"Maybe she's trying to keep her foes confused. If they are never certain who you are or what you want, they can't know what you are likely to do next."

"Is that Shakespeare?"

"*Game of Thrones*," said Windflower, laughing. "But talking about her reminds me that I need to take a look at the letters in the files we got from Crowder's house before I go to Marystown. Can you make some copies? We should send them in the package to HQ."

Evanchuk followed Windflower into his office, and he passed over the files. She made the copies and came back. "I'll get these off along with the other material," she said, handing over the copies. Tizzard came to Windflower's office soon after to give him the thumbs-up on the interviews in Marystown. After they left, Windflower got up and closed the door to try to guarantee a few minutes of quiet to go through the letters. He opened the envelope, laid the letters on his desk and started to read.

The letters went back a few years and, as far as Windflower could see, this was a one-way conversation. There was no reference to any correspondence back from the son, but the father clearly wanted to try and maintain some contact with his son. And he was kept from doing that by Elizabeth Crowder, at least according to the father. Bruce Crowder had a long litany of complaints against his former wife.

That was not surprising to Windflower. What was surprising was how explicit the father was in telling his son to be careful about his mother. In almost every letter he warned Jacob Crowder of the dangers he thought his son was in, and in one, dated the most recent, he said that "he should get out before she killed him." Unfortunately for Windflower, neither of the males involved could answer his questions about this perceived threat and what might lie behind it. Maybe Elizabeth Crowder could shed some light on the matter.

Windflower opened the door to his office and went to the front to see Betsy. "Can you call Charlene Parsons and see if Levi wants to go visit his dad? I'm going to Marystown and will drop him off at the hospital if he'd like a ride. But first I'm going to see a beautiful lady and a baby."

Windflower drove to his house and could see activity in the backyard when he parked in the driveway. He walked around the side and opened the gate. There was Sheila digging in one side of the garden, planting something. On the other side, Lady was burying something that she was clearly saving for later.

"I see Lady is being a big help, as usual," said Windflower.

Sheila pulled her hands out of the dirt and pushed her sun bonnet back to see him. "She is trying, in her own way," said Sheila. "Molly, on the other hand, is almost of some service."

Windflower looked over near the carriage where Amelia Louise was sleeping and the cat was curled beneath the stroller wheels.

"Our perfect little family. It's hard to tell who needs the most babysitting," said Windflower as first Lady and then Molly came up to be petted. He was rubbing both of them at the same time when he realized that the competition for his affection was over for now. Amelia Louise had just woken, and Windflower was convinced again that she was smiling at him.

He lifted his daughter out of the carriage. That seemed to drive both cat and dog into a nervous frenzy and soon both were racing around the yard. "Hey, Sheila. I think they're playing with each other."

"I think you're right," said Sheila. "Do you have time to change her? I need to get cleaned up."

"Absolutely. I'm heading to Marystown via Burin, but I can do that first." He took the baby inside and brought her upstairs. He got all his supplies out, including a clean diaper, wipes, and baby powder. Sheila had trained him well. He changed the baby and put on a clean pink onesie. Both he and Amelia Louise looked pleased when he handed her back to her mother who was sitting in a lawn chair in the shady part of the garden.

"Are you going to see Jeremiah Parsons?" asked Sheila.

"I'm mainly going to drop off Levi to see his dad. I'll only stay for a minute. His mom will pick him up. I'll be back later this afternoon if all goes well."

"Okay, Winston. Give us both a kiss before you go."

He bent to kiss his wife and gave Amelia Louise a peck on the cheek. Of course Molly and Lady came over for a piece of the action, too. Windflower patted both pets and was on his way. When he got back to work, Betsy came in to tell him that Charlene Parsons was happy to be called, and that Levi would be ready whenever he was. Charlene would be going over in the afternoon to bring Levi back.

"Inspector Quigley also called and said he would meet you for the interviews. He said he wanted a Double Double," said Betsy.

"I'm sure he would," said Windflower. "And so might I," he added to himself as he slipped out the door.

FIFTY-FIVE

Levi Parsons was standing in the driveway holding his backpack when Windflower drove up. He waved to his mother who was watching from the window. Windflower got out of the Jeep to let him in and waved back as well.

As usual, the first few minutes of the ride were deadly quiet. Windflower glanced over at his young passenger and saw him reach into his backpack. He expected to see the teenager whip out his headphones. Instead, Levi pulled out a CD. He looked at Windflower expectantly.

"I wanted to play you a song," said Levi. "If you want."

"Sure."

Levi looked relieved and put the disc into the player. The music that came out was hauntingly beautiful, first the acoustic guitars and then the chilling voice of the lead singer. If Windflower weren't driving, he would've closed his eyes and imagined himself being in the mountains back home. The lyrics were just as magical.

'And at once I knew I was not magnificent . . . . And I could see for miles, miles, miles.'

At the end Windflower was stunned, speechless for a few moments. Finally, regaining his voice, he looked at the kid next to him. "Wow, that was amazing. Who is that?"

"It's my favourite band, Bon Iver. Did you like it?"

"I loved it. What's that song about?"

"I think it means whatever you want it to mean. Sometimes songs are only words put together with really good music. But for me this song is about reaching a point in your life where things finally make sense. Where you can see what's going on around you."

"For miles, miles, miles. I get that. And I'm not perfect. That's a good lesson to learn, too."

"That's an easy one when you're a kid."

Both of them were silent for a few minutes after that as they processed their discussion. It could've been the end of their connection for the day but Windflower had an idea.

"Can you pull out my iPod and plug it in?" he asked the boy. "It's in the glove compartment."

Levi dug around, found the device, and plugged it into the system.

"Can you search for a song? It's by The Who? Did you ever hear of them?" asked Windflower.

"CSI. They always used Who songs."

"Really, why didn't I know that?"

"What? You didn't watch CSI? I thought all cops would watch that show. It's always on rerun."

"I'll keep that in mind. Look for 'I Can See for Miles.'"

Levi found it and turned up the volume. Windflower looked at him. "You have to turn up The Who," said Levi. "Everybody knows that."

Windflower smiled as the music kicked in. The distinctive windup guitar of Pete Townshend, the melodic voice of Roger Daltrey and the frantic drumming of Keith Moon brought back many memories of other days and other journeys. He also realized that what he had always thought was deep music was maybe a little bit shallow. He admitted as much to the young man next to him.

"I guess this was a pretty primitive attempt to say some of the things that your song talked about," said Windflower as the song died down.

"It's all good," said Levi. "It's just a different way to express the same things. I like it."

"Can we hear the rest of your CD?" asked Windflower.

This time Levi Parsons smiled and put his disc back into the machine. Soon after the music finished, they arrived at the Burin hospital. Windflower parked out front and walked in with Levi to see his father.

Jeremiah Parsons was more than alive and alert, he was happy, and very happy to see his son. He called Levi to him and gave him as big a hug as he could, considering his injuries. Windflower thought he could hear the father whisper "I love you" into his son's ear. For his part Levi looked confused and more than a little surprised, but even with his dazed teenager look, Windflower could see the kid was happy, too.

"There's a toonie on the table. Why don't you get a drink and let me say hello to the Sergeant?" said Jeremiah. Levi took the coin sheepishly and went outside to the vending machines.

"I want to thank you again, Sergeant, for the help you are giving to my family, to all of us. I know that's far above what you have to do. I want you to know that I greatly appreciate it."

"I'm happy to help. I do believe it's part of my job, though, to help families in trouble. Makes my job easier later on if a teenager turns around early."

"Well, thank you, Sergeant, in any case. I know that I've been given a precious second chance and I intend to make the most of it. If you need me to make a statement about the accident, I would be happy to do that now."

"I think we'll close the police investigation. But you won't be able to claim any damages through your insurance."

"What I have received is more precious than any truck. Thank you, again." He held out his hand and Windflower rose to shake it as Levi was coming back in.

"Your son has a great taste in music," said Windflower. Levi turned beet red. "I've learned a lot from him." He patted Levi on the shoulder and said goodbye to his father. "And not just about music," he added to himself. He was smiling about this last encounter as he left the hospital and was still smiling when he arrived at the Tim Hortons coffee shop in Marystown.

He ordered two Double Doubles, large coffees with two cream and two sugars. He also picked up a box of doughnut holes, called Timbits, as a gift for his boss and maybe a few for himself as well. He entered the nearby RCMP detachment and went directly to Quigley's office. The inspector was on the phone, but his assistant told Windflower to go on in.

He laid Quigley's coffee on his desk and opened the box of Timbits.

"I'm working on your next recruit," said Quigley. He reached for a couple of snacks from the box.

"Any progress?" asked Windflower as he popped another doughnut hole in his mouth.

"Soon," said Quigley. "'To climb steep hills requires slow pace at first.' Patience, my friend."

"That is true. But I would remind you that 'friendship is constant in all other things. Save in the office and affairs of love.'"

Quigley shrugged his shoulders at that last remark and let it go. "I'm doing my best, Sergeant."

"How are the prisoners this morning?" asked Windflower.

"Tutlow looks pretty relaxed, waiting. He's been through this before, and he knows he doesn't have much left on his breach charges. Elizabeth Crowder is steamed. She spotted me coming though and let me have it. I let her make a call. She says her lawyer is on his way. But he's coming from St. John's. So, we have a few hours to work with." said Quigley.

"Great. I'm ready to go."

"Who do you want first? I've got the interview room set up. I thought I would monitor from outside if that's okay with you."

"That's fine. Let's do Tutlow first. See what he has to say for himself."

FIFTY-SIX

Freddie Tutlow was brought into the interview room by a young RCMP officer who Windflower had seen before. Maybe it was at Frost's going-away party. He acknowledged him and indicated he should sit Tutlow across from him. That way Quigley would be able to see his facial expressions through the two-way glass behind him.

Tutlow did kind of look out of place in this situation. He was dressed in prison greens, but if he had a turtleneck and loafers, he would certainly be the preppy guy that Tizzard was talking about. His hair was short but professionally coifed, and he was indeed calm as he settled himself easily into the chair.

"Do you want some water?" Windflower asked.

"I'd love a coffee. One cream and a sweetener," said Tutlow, pointing to Windflower's cup.

"I don't think you're getting Timmy's for a while," said Windflower. "Although, your cooperation may speed things up."

Tutlow only smiled at that suggestion. "I don't have much," he said. "I don't mind doing my time here or back in Nova Scotia. It's all time served."

"Unless we add more charges down here. Like murder, for instance."

"Hang on a second," said Tutlow, his calmness fading. "I didn't kill anybody."

"Your prints were at the Crowder house, and I'm guessing they're all over the van where your buddy, Scott, was found. Tell me why we shouldn't charge you."

"I was at the Crowder house, but I didn't kill the guy. And I certainly didn't kill Jason," said Tutlow.

"Well, I'm willing to take my chances in court on either of them," said Windflower as he stood to leave.

Tutlow put up his hands. "Wait," he said. "Jason killed Crowder. He thought Crowder was holding something back on our deal."

"That's pretty convenient considering he's dead," said Windflower. "What was your deal?"

"We were in the computer import business. Crowder was doing the ordering and we were the delivery guys."

"We know that there was more than computers involved in your business. How about ordering and delivering drugs as well?"

Tutlow shrugged. "You can't prove anything on that, even if it were true, which it's not, and I had nothing to do with any of that stuff. Computer delivery guy, that's me. And I think I need a lawyer."

"Maybe you can use the same one as Elizabeth Crowder," said Windflower, going on a hunch. He watched as the blood drained from Tutlow's face. He looked like he was going to get sick.

"I want to call my lawyer," he said weakly.

"Okay." Windflower rose and knocked on the door. The young RCMP officer came in and took Tutlow back to his cell. "He needs to make a phone call," said Windflower.

Quigley came into the room soon after Tutlow had left.

"Interesting," said Quigley.

"That look on his face after I mentioned Elizabeth Crowder was something else," said Windflower.

"That was the face of fear. I think letting him have a lawyer is a good move. Plus, he won't know anybody, so he'll take a local person. That will move things along."

"Yeah, maybe the lawyer will let him know how much trouble he's in. We might be able to turn him."

"It will also be interesting to see Elizabeth Crowder's reaction when she knows we have Tutlow. Do you want her now?"

"Sure. Let's see what the lady has to say, too."

Minutes later a female RCMP officer brought Elizabeth Crowder into the room. She still looked great, even without her makeup and dressed in prison garb. But if her appearance was pleasing, her demeanor was not. She looked angry.

"Why am I here, and where is my lawyer?" she asked.

"I think your lawyer is on the way," said Windflower. "But we thought maybe you'd like to clear up some things for us."

"Am I being charged with anything? If not, I demand to be released. This is going to cost the RCMP a lot of money and someone's job. Maybe yours, Sergeant."

"We just have some questions right now. But we are investigating two murders and some other major crimes. Why don't we start with what you were doing in Grand Bank?"

"I was here to bury my son, at least his ashes."

"I mean before your son's death. We have fingerprints of yours at the house prior to his death.

"That's obviously some mistake. Police make them all the time, haven't you watched TV?" said Elizabeth Crowder snarkily.

"We know you were in Newfoundland before your son's death. What were you doing here?"

"What? You're not allowed to visit this province? I was in St. John's on business, personal business. Listen, Sergeant, I don't have to talk to you. Let me sit in my dingy little cell and wait 'til he comes and gets me out. Okay?"

"Okay. But you should know that we've talked to Freddie Tutlow. He had some interesting things to say."

For the first time that morning Elizabeth Crowder's confidence wavered as she took in that news.

"Do you know him? 'Cause he certainly knows you," said Windflower.

"I want my lawyer," was Elizabeth Crowder's only response.

Windflower called in the woman officer, and Elizabeth Crowder was escorted back to her cell.

FIFTY-SEVEN

"I think we've set the cat amongst the pigeons," said Quigley as he came back into the interview room.

"A very small chink in the armour," said Windflower. "Let's see where this goes. The truth is we really don't have much on Elizabeth Crowder. Even if she was at Crowder's house before he was killed."

"But we do have Freddie Tutlow and at least a case to make about his involvement in both murders. Let's hope his lawyer can help him see a way out of this situation," said Quigley.

"If need be, we'll take Tutlow. 'There's small choice in rotten apples'. Although, I have the feeling that the lady is more deeply involved in all of this than she pretends."

"Agreed. I do think that she does protest too much. Are you going to hang around for a while?"

"I think so. Can I have a spot to make a few calls?"

Quigley set Windflower up in a small, empty office near his and went back to work. Windflower phoned Betsy in Grand Bank.

"Hi Betsy, how are you today?"

"Good morning, Sergeant," said Betsy. "I'm doing well. How can I help you?"

"I'm just checking in. I'm going to be in Marystown for a while longer. Is anybody looking for me?"

"Constable Jones, sir. I'll get her on the line. Oh, and by the way, there's a nice write-up in the *Southern Gazette.*"

"I only talked to the guy yesterday."

"It's the online version. They post the stories as they write them now. Let me patch you through."

"Morning, Sergeant," said Jones. "I thought you'd want to know. One of the neighbours thought he saw Elizabeth Crowder in the house."

"When was this?" asked Windflower.

"Sometime this February. He wasn't sure of the exact date. He saw her get out of the back of a van late at night. He watched the house for a while but didn't recall seeing her leave. Then he saw her come back again, about a month later. Same deal, late at night in the van. Never saw her leave. He figures it must have been in the middle of the night."

"Interesting. Can you get him to make a statement for the record?"

"Already have, sir."

After Jones hung up, Ron Quigley came in to see him.

"When were you going to tell me?" he asked Windflower.

"Tell you what?"

"About Tizzard."

"He and Carrie are getting married."

"Not about that. Everybody knows that."

"I thought he should tell you himself. It looks like he did. That's good."

"I'm working on a plan for him to consider. But I wanted to talk to you about it first now that the cone of silence is lifted."

"What are you thinking?"

"He can get into university as a mature student and fast-track his bachelor's degree. That's the first step. If he's willing to do the courses remotely, with maybe one term a year in St. John's, I think we can keep him on."

"So, he'd be back in his old job?"

"Sort of," said Quigley. "The deal is, I would get Evanchuk as my assistant and Tizzard would transfer back to Grand Bank until he completes the degree. Can you accommodate that?"

"Absolutely. Does he know about your plan yet?"

"I thought I'd tell him at the party."

Windflower had no idea what his boss was talking about. "What party?" he asked.

"The one your wife is organizing at the B&B," said Quigley, and he walked away laughing.

Windflower's next call was to Sheila.

"There's a great picture of you in the *Southern Gazette*," she said. "Nice story, too."

"Thanks," said Windflower. "I hear we're having a party."

"Friday night. You sound surprised. We talked about it."

"True . . . never mind. That'll be great."

"I've got Moira doing a little spread for us. But we'll need a gift. Can you pick something up in Marystown?"

"Are you putting me in charge of getting an engagement gift? It's me you're talking to."

"You're in Marystown, and I don't have time to go. Plus, you'll do fine. You know both of them, and Eddie's as close to a younger brother as you'll ever get. Man up, Sergeant." Windflower could hear Sheila laughing loudly as she hung up the phone.

Now Windflower had some real problems to think about. All this crime and criminal stuff he understood. But engagement gifts. That was way beyond his comprehension. He puzzled about it and then fretted some more. Finally, he realized he needed help. Expert help. He phoned Betsy.

"So, you need an engagement gift?" asked Betsy.

"Correct," said Windflower.

"Give them something to share," said Betsy. "It could be a nice bottle of wine or fancy chocolates. It's not the gift but the thought that counts, anyway."

"Thanks, Betsy. But the thinking is what gets me into trouble. Those are great suggestions. I'll talk to you later."

Quigley came over again. "Tutlow's lawyer is here," he said. "They're together now. Wanna bowl of soup?"

"Might as well," said Windflower. "They'll probably take some time."

Lunch at the coffee shop was simple but satisfying: chicken noodle soup with grilled cheese sandwiches and a doughnut for dessert. Quigley had to hurry back for a meeting, but Windflower lingered with his coffee for a few more minutes. Then he remembered about his mission to find a gift. He started driving around town. The big place to shop was Walmart, but Windflower detested what he called the evil empire. He couldn't imagine buying a gift for Tizzard and Evanchuk there.

He drove to the mall and wandered inside. There wasn't much, but there was a small jewelry store. Windflower peeked in the window, and there among the glittering rings and watches was a tiny porcelain elephant. He remembered hearing somewhere that many people gave this as a gift to people who were moving into a new home. Or starting a new life, he thought to himself. He got it gift-wrapped and left the store.

On his way out of the mall, he saw a sign that said 'For Him and Her' in the window of Elaine's Massage Clinic. Wow, thought Windflower, that elephant has already brought me good luck. He went inside and got the package for Carrie and Eddie. Feeling pleased and more than a little lucky, he walked back to his car.

His cell phone rang.

"Tutlow's lawyer wants to talk to us," said Quigley.

"I'll be right there," said Windflower. This elephant keeps on giving, he thought. Maybe I should keep it for myself. He pulled up in front of the Marystown detachment and ran up the steps.

He went back to the interview room. This time Inspector Quigley was sitting inside talking to a slim young man wearing, what to Windflower looked like, an ill-fitting suit.

"Sergeant Winston Windflower, Colin Hanratty," said Quigley.

FIFTY-EIGHT

Colin Hanratty had a surprisingly strong grip for a man with such a slight build. Sometimes that meant people were stronger than they looked, thought Windflower as he took his seat beside Quigley.

"I hear you want to talk to us," said Windflower.

"Thank you, Sergeant," said the lawyer. "My client would like to be returned to Nova Scotia to deal with the misunderstanding about bail conditions."

"He's a suspect in two murder investigations," said Windflower.

"Are you charging him?" asked Hanratty.

"Why don't we try this?" asked Windflower in response. "We interview him on tape with you in the room and see what happens. If he can satisfy our concerns, we will take that into consideration."

"Let me talk to my client."

Quigley took the lawyer outside and got him an escort to see Tutlow. As he came back in, his cell phone rang. Windflower could only hear a series of "okays" from Quigley. When he hung up, he turned to Windflower. "The stakes just got raised. HQ wants to talk to both Tutlow and Elizabeth Crowder about something called Project Scorpion."

"That name came up a few times already," said Windflower. "Evanchuk said it was related to some dark web activity, maybe cryptocurrency. Jacob Crowder was involved somehow. And I didn't tell you about all the stuff we found in a safe at the house."

Windflower was explaining about the Swiss bank account and the files and letters from Bruce Crowder when the officer outside the door came in to tell them that Tutlow and his lawyer were on the way up.

A more confident Freddie Tutlow walked into the interview room behind his lawyer. He smiled at Windflower, but the Mountie was not disturbed at all. In fact, he made a point of smiling back.

"Let's get this tape rolling," said Windflower as he turned on the recorder and noted who was in the room. "Would each of you state your name for the record?"

After each man identified himself on tape, Windflower opened the interview by taking Tutlow back to the Crowder house on the night that Jacob Crowder died.

After looking at his lawyer and getting his approval he started talking. "I was there in the house that night. Jason and I were dropping off some computer equipment."

"That is Jason Scott you are referring to?" asked Windflower.

"Correct," said Tutlow. "Anyway, we were waiting to get paid by Crowder, and he started talking about not having any cash and that we'd have to wait. Jason just lost it on him. This had happened before, and he and Crowder were screaming at each other. Crowder went after Jason, and Jason pulled out his knife. He kept stabbing him over and over again."

"What did you do?" asked Windflower.

"I tried to stop him, but Jason was a wild man. He kept stabbing him until he was dead. I finally managed to drag him away, but by that time it was too late. Crowder was dead. I wanted us to get out of town, but Jason said he was going to go back and get his money. I split and left him there. I didn't see him again after that. Then I heard he was dead."

"Where did you go afterwards that night?"

"I spent the night in a cabin out in L'Anse au Loup. There's a place that nobody was using where we stayed sometimes."

"So, you broke into a cabin?"

"Well, it was never locked. It didn't have electricity or anything. Nobody was using it. We didn't break in exactly. We only borrowed it every so often. Listen, I didn't have anything to do with the killing part. I was only delivering computer parts, like I told you."

"We know that there was more than computer supplies. So do some other people from Headquarters and maybe from Europe. This scam is unravelling, and you are right in the middle of it. I've been told to hold you and Elizabeth Crowder until they get here."

Windflower let that last statement hang in the air for a few moments as he watched Tutlow process the information. The prisoner looked at his lawyer again.

"My client wants a deal," said Hanratty.

"Everybody wants a deal," said Windflower. "What's your client got to offer?'

"Maybe we should wait until your superiors arrive?" asked Hanratty.

"You could, although I would suggest that he needs all the help he can get. At the very least he's an accessory to murder and that doesn't go away unless we say so, no matter what transpires in other discussions," said Windflower.

Tutlow again looked nervously at his lawyer. "I need to get out of here," he finally said. The lawyer nodded again.

"Elizabeth Crowder was there," said Tutlow. "Although I knew her as Elizabeth Ryan."

"What was she doing there?"

"She'd been there before. I saw her a couple of times in St. John's and then again in Grand Bank. Jacob Crowder pretended to be running the operation, but she was calling the shots. He was afraid of her. We all were. Even my guys back in Halifax were afraid of her. If she knew I was talking, I'd be a dead man."

"She was there on the night Jacob Crowder died?" asked Windflower.

"She ordered the hit," said Tutlow. "I don't do that. Violence is not my thing. But Jason would do anything when he was whacked out on speed. I saw her pay him, and she was still there when I left. I took off as soon as I could. I stayed at that cabin overnight and then hitchhiked out in the morning. I was in St. John's waiting for the heat to die down."

"So, what do you think?" asked Colin Hanratty.

"A lot of pointing fingers the other way," said Windflower. "Depends on what Elizabeth Crowder has to say."

Again, Tutlow looked anxiously to his lawyer. This time there was no response at all.

Windflower stood and called in the officer who was standing

outside the room. A newly shaken Freddie Tutlow was led out with his lawyer close behind.

Ron Quigley came in shortly afterwards. "Feels like we are getting pieces of the story," he said.

"Indeed," said Windflower. "Breadcrumbs. I'm not sure I buy all of it. But I have a feeling that whatever we might want to charge him with is not going to stack up against what he might be able to share about Elizabeth Crowder."

"Speaking of the lady, I got word that her lawyer is here. I'm guessing he would like to talk with us, sooner rather than later."

"Happy to oblige."

The pair didn't have to wait long. Minutes later Quigley got the call, and soon after that Elizabeth Crowder's lawyer was escorted into the interview room.

FIFTY-NINE

Daniel Charron was the complete opposite of the lawyer who preceded him. He was well and expensively dressed. Windflower noticed that the gold pin in his crimson tie matched his monogrammed cufflinks. He was calm and confident and didn't bother shaking Quigley or Windflower's hand.

"I'm Daniel Charron," said the lawyer. "I represent Elizabeth Crowder. I would like my client charged or released immediately. My office is already aware of the situation and will be filing the papers any minute now." He paused and deliberately looked at his watch so Windflower could get a peak at his Rolex.

"Sergeant Windflower is conducting the investigation," said Quigley.

"We would like to question your client in regard to two recent homicides in Grand Bank," said Windflower. "So far, she has been uncooperative. Now that she has legal counsel, we hope that will change."

Charron smiled and shone his perfectly white teeth. Windflower had to fight himself to get the image of a crocodile out of his mind. "Always cooperative, Sergeant. But she has a few questions and conditions first."

Windflower composed himself and smiled back.

"My client would like immunity in return for her testimony," added Charron.

"We need to ask her a few questions," said Windflower. "Until she responds to this request, we will have to hold her. The Crown is aware of the situation, and I don't believe any judge will release her, especially when they are informed that we have a witness placing her at the scene of one of the crimes."

The lawyer smiled again. "My client would like to know the nature of any evidence against her and the names of any potential witnesses to events that she claims no knowledge of," said Charron.

"No conditions. No immunity. No further discussion until she agrees to provide a statement and answer our questions," said Windflower. This time he smiled, as broadly as he could.

"Very well," said the lawyer. "She will provide a statement and agree to be interviewed. Once." He added emphasis to the last word. "Then we expect your cooperation, or we go to court."

Windflower and Quigley watched silently as the lawyer rose and knocked on the door. The officer peeked in behind him for direction, but Quigley simply nodded.

After the lawyer left, Quigley said, "Very good, Sergeant. Cool in the face of fire."

"Those guys don't intimidate me," said Windflower. "I'm not much for the suits."

"He's pretty slick, though, and self-confident. Used to getting his own way."

"Sounds like he and his client have a lot in common. What's a body got to do to get a cup of coffee around here?"

"Let's go back to my office."

The two officers had just started drinking their coffee when Quigley's assistant told them that Elizabeth Crowder and her lawyer were ready.

A somewhat chastened but still proud-looking woman came in behind her always confident lawyer.

"My client is here to cooperate with your request. Once we complete this interview, we hope that you will agree to release her," said the lawyer.

Windflower decided on the direct approach. "Were you in Grand Bank before your son's death?" he asked.

"I was not," said Elizabeth Crowder.

"We have a witness who says otherwise. In fact, he says you were at the house on the night your son died," said Windflower.

"That's a lie," said Elizabeth Crowder. "The person you are relying on is a fraud and a liar."

"What is your relationship with Freddie Tutlow? How do you

know him?" asked Windflower.

"He was a friend of my son's. He was in business with him."

"Computer parts and supplies?"

"Exactly."

"How about drug smuggling and counterfeiting?"

"I object to that line of questioning," said Daniel Charron, recognizing the trap that Windflower was trying to create for his client.

Before Windflower could get to his follow-up, the door to the interview room opened, and Ron Quigley walked in. He motioned Windflower to come outside.

"Got a call from HQ. They want us to shut down our investigation. They're taking over. Orders from the top. Tutlow is being sent to Halifax, and we are to transfer Elizabeth Crowder to the women's jail in Clarenville."

"Okay," said Windflower, and he went back inside.

"It appears that our interview will have to be postponed. Your client is being transferred to Clarenville," said Windflower.

"That's outrageous," said the lawyer. He started to launch into a tirade when Elizabeth Crowder put her hand on his arm. He put his pad into his Italian leather briefcase and walked out of the room with her. The female officer led her back to her cell with the lawyer in tow.

"Looks like the web may be tightening," said Windflower after the pair had left.

"I guess our young friend, Hanratty, made some calls and got their attention. They're likely going to offer Tutlow something in exchange for his testimony," said Quigley.

"Sounds like they really want Elizabeth Crowder. I'm just as happy to be rid of the pair of them. My guess is that Tutlow is probably telling a portion of the truth, and while he may be a serial criminal, he's probably not a murderer."

"And Elizabeth Crowder is a whole lot of mean wrapped up in a pretty package. Anyway, I've got to go arrange escorts and make sure we deliver on our end."

"I'm heading back. Thank you for your hospitality."

"I'll see you at the party."

Windflower picked up one more coffee for the drive home on his way out of Marystown. There were still plenty of questions and very few answers. But sometimes cases, and life, were like that. For now, he was more than happy to head home to see his beautiful family.

SIXTY

The drive back was perfect. There was little traffic and no animals on the highway, and "Summer" from Vivaldi, performed by a small orchestra with a fabulous violin soloist, was playing on the radio. The music enlivened him and he tapped his fingers along with the exhilarating notes from the violin. It was the perfect accompaniment to the picturesque scenery, and the music slowed as he reached the crest of a hill that brought Grand Bank, and home, into view.

Windflower didn't bother going into work. He drove past the detachment and straight to his house. This was going to be a quiet night at home. Everyone, especially Sheila was happy to see him. They talked casually about their day while the pets circled in competition for his attention, and he carried Amelia Louise around until she started to doze off. Sheila put her down for a nap, and Windflower took the animals outside.

He fired up the barbecue and went inside to see Sheila.

"Hamburgers and salad?" he asked when she came back down.

"Perfect," she said. "I'll make the salad."

Windflower took three burgers out of the freezer and put them on the barbecue. He watched as the two pets explored their own regions of the backyard. Lady was busy sniffing near Sheila's rose bushes, while Molly was creeping through the grass like a stealth hunter. "Good work, Molly," said Windflower. "Get your practice in." When Lady heard his voice, she ran towards him. "You're doing great, too," he said.

"Who were you talking to?" asked Sheila when he came in to get the buns for toasting.

"My friends," said Windflower with a laugh.

Minutes later they were sitting at the kitchen table eating their hamburgers and passing around the green salad that Sheila had prepared, along with a tub of potato salad that she'd found in the fridge. Windflower showed Sheila the gifts he had purchased for the engagement party. Sheila was impressed, especially by the elephant. Windflower was more than relieved that he had passed another test as husband. Although he pleaded not to be asked to do anything like that again.

Sheila laughed and got them a slice of pie and a cup of tea. The rest of the evening passed calmly and without major incident or accident. A perfectly normal family evening, thought Windflower as he turned off the lamp next to his bed. A perfect evening.

Windflower was up and out early the next morning. He took Lady for her constitutional and was coming out of the shower by the time Amelia Louise and Sheila woke. He changed the baby and passed her to her mother before heading straight over to work.

Smithson was coming in from his last round, and he and Windflower shared a coffee and a muffin from the fridge. The young constable left, and Windflower had a few quiet moments in the office before the day officially started. His morning reverie was broken, as usual, by his cell phone ringing.

"Good morning, Ron," said Windflower. "You're up early."

"She's dead," said Quigley.

"Who's dead?" asked Windflower.

"Elizabeth Crowder."

"What? How'd that happen?"

"That's what I'm on my way to find out. We packed Tutlow off to Gander, and he's on a flight to Halifax this morning. Elizabeth Crowder didn't make it to Clarenville. Died on the way. The paramedics said they thought it was an overdose."

"That's freaky. How would she get drugs while she was in custody?"

"Great question and one that I, and my superiors, would certainly like to have an answer for. Anyway, I thought you should know."

"Thanks for telling me," said Windflower, but Quigley was gone.

Windflower sat in his office in a bit of a stupor, trying to process the information he had just received, when a visitor appeared at the doorway.

"Good morning, nephew. You look like you're a million miles away," said Uncle Frank.

"Sorry," said Windflower. "Just received some strange news."

"Good or bad?" asked his uncle.

"Bad for the person involved. But I'm not really sure what it all means yet. How are you this morning?"

"I am grand, just like the morning. I'm taking the taxi to St. John's this morning. I wanted to say goodbye for now."

"I'm sorry you're leaving. It's nice to have you around, and you were especially helpful with security."

Uncle Frank laughed. "That was easier than the pogey," he said. "But it's time for me to go back and look after my lady. I've already been by to see Sheila and your little angel. I've got lots of pictures to take with me."

"We'll be out in the fall," said Windflower. "Then, Auntie Marie will be able to see her for herself."

"Well, here's my taxi," said Uncle Frank, pointing out the window. "Goodbye, Winston. I love you."

"I love you, too, uncle," said Windflower, standing to embrace his relative in a warm hug. "Be safe on the road."

"I travel slowly these days. Wisely and slowly. 'They stumble that run fast.'"

Before Windflower could respond, Uncle Frank waved goodbye and was outside the door heading to the van that would take him on the first leg of his journey. Windflower walked to the front and waved him goodbye as Betsy came in for the day.

"Good morning, Betsy, how are you this morning?" he asked,

"I am wonderful, Sergeant. Do you have anything for me today? I was thinking about leaving early to enjoy the sunshine."

"I think things might be a bit slower," said Windflower. "And you know what? I might do the same."

He went back to his office and did up some memos on both murder investigations, noting what had happened to date and where the main players were now. His final paragraph contained his preliminary conclusions that the Jacob Crowder and Jason Scott homicides were to remain unsolved for now but were to be filed as cold cases until any new information became available.

He did a separate memo on all the other outstanding issues surrounding these cases, including the materials found at the Crowder house and what they had collected from their investigations. Someone higher up in the chain of command would be looking for that information. He attached both memos to an e-mail that he sent to all the staff, including Betsy, for comments.

Betsy came in first to talk about Elizabeth Crowder's unfortunate demise, and throughout the morning the other staff came in one by one to talk to him about the case and wonder about the late woman and questions they still had. Windflower, too, had mostly questions and few answers. At the end of the morning he put his computer in sleep mode and told Betsy he was on his way out. She was doing the same, and they both shared a smile together in the sunshine as they left for the day.

He was driving home to surprise Sheila when he saw a familiar face on the side of the road. He pulled his Jeep over and got out to talk to Herb Stoodley.

"Good morning, Herb," said Windflower.

"Hello, Winston. Beautiful day for a walk," said Stoodley.

"It is indeed."

"Too bad about Elizabeth Crowder."

Windflower thought about asking how he'd found out about the woman's death but realized that bad news really did travel much faster than the formal channels. He just replied, "Yes, it's too bad when anybody dies before their time." He started to head back into his vehicle when he remembered something that Sheila had said. Two things, actually.

"Sheila's thinking about asking you for some painting lessons," said Windflower.

"I'd be more than pleased," said Stoodley. "But I'm hardly an art teacher."

"You're very good. I also wanted to know if I could change my order about the painting I talked to you about."

"Absolutely. What did you have in mind?"

"I'd like a portrait of Diane Matthews to hang in our dining room at the B&B."

"You mean the ghost lady?"

"Yes. I'm not sure what I believe, but I'm trying to keep an open mind."

"It's a great idea to give the wandering ghost a welcome and a place for her to rest. I'll start on it right away. Should be ready in a month or so."

"Perfect," said Windflower as he jumped in his Jeep and resumed his short trek home.

SIXTY-ONE

Sheila was pleasantly surprised to see Windflower show up that early, and when she heard that he was there for the day, she was more than pleased. The baby was having a nap, so they had a chance to sit out back with their pets and enjoy a sandwich together. Later, they drove to the L'Anse au Loup Trail where all of the family got to get out and enjoy the beautiful weather.

Lady went directly out onto the rocks to bark at the seals whereas Molly was content to curl up on a large, warm beach rock and bask in the sunshine. Windflower carried Amelia Louise in the baby carrier so he could see her face as he and Sheila walked along the path.

"I'm guessing you heard about Elizabeth Crowder," he said.

"They said she overdosed. How is that possible?"

"Everybody's asking the same thing. Either somebody inside gave it to her or she had it hidden on her body somewhere. I feel sorry for Ron because they will certainly not be happy with him or his section. But I have mixed feelings about Elizabeth Crowder. Maybe the noose was tightening, and she knew it."

"I understand. Maybe she couldn't imagine going to jail. I know she had a tough exterior, but jail would have likely killed her anyway."

"Maybe. In any case, it clears up a whole lot of paperwork and frees me up to enjoy more days like this."

"I can certainly go for that," said Sheila as she called Lady back from near the water. Molly came as soon as she saw the dog head back towards the Jeep. They drove home where Windflower and Amelia Louise had a wonderful nap. Windflower offered fish and chips takeout for dinner, and Sheila readily agreed.

They took their meal with lots of salt and malt vinegar. "Not as good as Leo's," said Windflower. "But not bad at all b'y."

A cup of tea and a game of crib rounded off their evening, and an early and romantic night capped off a perfect day for Windflower.

"Good night, my love," he said as he turned out the light. "Thank you for a great evening."

"Thank you, Winston," said Sheila. "We are lucky."

The luckiest couple in Grand Bank, thought Windflower as he drifted off to sleep.

The morning came with gray clouds and showers, but that did not dampen Windflower's spirits one iota. He did his smudge quickly and took Lady on a full tour of downtown Grand Bank. Sheila had coffee and scrambled eggs ready when he got back. After breakfast he was coming out of the shower when he heard his cell phone ringing.

"Good morning, Inspector," said Windflower.

"Well, we know how she got the drugs," said Quigley. "She had them concealed in a filling inside her mouth. When she knew she was going to Clarenville, her lawyer must have found out what we had on her."

"Wow, that's a new one."

"Carfentanil. It's some evil combination of heroin and elephant tranquilizers, 100 times more potent than fentanyl. A few grains can kill you. They did for Elizabeth Crowder. That gives us a bit of breathing room on the investigation that's coming. They're already asking for our notes."

"I'm on top of things on this end. I'll send you my stuff later this morning. I was just waiting to get Tizzard and Evanchuk's input."

"Great. I spoke to Tizzard and told him I had a plan. I said I'd tell him and Evanchuk tonight when I come over for the party."

"Okay, see you tonight."

Sheila was carrying the baby in as he was coming out. "Was that Ron? Is he coming tonight?"

"Yes," said Windflower. "And he's bringing good news. Eddie's going to be transferred here while he goes to school, and Carrie is going to be in Marystown."

"That's great news. I have that meeting with Eastern Health this morning at 10. They are coming over to the Town Hall. Do you think you could hang around here until afterwards?"

"Sure. Amelia Louise and I will be fine."

"I'm sure you will," said Sheila. "But if she kicks up a fuss and needs to be fed, bring her over and I'll skip out of the meeting, or I'll just feed her right there and people can think what they want. Why don't you clean her up, and I'll have my shower?"

She handed Windflower the baby and he could smell that the little creature needed changing. He cleaned, wiped, and dressed Amelia Louise. He took her into the bedroom and played with her on the bed until Sheila kissed them both goodbye.

"Wish me luck," said Sheila.

"Good luck," said Windflower as the baby gurgled. "Amelia Louise wishes you good luck, too."

He played with the baby and snuggled with her on the bed until she got dozy. Once she was gone he read his book for a while and then went back downstairs. He absent-mindedly turned on the TV to the all-news station.

There on the national news was a picture of the now late Elizabeth Crowder. She was identified as the key suspect in an international drug smuggling and counterfeiting scheme. They called her Elizabeth Ryan, and the spokesperson from the RCMP talked about cooperating in the investigation Operation Scorpion. They said they had shut down a dark web organization with its headquarters in Canada. They didn't mention Grand Bank or Newfoundland, but Windflower had learned long ago that credit or attention wasn't worth the amount of work that came with it.

"What are you watching?" asked Sheila. "I thought you'd be watching cartoons."

"My daughter is much smarter than that. Like her mother," he quickly added.

"Well her mother, with the help of Richard Tizzard and Constable Jones, has convinced the department to send us a mental health worker for six months on a trial basis," said Sheila. "They are coming next month to do an evaluation and the program should be up and running by September when school comes back."

"Congratulations, Mayor Hillier. Another feather in your distinguished hat. Come closer so I can thank you more personally."

Sheila cuddled up to Windflower on the couch and allowed him to pull her in closer. "I could get used to this," she said.

"Good. 'Cause I plan to keep doing just that. But for now I probably should go to work. What time is the do tonight?"

"Come any time after five. Moira and Beulah will be there at four to set up and then Beulah is going to take our little one upstairs."

"Perfect. I'll see you then." Windflower drove over to work still buzzing from the glow of his morning and last evening off.

The detachment was busy as a beehive with people coming and going, and almost all of them dropped in for a moment to say hello to Windflower. Normally, that would have driven him crazy. But somehow today everything was fine. He remembered Uncle Frank telling him one time that happiness was an inside job. If that was the case, Windflower's insides felt pretty good.

After everybody but Smithson had left for the party, Windflower drove his Jeep home and walked to the B&B. Smithson had volunteered for the overnight shift, and none of the other officers had objected. They all wanted to be there to celebrate Tizzard and Evanchuk's engagement. When Windflower arrived, Sheila handed him a glass of champagne. She didn't have to tell him where the food was.

On his way to the buffet table, he noticed Molly prowling around the premises. Sheila must have brought her over. He piled his plate high with salad and sandwiches and joined Jones and Richard Tizzard at the table in the corner. Soon afterwards, the happy couple entered, and they made the rounds of the room before stopping at Windflower's table.

Evanchuk was showing off her ring to Jones as Tizzard sat next to Windflower.

"Get a plate, Eddie," said Windflower.

"I'm too nervous," said Tizzard.

"Getting married is no big deal," said Windflower.

"I'm not worried about getting married. The inspector said he wants to talk to me about going back to school."

Windflower noticed Ron Quigley and a few of the Marystown officers come into the B&B. "Well, here he comes right now. Why don't you go ask him?"

Before Tizzard could move, Quigley motioned him over.

"Good luck," said Windflower as Tizzard went to talk to Quigley.

Windflower resumed eating his meal and was contemplating seconds when he saw a beaming Eddie Tizzard, holding two glasses of champagne, come back towards their table. He handed one to Evanchuk and whispered in her ear. Then, he looked at Windflower who was smiling. "You knew, didn't you?" he said.

Windflower continued smiling. "Since you have your glass, why don't you get up and propose a toast to your bride-to-be?"

Windflower clinked on his glass to get everybody's attention.

"Ladies and gentlemen, let me present the happy couple, Eddie and Carrie." The room exploded with applause, and Tizzard and Evanchuk stood in the middle of their circle of friends.

"First of all," said Tizzard, "I want to tell you how happy I am that Carrie has agreed to be my wife. I know she will make me a better man. To Carrie," and he raised his glass to his future wife. Everyone cheered and toasted Evanchuk with their champagne.

"I also want to thank all of you for coming today to help us celebrate this new beginning," Tizzard continued. "Thank you to my Dad. I love you, Dad. And to my best friends in the whole world, Sheila and Winston. I also want to share with you some more good news. I am going back to school, but I will do so while maintaining my position with the RCMP right here in Grand Bank." An even bigger cheer erupted from the audience. "Now, here is the intelligent and beautiful Carrie Evanchuk."

Evanchuk looked like she was going to cry but started speaking in a surprisingly calm voice. "I also want to thank everyone here for your support, Yvette Jones who has agreed to be my maid of honour, and all our friends who are here tonight. Thank you to Richard for welcoming me into your home and heart. I love you, too, Dad." At this point many eyes in the room grew moist.

"I also want to thank our Sergeant Windflower for his ongoing support," she continued, "and to let you know that I, too, will be staying in the area as assistant to Inspector Ron Quigley in Marystown. Eddie, I want you to know that I am grateful to be your partner and that I will always love and support you. To Eddie."

Everyone toasted Eddie, and soon after he declared that he was starving. Everyone laughed at that, and Windflower knew at that moment that everything was right in his world. The party continued for a few more hours. Afterwards, Beulah came down with the baby and everyone took turns holding her while Windflower and Sheila cleaned up.

The goodbyes were pleasant and extended, and when Eddie and Carrie left with the Stoodley's close behind, Windflower sat in a big armchair in the parlour with Amelia Louise in his arms. He was looking down adoringly at her when Molly came in and laid something at his feet. Then she turned and walked back out to the kitchen.

Sheila came into the room and almost shrieked before she realized the mouse was dead. "Molly?" she asked.

"Her application for chief mouser at the B&B," said Windflower. "I think she's got the job." He gave Sheila the baby, wrapped the tiny animal in a handkerchief, and got up to dispose of it. He said goodnight to Beulah, who was leaving for the night, and went to find Molly. He gathered the cat up in his arms, and the two of them joined Sheila and Amelia Louise at the front door.

"Time to go home, ma'am. Our mission here is done."

"Yes, Sergeant. I believe it is."

SIXTY-TWO

ONE MONTH LATER.

Windflower was carrying the baby down from upstairs in the B&B, and Sheila was saying goodnight to Beulah. Levi Parsons was in the kitchen mopping the floor. He would stay overnight at the inn in case anything went wrong and then would sleep most of the day once Windflower got back to start breakfast in the morning. It suited his teenage lifestyle perfectly, and his friends were amazed that he got paid to stay up late and watch videos on his iPad.

This system worked for Sheila and Windflower, too. Windflower cooked dinner every night and breakfast six days a week. Beulah did the cleaning, and Sheila looked after registration and check-out. Levi would let people in when they arrived late and help them with their bags. The kid was careful and responsible and looked after the cleaning up after meals as well. What's not to like, thought Windflower.

He yelled goodnight to Levi, and the boy shyly waved back. Their budding friendship was still a little awkward, but it was coming. The boy even talked to Windflower about his father once, which was another minor miracle. Maybe over the summer they could grow even closer. Windflower had the time. He arranged for all July off from work and a reduced schedule in August. Sheila was happy with this arrangement, too.

She was in the dining room, ready to turn off the lights when Windflower, with a sleeping Amelia Louise in his arms, came up behind her. "It's a beautiful picture, and it fits in here perfectly," she said.

"Well, it seemed appropriate to give the ghost lady a place

to rest," said Windflower. "Diane Matthews has been wandering around for years and now she has a room of her own. At least when we're not here."

"This was a great idea," said Sheila. "But I didn't think you believed in ghosts."

"Who am I to believe or not believe? This lady is part of the history of this house, and maybe, you know, you really do have to be open to possibilities. Let's go home and leave this place to people who want to get some sleep. Maybe we can, too."

"It's funny how so much happens in a short period of time and then nothing."

"That's part of the charm of this place."

Amelia Louise was still out cold when they went outside. Windflower put her in the stroller, and she didn't stir a peep.

"I still can't get over the fact that three people just died, two of them in our little town," said Sheila as they started to walk home. "I even feel a bit sorry for Elizabeth Crowder."

"You're too kind," said Windflower. "It looks like she may have killed her husband and been involved in the death of her only son. And it now looks like she really was the mastermind of a massive online drug-smuggling scheme."

"Maybe you're right. Why would she want her son killed? As a mother, that is the worst thing imaginable."

"According to what I heard, Jacob Crowder was diverting some of the profits into bitcoins and then stashing them away in Swiss banks. She found out and freaked. That's what Freddie Tutlow told the investigators. Ron Quigley told me."

"I bet Tutlow got a deal for his efforts."

"Probably. But that operation they were running was bringing in a ton of synthetic fentanyl and the even worse stuff, that carfentanil. He would have helped shut that down and saved hundreds, if not thousands, of lives. That may have been worth letting one snake slither away."

"Doesn't all of this make you want to just give up being a policeman? I can't imagine having to deal with all of the stuff that you see."

"It's an important job. But I do have doubts sometimes."

"I think we all do. I know, for me, that I have done my share as a mayor, as a politician. There's more in life than that. I really admire Eddie for his decision, too."

"I think Carrie may have had a part in that, as well. They are such a cute couple, and he's head over heels in love with her, like I am with you."

"I love you, too," said Sheila. "Look, it's a full moon tonight. We can see it now that the wind has blown the fog back out to sea."

"It's beautiful," said Windflower. "Back home we would call this a Raspberry Moon. Auntie Marie says that it is a time when great changes begin in the natural world and in our hearts. The raspberry is known for its thorns and brambles, but with gentleness and kindness we can harvest the fruit and knowledge that helps us to raise our families."

"Wow. We have to go see her again. I want to learn more about those moons and her teachings."

"This fall you and I are taking Amelia Louise to Pink Lake," said Windflower as they arrived at their front door. As he opened the door, Lady bounded out and lapped Windflower, Sheila, and the stroller. Sheila laughed and went inside with the baby. She threw Windflower the leash. "Another lady needs a walk," Sheila said.

"Come on, girl," Windflower said. "Let's see what's happening in Grand Bank tonight, shall we?"

Lady, as always, was happy to oblige.

THE END

ACKNOWLEDGEMENTS

I would like to thank a number of people for their help in getting this book out of my head and onto these pages. That includes beta readers and advisers Mike MacDonald, Andy Redmond, Denise Zendel, Barb Stewart, Lynne Tyler, and Karen Nortman, and Bernadette Cox for her copy-editing and advice.

ABOUT THE AUTHOR

Mike Martin was born in Newfoundland, on the east coast of Canada, and now lives and works in Ottawa, Ontario. He is a long-time freelance writer, as well as the author of *Change the Things You Can: Dealing with Difficult People*. His short stories have appeared in various publications, including *Canadian Stories* and *Downhome* magazine.

The Walker on the Cape was his first novel, and the premiere of the Sgt. Windflower Mystery Series. *Darkest Before the Dawn* is his seventh book in the series. You can follow the Sgt. Windflower Mysteries on Facebook at https://www.facebook.com/TheWalkerOnTheCapeReviewsAndMore/